DEATH AND TAXES

by

Galen Surlak-Ramsey

A Tiny Fox Press Book

Tiny Fox Press LLC
North Port, FL

*For my brothers, Michael and Sean,
who got me hooked on Night of the Living Dead at the tender
age of 5*

Chapter One

Of the two things in this world that are an absolute certainty, death and taxes, Ryan Conner ended up with a career in the latter. He had thought about pursuing a career as an embalmer, a funeral director, or even as a doctor. After all, people would always get sick and die, and even if they skipped the first stage, all three professions would still be involved in the second. There was tremendous job security in death. But none of those careers held any lasting interest. They lacked power. They lacked excitement. They lacked the frequent use of cheap, red, ballpoint pens and rubber stamps.

Thus, Ryan Conner had settled on being a tax collector.

"Ms. Clarice," he said without looking up from his desk.

There was no immediate answer, and he tired of his new secretary's newness.

"Ms. Clarice!" he bellowed as he glared at the door. He glanced down at the plethora of unstamped paperwork and groaned. Sure, he had a stamp nearby—in hand, actually—but recent use had exposed a flaw, and whereas he could always use a cheap, red, ballpoint pen, a cheap stamp would never do. Not in a tax office and certainly not in his.

As such, Ryan decided, if his secretary did not appear by the time he counted to ten, he might just have to kill her.

Clarice, having heard the disturbing edge to her new employer's tone, abandoned the yet-again-malfunctioning copier, dashed through the busy workplace on two-inch heels, and skidded into Ryan's office. "Yes, Mr. Conner?" she asked.

"My stamp is deficient," Ryan said, giving it a press with his hand and then wiggling it once for good measure. Slowly, he lifted the stamp and inspected the paper below. His spidery fingers traced the ink mark. "As you can plainly see, it's not conveying the mood that I want."

"I'm sorry, Mr. Conner," she said, leaning in for a better view. "Is there anything I can do about it?"

"Yes. Yes, you can," Ryan replied, slowly backing away from the stamp and eyeing it from afar. "First, I'd like you to draft a notice."

"A notice?" Clarice's face scrunched. She wasn't sure what sort of notice could attend to a non-mood conveying stamp, but she would try nonetheless. Hopefully, there was a form for it somewhere. The office seemed to have forms for everything.

"Yes, a notice," he reiterated. He hunched in his leather chair, putting his eyes a hair above the level of the desk, and continued his inspection of paper and stamp. "I want you to draft a notice making an appeal." He paused and straightened his posture before moving on. "I want this sent to Mr. Whittam in regards to his assertion that his company makes the best stamps."

"Yes, Mr. Conner," she said. Her voice hesitated as it tried to decide whether or not her brain should catch up. "I don't think that's necessary," Clarice added. "He's my friend."

"Your friend?" He raised an eyebrow at the thought. "Am I supposed to grant him some sort of leniency? Perhaps you should think about with whom you associate."

"No, sir," she quickly backtracked. "It's just that I was thinking I could call him when he got back. Maybe that would be less, um, intimidating, and he might want to do more to rectify the situation?"

"Back? Back from where, exactly?"

"I'm not sure," she said, chewing on her *welcome to the team* cheap, red, ballpoint pen. "Somewhere in the Blue Ridge Mountains, to fill a custom order or something like that."

"Clarice," he said as he folded his hands together. "Take that instrument out of your mouth at once. I don't appreciate being distracted by your lack of manners."

"Sorry, sir," she said, snatching the pen and tucking it into one of her pockets.

"Now then, how long will this friend of yours be gone?"

Clarice shrugged. "I'm not sure."

Ryan leaned back in his chair. The expression on his angular face made it clear he was contemplating how he wanted to handle the dilemma. Either that or she was about to get fired. Given that it had taken her three months to find this job—any job—the latter would be especially bad. Even more so with student loans now due.

Clarice sucked in a breath and held it. She wanted to appear as professional as she could and did her best not to fidget as she waited. Her hair was fine. The bun had been smartly made. Her skirt had been pressed that morning, and there was no need to smooth it out. Unless of course, she had wrinkled it when she sat down? Her hand drifted behind her back, and her eyes glanced over her shoulder.

"Do you have something more important to attend to?" Ryan asked, snapping her attention forward. "I thought I made it clear when I hired you that we are a disciplined group."

"You did, Mr. Conner," she replied. "I didn't mean to be distracted."

"Good. Then let me be a little frank with you, Ms. Clarice, and excuse the fact that I'm going to slip out of my usual charming character," he finally said. "I'm now in a funk as I did like the prospects of this stamp. Your Mr. Whittam made a number of promises to me. Granted, most turned out to be true. In the end, however, this stamp hasn't measured up to his claim. And getting it mostly right never works around here, now does it?"

"No, sir."

"So now my day will suffer, and as my day will suffer, inevitably yours will as well. But more important, all of us as a whole will suffer. Do you know why that is?"

Clarice shook her head timidly. She wondered how much of this was standard secretarial knowledge. Maybe there was a *Dummies* book on the subject.

"Because if I can't stamp well, I can't collect well," he replied gravely. "And then everybody loses. Imagine a world that might exist without taxes. What would we do with all those rules? They can't just be slapped anywhere haphazardly, now, can they? And think of the bubbles that wouldn't be bubbled! The pencils not sharpened! Think of the computer programmers who would weep for nights because they can no longer add in that last bit of code for the next tax year! A world without taxes, my dear, is a world that's frightening indeed."

Clarice nodded politely as she was growing accustomed to doing. "What might I do to help move things along?" she dared ask again.

"Yes, yes," he said, sinking back into his chair. "You can do something. I'd like you to do two things. First, I'd like you to get me a number where I might reach this friend of yours. And second, I'd like to know exactly where he went."

"Yes, Mr. Conner. Is there anything else?"

"No," he replied. "But time is of the essence, Ms. Clarice, especially regarding your employment status."

"Yes, Mr. Conner," she said again and slipped out the door.

While Clarice thought that Ryan's objection and obsession with the stamp was a little borderline, she, like most of the world, failed to appreciate precisely how important a good stamp was. It went far beyond the simple clarity in the impression that seemed to satisfy everyone else. A stamp needed solid, well-defined lines that were neither too fat, which implied laziness and wanton use of resources, or too thin, which implied weakness and a lack of character. It needed the perfect handle, one that was comfortable to fend off metacarpal-phalange fatigue, yet it also needed to be strong enough to absorb the shock of repeated slamming. Nothing quite says, "I'm not kidding," as a slammed stamp.

Then, of course, it needed to be able to convey whatever mood the stamper was in. Decent stamps were able to do one or two moods, sometimes even three. But to craft a stamp that could articulate precisely what the stamper wanted, in the exact tone and voice intended, was indeed a work of art. And that was what Mr. Whittam had promised when he had filled the order placed by Ryan Conner, Tax Collector.

Ryan leaned back in his chair and continued to examine the wares sold to him, occasionally glancing up at the wall clock and wondering what was taking Clarice so long. After about ten minutes, or an approximate 8.3 lost stamps given his current rate, he had dire concerns as to the abilities of his new hire and shuffled through last week's list of job applicants.

Once out of Ryan's office, Clarice zipped over to her cluttered desk, found the number to Whittam's Stamp Emporium, and spent several agonizing minutes trying to figure out how to dial out of the building. Her first attempt called the desk next to her, which was forgiven and remedied easily enough. Her second attempt reached the county's emergency services, which took a bit of coaxing on Clarice's part for them not to send a squad car as a precautionary measure. Finally, her third try yielded Whittam's, or rather Whittam's automated phone system. After pressing the proper combination of buttons on her touch-tone phone, she reached a live person and obtained the information she so desperately sought.

Clarice darted through Ryan's door once more. "I have the number and address here for you, Mr. Conner," she said, handing him a note.

Ryan took the paper in one hand and picked up and dialed the phone in the other. After a few rings, someone picked up. "Hello, this is Ryan Conner," he said. He then added for additional effect, "Tax Collector."

Clarice waited patiently, trying to put together what was being said on the other end of the conversation.

"I'm glad to hear you're up to date with your filings," Ryan replied, annoyance crossing his face. "I'm looking for someone, a Mr. Whittam to be precise. He was reported to me as staying at your fine establishment."

There was a pause in the exchange, and Clarice picked up on someone yelling to a third party. Finally, the conversation resumed. "No, I'm not mistaken about this," Ryan replied. "He drives a..." He stopped, looked up at Clarice who mouthed the answer, and then continued, "a black and brown Blazer. From Kentucky."

Ryan rolled his eyes and doodled as he was put on the impromptu hold button. More yelling. When the person came back to the conversation a second time, Ryan became attentive once more. "Look, I appreciate your help in this matter, but this is costing me stamps," he interjected. The Tax Collector's grip tightened on the phone. "I'm aware that the phone company doesn't charge postage." He took a deep breath and continued, "I mean rubber stamps. Mr. Whittam traveled to your area to sell some of his wares, and I need new rubber stamps from him."

That seemed to spark the memory of the other person. A bunch of chatter ensued. Ryan smiled, frowned, looked puzzled, smiled again, and ended with frustration. "What do you mean he didn't stay there long? And why won't he be returning if his car is still there?"

There was more chatter. Ryan rattled off a few more questions, answers being given in between. "Where exactly is he? Well, how did he get there? He walked? What county is this in? What do you mean, there is no county? Who collects the property taxes?" Ryan jumped out of his chair at the end of the final question.

"No taxes!" he exclaimed, eyes wide with excitement. He took in several deep, deliberate breaths before sitting down.

Ryan asked a few more questions ending with, "And you're positive it's one private lot?" He ended the conversation after a few more minutes, saying, "I see. Thank you for the information and have a good day."

Clarice stood still, her mind latching on to her voice to keep it from running out of her mouth. It soon became a daunting task as she wanted to know the cause behind her employer's growing elation.

"It seems that Mr. Whittam has taken up a new residence, and the locals think he's there to stay," Ryan said. He stood, went over to a large bookshelf, and pulled out an atlas of the United States. Pages flipped by until the book yielded to his search.

"So you'll be getting your stamps then," Clarice guessed.

"Yes, yes I will," he replied, putting up his atlas and grabbing another book. A big book. A big, heavy book filled with countless columns of numbers and counties and years. It was a book that no one would ever buy, except a tax collector such as Ryan Conner.

His finger traced down through a few columns and finally stopped. "We'll also be doing what we do best," he said, grabbing his calculator.

"Come again?"

"Collecting taxes, of course!" His fingers punched the keys in rapid succession, making small pauses as he jotted down parts of his calculation on a Post-it note. Finally, both the punching and the jotting stopped. Ryan sat back, his eyes never leaving the little red marks. "Mr. Whittam has stumbled upon a small town that owes a bit of money."

"It's not even in our state, though, is it?"

"They don't seem to want to collect," Ryan said disapprovingly.

"That can't be right," she replied. "There must be some mistake."

"No one lives there," he explained. "No one has lived there since before the Civil War apparently."

"Well, that makes sense then."

"No, Ms. Clarice," he said. "It doesn't. But we will rectify the situation this very moment. If they don't want to collect taxes, we will."

"But you just said no one lives there."

"Look, you can't not pay taxes," he said as he leaned back in his chair. "At best you can file for an extension, and I'm willing to wager no extension has been filed. Even if it has, it expired sometime in the last hundred and fifty years."

Clarice knew her face was giving a blank stare, but her mind, unwilling to make sense of what he was saying, could offer no other response. She wondered if this marked a new low for government stupidity and then recoiled at the thought that this might be par for the course.

"Do you know what the taxes, fines, and interest come out to be after a hundred and fifty years?"

Clarice shook her head, "I have no idea, Mr. Conner."

"Eight hundred and thirty-two million, six hundred and nine thousand, four hundred fifty-nine dollars and twenty-one cents!" Ryan exclaimed. "Imagine that! Over eight hundred million in uncollected property taxes!" He then dove like a hawk into the drawer on the left side of his desk. "Blast it!" he said, coming up empty-handed. His eyes circled the desk twice before giving up with a sigh. "Well, you know what to do. Get a demand letter written up for this place, Colmera Springs, and have it on my desk so I can sign and stamp it with this inferior stamp. I suppose it will do for one last notice. I want this out on registered mail by this afternoon."

"I don't think anyone will be there to sign for the receipt, sir," she pointed out. The moment the words passed her lips, her mind disciplined itself for relinquishing control of her voice.

"Fine thinking!" praised Ryan. "You have no idea how happy I am that you are already starting to look ahead in your work. Not like that last girl I had. We'll deliver it ourselves then. It should make an exciting trip, not to mention justify a write off for what will be in essence a vacation."

"Sir, I don't think—" but that was as far as Clarice got.

"You disagree with my decision?" Ryan asked, arching an eyebrow.

"Confused is more like it," she said after she took a moment to find a choice of words that wouldn't commit her to revising her resume.

"I'll make this simple for you," he said. "Your Mr. Whittam obviously knows something about this Colmera Springs that the local municipality does not. Tax evaders can be quite clever when it comes to hiding assets. So after we tour this Colmera Springs, we'll track down Mr. Whittam and see what he has to say on the matter—not to mention get some restitution for these mediocre wares he's peddling."

Clarice knew her facial expression hadn't changed in the least, despite her attempt to appear less confrontational. In the end, she decided to go with her inner turmoil and hope for the best. "I can't imagine there's not an easier way."

"Is there?" he asked. "Do you have some sort of grand idea I'm unaware of?"

Clarice shook her head. "No, Mr. Conner."

"Perhaps then you simply think you are smarter than I am?"

Again, Clarice shook her head. She'd certainly never claim that with anyone. Well, maybe she would if she were up against a Darwin Award winner, but that was about it. After all, she'd never think chewing on a blasting cap would ever be a good idea.

"Do you like your job here, Ms. Clarice?" Ryan asked, cutting into her thoughts as he leaned forward and lowered his tone.

"Yes, Mr. Conner," she answered, even though at this point in time it was a resounding *no*.

"Am I right to believe then that you wish to remain employed?"

Clarice took a moment to reply. The position at the vet's office hadn't been filled yet, but it didn't pay as well. And there would be cats. Lots and lots of cats. Shedding, meowing, clawing little need machines with an infinitely large god complex. "Yes, I'd like to keep my job, Mr. Conner," she finally said.

Ryan sat back in his chair. "Good," he said. "Now stop arguing with me and do as you're told. And since this endeavor is tied to your friend, I'm holding you personally responsible if anything goes wrong. Aiding and abetting tax evasion is a serious crime. Is that understood?"

"Yes, Mr. Conner."

Ryan glanced at his wristwatch. "Now that we're clear," he said. "I want you to go home and pack your bags. Also, you need to learn your forms. I have a book that will help you in that regard. We leave promptly tomorrow at seven in the morning."

Chapter Two

Clarice fishtailed her sky blue Datsun 260z around the last bend in the road before her condominium entrance. Edgar, the security guard posted at the gates, would undoubtedly shoot her a *please-stop-doing-that* look as she passed by, but she didn't care. Her weekend was now ruined, and no rent-a-cop was going tell her what she could or could not do. She pressed the remote control that hung from her sun visor, and as the black iron gates of the complex swung open, she tightened her grip on the steering wheel.

"I hate this place," she muttered, pulling through the entrance. Her feelings for where she and her fiancé Nick currently lived were hardly a secret, despite the "great rate" they got on it. She hated the security posted and the six-foot walls that encircled the compound—a term she preferred to call it instead of home, and she usually had an expletive or two attached as well. She hated the neighbors who felt it necessary to enforce every jot and tittle of the association rules and was convinced they had their own SS brigade on patrol.

Nick, on the other hand, would call it safe, peaceful, and affluent. But Clarice knew what it really was, upscale neighborhood or not. It was a prison that people paid to be in. And with that thought she whipped the car into her tiny, designated parking space, stepped out and slammed her door shut. It felt good. So when she had run up the stairs to her place and went inside, she made sure she slammed the front door as well.

"You're home early," said Nick, who was seated in their living room, surrounded by two laptops and a disemboweled desktop whose electronic guts were strewn about the floor. He was wearing his usual business casual attire, khaki pants and a well-fitted, yellow polo shirt that accentuated his good physique. "And you're in a good mood to boot."

"Not interested in your sarcasm," Clarice said and tossed her denim purse on their couch. She headed for their one bedroom, flicked the light switch, and glanced down at the piles of clothes on the floor. She was reasonably sure what she wanted wasn't in any of them and went through the oak drawers in the corner instead. "I'm going for a run," she announced when she pulled her sports bra, white tank top, and blue running shorts free from the pile of socks they were smothered in. "I'll be back in an hour or so."

"Today is rest day," Nick called back. There was hesitation in his voice, and Clarice couldn't help but mentally pat herself on the back. His training was almost complete, but there was still too much micromanaging for her likes. The perfect relationship needed to run smoothly. Hopefully, all the kinks would iron out before the wedding at the end of the year.

"Tomorrow is your long run," he added when she didn't respond. "It's not a good idea to mess with the schedule. That's how injuries happen."

"Yes, I know that's how injuries happen," she said, putting a bite into her tone while changing clothes. "I was running long before I met you, you know."

Clarice trotted back to the living room and lightly bounced on the balls of her feet a few times in order to get her blood pumping. When she finally came to a rest, she crossed her arms and shot Nick a glare. "Well?"

Nick looked up from what he was working on with confusion splashed across his face. "Well, what? You look fine."

"You're not going to ask me why I'm home early?"

"Should I?" he asked hesitantly.

Clarice groaned and rolled her eyes. "Of course you should. What kind of insensitive fiancé are you?"

Nick's shoulders went up. "The kind that figured asking why you got canned would make you more upset?"

"I wasn't fired, thank you." Clarice grabbed a pillow from the couch and beaned him in the head playfully. "You think I can't hold a job for a day?"

"No, no," he replied, grinning with his hands in a defensive position mid-air. "It was just the first thing that came to mind as to why you'd be home early and pissed off is all. I mean, I thought this was a regular eight to five kind of deal."

"Yeah, a normal person might think that," she said. "Apparently, it's an eight to five kind of deal, except when you have to go away for the weekend and work some stupid claims case that even a lunatic wouldn't chase."

"Away?" Nick's arms fell, and his tone deepened. "What do you mean by away?"

"Don't even start with that overprotective crap," Clarice said and headed for the kitchen.

"I'm not being overprotective—"

"Or the jealous crap," she added. She grabbed a plastic Oakland Raiders cup from the cupboard and downed some water from the fridge. "I can take care of myself, thank you, and I'm not interested in some skinny old guy on a power trip."

"Concerned for your safety, is all," Nick replied sincerely. "It's not the same thing. It's a good thing, really. You should like it."

"Whatever it is, I don't. So please cut it out."

Nick closed his laptop and gave her his undivided attention. "Where are you going on this trip, exactly?"

"Blue Ridge Mountains to hunt down non-existent tax evaders." Clarice tossed the now empty cup into the sink before going on. "So since I'll be away for the weekend, trapped with my boss doing errand after errand, I'll be doing my run now since I can't very well do it tomorrow."

Nick sat a moment and drummed his fingers on his thigh. "I really don't like the idea of this."

Clarice began stretching her leg muscles, starting with her quads, one hand pulling her ankle to her buttocks and the other on the kitchen counter. "It's not as if I have much of a choice, now do I?"

"You could say no," he suggested. "Or quit if you think that won't fly. Something's not right with this."

"One of us needs a real job," she shot back, more forcefully than she intended. She took the edge off her voice as she continued. "That came out wrong. I'm sorry. Look, my student loans are due, and mortgage will be in a couple of weeks. We have to have a paycheck by then, no matter how close you are to finishing your software package. Almost working isn't going to pay our bills."

"What about the vet office?"

"There's no guarantee I'd get it, and I don't want to risk being out of work," she said.

"We can manage a bit."

Clarice shook her head. "No. I have to know we've got money coming in. I'd rather be in a padded cell with a snuggly jacket than worry how we're going to eat."

Nick, patient as ever, continued to spitball ideas calmly. "I'll come with you then. I can finish this communication suite on the road. It'll be fun."

"I can't see that happening," Clarice said. "Mr. Conner is obsessed with being professional and having my fiancé tag along is decidedly not so much."

"You could ask."

"Ask and get fired? No thanks," she said as she headed for the door. "Look, you're simply going to have to deal with the fact that I'm going by myself, and I'll be fine."

"We'll see," he said with a grin.

"Nick, I love you, but if we're going to make this work, you've got to trust me to handle things. I got enough of the watchdog from dad growing up. It's one trip."

"I'm not your dad."

"I know," she said as she trotted over and kissed him. "I'm trying to keep it that way."

An hour and a half later, Clarice returned from her run, hot, sweaty, and pumped with endorphins. Her muscles ached, and her stomach growled in hunger, the latter being accentuated by the sight of a Rueben sandwich and sliced apples waiting for her on the kitchen counter.

"Thought you might like something to eat when you got back," Nick said, seated on the floor in the same spot as he was earlier.

Clarice studied the food-laden platter and gave a wary smile. "Thanks."

"Thought we might make some sushi tonight too," he added, trying to manage a poker face. "Spider rolls, maybe?"

Clarice smacked her lips, and despite the growing deluge in her mouth, she did not reach for the sandwich. Instead, she folded her arms and leaned against the wall, smiling as she did. "You fight dirty."

"Love you, too."

Clarice's eyes met his, melted, and surrendered—partially at least. She pushed off from the wall with her shoulder and made for the telephone hanging on the wall. "Okay, okay," she said. "I'll call and ask. But I'm just asking. I'm not pushing this one bit."

"Never said you had to."

"And either way, you owe me a massage when I get out of the shower," she said, drawing the corner of her mouth back.

"Oh, I do, do I?"

"Yes, you do."

"You're really going to milk this, aren't you?"

Clarice went over and kissed him softly. "I am," she said. "But I'm worth it."

"Sometimes," Nick replied with a wink. "Truth is, I just can't resist a redhead. Other than that, you're not all that."

Clarice playfully punched him in the arm before heading back to the kitchen, grabbing the phone, and dialing the office. "Mr. Conner?" she said once the line was answered. "It's Clarice. I have a question." She stopped and listened intently as her boss took the conversation over.

"Yes but—" she tried to get in, but was quickly drowned out.

"I'm sorry it's not—" Clarice put the phone down, ran her fingers through her hair, and rolled her eyes before picking it up once more. "Mr. Conner!" she shouted.

When the conversation had come to a definitive pause, she took a deep breath and continued in a more civil, hopefully still employed, manner. "Mr. Conner, I know someone who can fix your laptop faster than anyone else in the world. But if you want it ready for tomorrow, he'll have to come with us."

Five minutes and fourteen praises later, Clarice hung up the phone.

Chapter Three

Colmera Springs had but one dirt road that led out of town. It ran a short stint south but eventually turned east for the view. Due to years of neglect, the road had become overgrown with all manner of vegetation and was little more than a weed-infested footpath that limped its way down the mountainside. At the end of its run was the small town of Seraville, which sat on the side of a county road. According to the most recent census data, Seraville consisted of four people, three buildings and one car. There was at this time, however, at least one change: the recent addition of a black and brown Blazer from Kentucky.

Clarice was sitting in the back seat going over her notes when Ryan Conner, Tax Collector, pulled his Pathfinder alongside this new addition. Her mind was still trying to catalog the myriad of forms and procedures Ryan had been rattling off for the past hour, and as such, she was surprised when their journey came to an end. Part of her was grateful to be free from such a long car ride, but another part dreaded the day to come. With a little luck, she prayed, her boss would realize the wild goose chase they were on and they could return home posthaste.

"Let's get to work," Ryan said, eagerly stepping from his vehicle. "There's much to do and little time to do it."

Clarice, with less pizzazz than her employer, exited from a rear passenger door and stretched her limbs, ignoring his continued ramblings. At the start of the trip, she had remained attentive to her employer's needs. The long drive, however, had taken its toll. Her mood had changed, and she was now as amicable as a stomach pump. Fortunately for the future of her employment status, Ryan was too excited to take note.

"Just imagine, a gold mine of taxes mere miles away, and these poor sods won't even collect on it," Ryan said, taking in a deep breath. He took a pause from his self-induced ecstasy and studied the buildings. They all needed tending to, the rusted boathouse especially. The tax collector slumped and shook his head. "Property values around here must be atrocious."

"God, I hope this doesn't take long," said Clarice. "I still say we could've just sent them a letter. Or a phone call."

"First, it would take too long, and second, as you, Ms. Clarice, pointed out earlier, who would sign for it?" Ryan said, turning back toward her. "Besides, I want to be able to tell the judge later that we personally ensured its delivery. Going the extra mile like that can make a big difference in the courtroom, not to mention solidify our claim for a whistleblower's reward."

Nick, only a step behind Clarice at this point, slung his laptop bag over his shoulder before weighing in on the conversation. "Fed Ex does overnight, and you can track it every step of the way." When Ryan shot a glare toward him, he quickly amended, "But I'm stating the obvious, aren't I?"

Clarice sent him a disapproving look of her own. His job was to fix a laptop, no more, no less. The less he talked, the less he rocked the boat, and the greater the chance she might survive this weekend with her job intact.

"Yes, you are," Ryan said, apparently ignoring his secretary's reaction. He looked around again, and his eyes drifted from the town proper to where someone had arranged countless small, carved rocks into long rows that extended down the hillside. "Now where do you suppose Mr. Whittam went?"

"We could ask," Clarice offered. She motioned toward an aged man sitting on a nearby porch, whittling in his rocker. "I'm sure he knows."

"Come again?" Ryan said, eyes scanning. "Oh, yes!"

Quick in step, the three approached the town's reigning whittling champion. His skin looked like the piece of basswood he had in his hands, and his overalls looked like they had been under one too many leaky engine blocks. His smile was warm, but his eyes looked lifeless, as if the tenant behind them stepped out for frequent vacations.

"You the guy who uses stamps for the phone?" the old man said once they reached the foot of his porch. "You look like the sort that might."

"I'm the man you mistakenly thought was trying to use stamps for the phone, yes," Ryan corrected. "I am Mr. Ryan Conner, Tax Collector. This is my assistant, Ms. Clarice, and her computer technician, Nicholas."

The man gave a friendly wave to all three. "Name's Martin. Ma is upstairs, taking a nap. Everyone else ran to the store. Have yourself a seat if you like."

"I don't mean to be rude, but we haven't the time," Clarice cut in before anyone could take him up on the offer. "We need to deliver a notice and get moving."

"Good to be productive," Martin said and returned to his woodwork.

"So, if you could point us to where Mr. Whittam ran off to, we'd appreciate it," Nick chimed in after a lull in the conversation.

"Won't do you no good," Martin replied. He pointed toward the mountain with his pocketknife and gave it a wiggle. "No one lives there, and if your friend ain't back by now, he ain't ever coming back. You might as well go home now while it's still light out. Lot safer that way, too."

Ryan cleared his throat and squared himself in front of Martin. "I'm here to collect, Mr. Martin, and no one will stop me, not even death. The best one can hope for is an extension, but payment will be made in the end. And I think it's safe to say these people have already been granted quite the extension, wouldn't you agree?"

Martin blew sharply on his piece of basswood and continued whittling. "I ain't here to argue with you. But my conscience wouldn't be clear if I didn't at least say something."

"Well, thank you," Clarice cut in. "But could you please just tell us where we need to go?"

For the moment, Martin ignored her request. "If you'd like, you can borrow one of my shotguns," he offered the three. "All sorts of things run around the mountains. Some ain't too friendly."

"Thank you, but no," Ryan said.

"Rifle then?" he offered. "Old Betsy kicks like a mule, but I got a couple of others that ought to be okay for folks like you. I even have one for the pretty little lady. Won't put down a bear or nothing, but that ain't your worry here. Folks up that way ain't right in the head. They like to eat, if you understand me."

"I'm not interested in their eating habits," Ryan stated. "And more importantly, I don't want the responsibility of caring for someone else's possessions."

"We only want directions," Clarice tacked on. "And if there aren't any lions or bears or crazy people trying to shoot us, I think we'll be fine."

"Nope. Bears and lions ain't around here. In fact, most of the critters we used to see have gone. Ain't no one with weapons there either." The old man grunted and then motioned toward the woods with his hand. "Well, off you go then and have yourselves a look. Take that old dirt trail up into the mountains. A few hours hike maybe if you're fast; little less coming back, of course. I've painted crosses on the trees where the path gets a little hard to follow, but you ought to find the place good enough."

"Thank you," Clarice said with a great exhale. Her muscles relaxed and hope for a quick day's work bubbled from within.

Martin pointed with his knife toward the field of gravestones. "When you meet them, keep your distance and don't be looking to make friends. They don't take kindly to people from the outside, and I hate cleaning up the mess and making things right."

"I'm not here to make friends," Ryan said. "I'm here to do my job in a proper and efficient manner. I assure you that whatever their reaction may be, I carry the full authority of my position as tax collector. They will respect that authority."

In the beginning, Martin tried to warn newcomers about Colmera Springs. He told them that it was a dangerous place, filled with people that were centuries old and never seemed to die. He told them of acts of cannibalism and deadly disease. He told them all of these things, and in the end, for his efforts, Martin was fitted in a warm, snug, white jacket and given a padded room to sleep in, both of which made whittling a difficult task.

To make matters worse, more people came with lovely white jackets and black stethoscopes and did anything but listen, despite their claims they would. Each time he told the truth about what he had seen, whittling became more and more difficult. Finally, Martin gave up, and a few weeks later he was released with a lifetime supply of prescriptions.

From that point on, his wife and three children lived a good Christian life, all the while staying clear of their ornery neighbors. They decided to keep running the gas station and gift shop, to close each day of business with devotion, bible study, and prayer, and take solace in the fact that they tried their best. After all, what more could be expected of them?

Occasionally one of Colmera Spring's inhabitants managed to work its way down the path. Usually, it wouldn't get within a hundred yards or two of the house before it was given a proper shot in the head and decent burial. Ma was always first to volunteer to officiate the memorial service, mostly because she felt it was the motherly thing to do for one who had been without a mother for so long. Pa had challenged her on how she knew they were without a mother in jest one day, to which she in all seriousness had replied, "No momma would let them out dressed like that."

As Clarice, Ryan, and Nick took to the path, Martin watched and said a little prayer for the three as they disappeared into the tree line.

Chapter Four

Almost a hundred and sixty years before Ryan Conner, Tax Collector undertook his crusade to Colmera Springs, some men found a few shiny rocks in a nameless river near the West Coast. Shortly after this discovery, thousands and thousands of people—people who weren't satisfied with their own rocks—took to ship, horse and foot in order to join the fun. Some made it; some didn't. A number of those who didn't had decided to feed the local wildlife, namely bacteria and carrion eaters. Other travelers performed the same job, only in a marine environment.

The founders of Colmera Springs, however, took a different approach to those involved with the California Gold Rush. The philosophy these pioneers had was simple: Why travel thousands of miles to grab rocks and play in water when perfectly good rocks and waters were much closer? With that in mind, these brave men and women loaded their wagons, shoed their horses and ended up a few hundred miles south of Pennsylvania.

The first few months of the town's settlement saw tremendous growth. Houses, shops, stables, and a first-class saloon, complete with lodging above and an affable bartender below, were quickly built. Though these were all needed, the population also felt that they should keep up with the progress in California, and so they dug a pair of mines and constructed a few sailing ships, but by the year's end they were abandoned (fashion trends were fickle in the 19th century, and more than one person had theorized that the townsfolk had lost their sanity due to some unknown virus running rampant).

Time marched on. Town residents grew ill here and there, and more than one became a touch mad—well, madder than they already were when they built the marina. Funny how something that affects the mind keeps making things worse and worse.

One particular day, no mail came from the disheveled mountain town. No one on the outside thought anything of it, and even if they did, no one cared enough to find out why. A short while later, a nameless postman delivered two parcels to Colmera Springs, but to no further place on his route. From that point on, the town faded out of people's minds—primarily since no one had ever found a rock worth bringing back.

Of all of Colmera Springs' citizens, Jack was one of the youngest when the twenty-first century dawned. He sported an eighty-something-year-old body that was the envy of all. It was free from rot, save for a small patch in his abdominal cavity that allowed him to keep his pet rat Mandi close to his heart. His skin was a pale moon white, blotched here and there with hues of purple and blue, and it was nearly intact as only a portion of his scalp was missing where his left ear had once been. Aside from the Van Gogh look, the only other thing Jack was missing were two toes from his right foot. Despite this lack of piggies, all four of his appendages were in good working order, which made grabbing and chasing meals simple.

Though Jack had the one up on all the other zombies in terms of physical fitness, there were two things that they all shared in common: First, they could each only remember two things at any one point in time (three with a pair of half-truths). And second, no one had the desire to explore outside of the town proper. Meals came from time to time, and a good game of Eats was had and enjoyed by all, which was all that mattered. Thus, the inhabitants of Colmera Springs kept to themselves.

A few times in the past, however, Jack had explored the countryside. Each time he left, all that he found were more of the same rocks he'd seen before, which sat near the same tall trees and the same short bushes. There were also the same streams that never left, and since their vocabulary was even more limited than his own, it made for boring conversation.

The one time Jack did find something unique to the area, it only served to annoy and teach him all he needed to know about humans: they were fickle and contradictory, especially about their attitudes toward the walking dead.

The incident started while Jack was taking a nap along a country road. His restful sleep was disturbed by a passerby who ran off in a hurry. This passerby soon returned with not one, or even two or three, but dozens and dozens of others who were all intent on not letting Jack sleep one iota, try as he might.

Some came with lights on their cars, chalk in their hands, and radios on their shoulders. Others were dressed in lab coats, rubber gowns, masks, and latex gloves. Some held cameras and snapped off pictures faster than a rampaging herd of paparazzi, while still others insisted that they move Jack on their stretcher to someplace new.

As far as Jack could tell, everyone was fine and dandy as they went about watching, prodding, giving sympathies, and making outlines of his sleeping quarters. But when Jack had decided enough was enough, and it was time to go home, all they wanted to do was run around and scream.

First, they yelled at Jack, then at each other, and then back at him. Eventually, there was too much screaming, and like any loud argument, it left Jack stressed. So he ate, starting with a supple, young brunette that was within arm's length. Then there was even more screaming, which led to more eating as well as a few dozen gunshots. By the end of the episode, Jack had made a new friend, Danita.

Danita was a clever sort, and once she returned with Jack, she was the new envy of all the other zombies. For whatever reason, the Lord had blessed her with the ability to remember three things at once (four with a pair half-truths), which enabled her to become quite the philosopher, theologian, and game maker.

The position of game maker was markedly more difficult to fulfill than others. Games had to be entertaining and have clear rules that could be understood. They had to have fine packaging, smart names, and impressive marketing to compete with all the other games that were available to the undead populace such as Rock-Paper.

As wonderful as all the games were, they did little to progress the zombies as a whole. It was the study of theology and philosophy that spurred the evolution of zombie communication. Before Danita had been introduced into their ranks, the language they spoke, which was more of an intricate gesture-by-standing, was incomplete. In her discussions, she brought in the missing key—syllables.

This new component brought to life all sorts of fantastic conversations between the inhabitants of Colmera Springs. Jack had already been fond of picking the brains of others and now enjoyed what Danita had to offer.

On this particular, present day, it was during an intense debate of whether or not there existed life before death that Jack spotted a figure approaching the town. Soon a few other shapes appeared behind it. They all stank of freshness.

With a grunt and a gesture, Jack pointed the group out to Danita. She stood in response. They both agreed that the leader held a particularly strange aura about him, one that exuded confidence. Jack started to shuffle toward them. Danita said she had a thought to spare and felt it might be a good idea to utilize it. Apparently, she wanted to lead them closer.

Jack growled, and his stomach agreed. Anytime was a good time to eat. And if these people were going to walk right at him, he saw no reason to try and hide, despite Danita's protests about spoiling a good ambush.

He got only a few steps before his zombie friend spun him around and drew his attention to the parlor with one of her partial, withered fingers. She then reminded Jack how pleasant it would be to have a good nap. Jack, of course, was never one to turn down naptime. And even though he had already been sold on the idea of going back inside, Danita added a bit of icing on the cake by pointing out that inside the parlor, he wouldn't be disturbed by people with chalk.

Jack grunted with pleasure, and with all thoughts removed of the approaching humans, he shuffled into the parlor with Danita right behind.

Clarice had opted to take the lead as they progressed up the mountainside, and her attitude continued to brighten that this would soon all be over. And when it was, she decided, she'd treat herself to a pleasant day at the spa, followed by snuggle time and a movie to smooth things over with Nick. Maybe she'd dig up her French maid outfit for him, too, as an added bonus for putting up with her abuse the past day or so. She knew she could get a little bitchy under a lot of stress, and she was grateful he had the patience of a saint with her.

She also decided, as they traveled, that her employer, Ryan Conner, may have been built for collecting taxes, but he was not built for climbing mountains. Whereas she and Nick traversed the terrain with little difficulty, he made his ascent with the grace of a tipped cow. After three hours of watching him stumble over rocks, logs, and pseudo-pitfalls, the three arrived at a strange construction of timber. The path, having seen all of it before, ran ahead, over a river and through the woods.

Clarice stopped first and asked what she assumed everyone else was thinking. "What is this?"

"Ruins of something," Ryan said with a dismissing hand. After a moment's rest, he added, "Let's not stare at poor caretaking all day, even if such bad practice is going to lower the land value."

Nick circled the nearest clump of wood. He tapped it twice and then pushed hard with his thumb. "I think..." he said hesitantly. "I think it's a mast. But it's preserved by something, almost petrified."

"From a ship?" Ryan said, without looking twice. "I think not."

"I'm pretty sure it is," Nick said, crouching down and examining the ground. "I don't really see what else it might be. This right here has to be a mast."

"It's not a mast," said Clarice. "I really didn't mean to stop us for an hour while we figure this out. Let's get going."

Nick ignored the request. He paced about the immediate area, measuring distances with his arms and stride as he did. "I bet those are booms and gaffs," he continued. "And that's got to be a block, or what's left of one. They're all in the right places."

Clarice, having had her hope of a quick exit from the mountains snatched from her by an overly curious fiancé, prayed for an end to the insanity. "Yeah, I'm sure someone just dropped off a frigate as they were hiking through."

"No, really. I mean it," said Nick. With his hands pointing to spots on the ground on either side of him, he tried his best to show what he explained. "Look, there's the bow—the front of the ship. The aft—back end—is over there. You can even see the entire hull if you just imagine it not so covered with moss and plants, and not quite as flat."

"And how did it get up here, mister smarty-pants?" she asked.

"I don't know. Maybe it ran aground."

"Aground!"

"Why not? A careless skipper is all it would take."

"It ran aground on top of a mountain!" she exclaimed.

Nick's face tangled in a giant ball of confusion. "It's been known to happen."

"No, it hasn't," she retorted with force. "Not once has anyone ever hit the top of a mountain!"

"Well, Noah did."

Clarice blinked, stupefied and unsure if he was being serious or a smartass. "Excluding Noah, no one has ever done this," she said, enunciating every syllable. "And I don't see a petting zoo around, so let's assume it wasn't him, okay?"

Nick sighed. "Look, I'm not saying that I know how it got here, okay?" he said. It was clear he was trying to placate her as best he knew how. "I just know what I'm looking at, and I'm telling you those are the remains of a ship right there." He then looked a little farther off. "And I would wager that's another one, too."

"You're saying there are now two ships here, son?" Ryan said with a calm voice.

"Yes," Nick replied. "At least, I think so."

"But you aren't sure?" Ryan asked.

"I'm not completely positive, no," Nick admitted. "But if I had to place a twenty on it, I'd say those are boats and would be something to at least check out later."

"For what, sunken treasure?" Clarice mocked.

"Well, you'd need to be certified for wreck diving first," he said with a grin.

"Gah!" she yelled. With that, Clarice stomped away a dozen paces and sat on a fallen tree. A fallen tree, she told herself, not a broken mast—a fallen tree that just happened to have been gnawed upon in a few curious places. By beavers. Curious beavers. Satisfied with the explanation, Clarice thought to pursue it no further.

"Clarice," Ryan called to her. "Don't you know what this means? This is fabulous news if it's true!"

She turned her face slowly toward him. "What, exactly, does this mean?"

"A marina means higher property values, Ms. Clarice," he beamed.

"It's not a marina," she replied. She turned toward Nick whose mouth was partially open and eyebrows slightly arched. She knew that look. "What? What are you just dying to spit out?"

Nick gave a sheepish shrug. "Well," he said with hesitation. "It could be a marina. Or could have been, rather."

Clarice grabbed a nearby, fallen branch and threw it at his head. "It's not a goddamn marina," she barked. She took a deep breath and exhaled sharply. "It's not a marina," she said once more, softening her tone. "Sorry about the stick. I'm tired and just want to get home. None of this is helping."

Nick gave it a kick across the forest floor and sent it flying to some bushes. "No worries," he said. "Your aim is horrible."

"Why would there be a marine in the mountains without at least it being on a lake?"

Nick shrugged. "I don't know. Maybe they were going to make one or thought they could. Maybe everyone's brains shriveled up, and they thought it was a genuinely good idea. Who knows? I'm only saying what it looks like."

"Fine. I don't want to argue about it anymore, but if you could think of something else it might look like—something else that at least feels somewhat normal—I'd appreciate it."

"Ms. Clarice," Ryan said, drawing her attention back to her employer. His arms folded across his chest and his brow furrowed. "Do you like collecting taxes?"

"Yes," she lied.

"Good. Because I would hate to think you are purposefully trying to lower the land value around here and sabotaging our collection efforts."

"I'm not."

"Good, because if I say this is a marina..." his voice trailed as he raised an eyebrow.

"It's a marina," finished Clarice, who at this point was pretty sure Ryan Conner, Tax Collector would have been sprawled out on the ground had he been within arm's reach at the end of that statement. But luckily for her employment status and his nose, he was still a few paces away.

A short while later, long enough to put the newfound marina out of sight but not out of memory, the trio reached Colmera Springs. They paused and gazed upon what no living mortal had seen in over three days' time.

The path dodged between a number of scattered, dilapidated buildings. It found its end surrounded on three sides by some of the larger constructions of the town, taking on the shape of a deflated tire. Standing near one of the buildings was a couple who took brief note of the new arrivals before ignoring them and sloughing off toward one of the larger, still standing structures.

"You there!" Ryan called out, picking up his pace. "I would like to talk to you!"

His attempt to gain the inhabitants' attention failed miserably. The two people continued on their way and soon pushed through a rickety door and disappeared from sight.

Ryan stopped in his tracks for a minute. "Hmph," was his only comment. His skin turned a bright red, and his brow furrowed.

"Not the most hospitable folk, are they?" Clarice said, catching up from behind. "Maybe they're pissed off they weren't hired as deckhands," she teased, turning toward her fiancé.

"Not funny," Nick replied. "You'll see I'm right."

"No, I won't," she said quickly. "I'm not coming back to this stupid place."

"As long as we get everything done that we need to do, yes," Ryan interjected. "But we might need to return later if Mr. Whittam has decided to stay here. I want my stamps, and I want to know what his involvement is here." He then paused, looked down at his empty wrist and asked, "What time is it, Ms. Clarice?"

"Three-thirty," she said, checking her sports watch.

"Mark it down." Ryan reached into his right pocket for one of his cheap, ballpoint pens and eagerly twirled it in his fingers. His other hand reached into his left pocket, pulled forth a rubber stamp, gave it a squeeze several times, and then returned it. His posture straightened, and his chest moved forward an inch before he started his march to the parlor door. "Let's get this thing rolling and get out of this blasted heat."

Clarice wiped her forehead and glanced skyward. The sun had gone from hot to scorching in the last ten minutes. She pulled her hair back into a ponytail, using her favorite Buccaneer's scrunchie to complete the maneuver. "I can't believe these buildings are even standing. You'd think the heat would melt them in a day. How can anyone live in such a craptastic place?"

"What do you think Martin meant about them not being too friendly?" Nick asked. His eyes darted from building to building and from shadow to shadow. "I have a feeling I'm going to regret being here."

Clarice followed her fiancé's eyes, and the more she looked at the ruined structures, the more she wished she wasn't there either.

Ryan's expression was the only one that did not change. "Not many are terribly friendly in this job," he said. "Does it matter?"

"I don't want to get shot by some crazed hick," Nick explained, turning to face Ryan. "I've been shot before, and it's not fun."

"You got shot by a pellet gun when you were nine," said Clarice. The ridiculousness of his statement brought welcome, temporary relief to her anxiety. "Let's not pretend it's some grand war wound."

"Oh sure, when you put it like that it's not nearly as heroic," Nick replied, showing no signs of offense or embarrassment at getting called out. "And when you're nine, it might as well have been a shotgun blast. That thing hurt like a bitch."

Ryan looked over at both of them, his face chiseled with determination. "I can assure you beyond any sort of doubt, you won't be shot today."

"How do you know?" Nick asked. He stuffed his hands into his pockets and an eyebrow raised.

"As sure as I am a tax collector, it will not happen," he said, marking the end of the conversation. Ryan rapped on the half-open door, using enough force to make it swing open. "See?" he said with a crooked smile. "They've invited us in."

Clarice rolled her eyes at the skirting of legalities. "No electricity it would seem," she said, peering inside at a world of shadows. "You'll never get any real land value out of this."

"Doesn't matter," her employer said, pushing the door open a few more inches and stepping in. "We collect anywhere and everywhere, Ms. Clarice. With these many years in default, the interest and penalties are the sources of all the monies owed."

Clarice followed, only to stop and start gagging. "Good god! Don't they have plumbing?"

Nick brought up the rear, hands over his nose and mouth. "Thanks for the warning."

The inside of the building looked like it was the home of a family of disgruntled rhinoceroses. The walls, floors, and ceiling all had various holes in various places. A dozen pieces of furniture lay scattered about. Most were broken. A few looked rotted. All, however, were beyond any sort of repair. At the far side of the room, shrouded in darkness, was a body—a human body. It lay on its back and twitched occasionally, but did not seem to take note of its new guests.

"Sir," Ryan shouted. "Might I have a word with you?"

When the person didn't answer, Ryan called out to him again and received the same response.

"Give me a flashlight," said Ryan.

Clarice shrugged, as did Nick.

"Christ," Ryan swore as he patted his pockets. "I thought you were going to come prepared. What the hell kind of assistant are you if you can't assist?"

"No one said anything about needing flashlights," Clarice replied, her defensive edge ringing in her voice. Her gaze shifted from her employer to Jack, who was still motionless on the floor. She tried to ignore the weird that was settling in. "Do you suppose he's alright?"

"Isn't he the one we just followed?" Nick interjected. He took a tentative step toward Jack and tried to peer through the darkness. "That has to be him."

"Doesn't mean he might not have had a heart attack or something," she replied. "Or tripped and hit his head."

"Sir!" Ryan said a third time. He turned back to his companions, motioned for them to follow, and then approached. With a prod of his Timberlands, Ryan addressed Jack a fourth time. "Now, sir, I am done being polite with you!"

The man on the floor opened an eye socket and regarded his visitors. "Urrhhh?" he moaned inquisitively, still in a half sleep.

Ryan turned back toward Clarice. "See? He's fine."

Clarice's hands trembled. Soon, the rest of the muscles in her body joined the mutiny as the light illuminated a rising corpse. "Oh, my god," she said, backing up. Her brain stalled as it tried to make sense of what her eyes took in. Despite being covered by tattered combat fatigues and smothered in shadow, Clarice could still see well into the creature's abdominal cavity. And when a curious rat poked its head out from inside, Clarice went into a full panic.

"Get out!" she yelled. "Get out now!"

Both Nick and Ryan stood confused, neither reacting to Clarice's shouts. They did, however, see another zombie approach from behind the door and lunge at Clarice.

The young woman had already spun around to make a run for the door when a second withered—but very much animated—corpse fell atop her. Clarice stiff-armed her attacker, turned with the momentum generated by the zombie and smacked it with the leather-bound portfolio she was carrying as she dashed out.

Nick had been with Clarice long enough by this point and had learned his lessons well. Consequently, whenever she made her exit for whatever reason, he did the same.

Ryan was slower to leave than the other two, but he stormed outside for different reasons. "Ms. Clarice!" he yelled, pushing past the now off-balance female zombie. "Get back here at once with that demand notice!"

Clarice stopped and spun on her heels. Nick came to a rest at her side, and her eyes widened. She stared as the two corpses lunged from behind her employer and grabbed Ryan firmly by the shoulders. She watched herself pull Nick back when he went to go help as other figures oozed from the buildings, groaning with each step they took. She wasn't sure what she yelled at her fiancé, but whatever it was, it was enough to keep him with her as she took off down the mountainside.

Chapter Five

Few children when questioned about what they would like to do when they grow up ever answer ballpoint pen salesmen. Nor will they usually answer with something such as ballpoint pen engineer. Certainly some unique individuals have replied with something akin to, "I want to be a ballpoint pen." But the actual designing and marketing of ballpoint pens is utterly dull to the world's population.

This was the slump that Henry Bollivor was in during World War II. Several companies had enjoyed success when it came to engineering and selling their particular brand of ballpoint pen; one hundred and seven other companies by Henry's last count. What few ballpoint pen engineers there were to be had were already employed elsewhere, which made designing structurally sound pens difficult for the entrepreneur. As luck would have it, Henry Bollivor did manage to win two in a game of pinochle, and his company's future brightened.

Henry was a diligent and fair man. He kept his two engineers well paid and happy as he expanded his small company. In a meeting with the company's nine shareholders, it was decided that sales might improve if they marketed pens that were more than just pens. Everyone could make pens that could write. Some of the pens even wrote well. But to the best of Henry's knowledge, there wasn't an established multi-functioning pen market, something like a Swiss Army pen.

The actual design of the pen was a difficult task, at least in terms of keeping the desired product pen-like. It was easy to add things like a magnifying glass, or saw, or knife in addition to the pen, but it always produced at best, a boxy, Swiss Army knife-looking pen, which Henry decided he did not want. One version that remained true to the pen form was the luncheon pen. Sadly, it was found lacking in taste and had the habit of asphyxiating the user.

Everyone agreed that that particular line should be closed until R&D could revamp it, which they never did. But they continued to push the envelope, attempting to go where no pen engineer had gone before.

After a series of failed design attempts, six hundred and thirteen by Henry's last count, it was settled that perhaps instead of changing the overall design of the pen, the company's product could be marketed with instructions that included a variety of other handy things the pen was capable of other than writing.

The chief ballpoint pen engineer found this job much easier since he could pass the task off to the marketing department. With his mornings now free, he could spend them working out the plans for a perfect glass, one that would never be half empty.

Of the seven hundred and ninety-nine uses that were spitballed during the final roundtable for the catalog product number 31A, green metallic shell ballpoint pen, not one made mention of "self-defense against the walking dead." Nor did they come up with a variation of "distraction object for the easily distracted." The latter Henry's company would have considered had they, when looking for use eight hundred, not all become completely enthralled with how the reflective surface of number 31A caught the ceiling lights.

Yet despite not knowing any of this, or caring if he had, Jack watched his newest meal pull out a 1941, catalog product number 31A, green metallic shell, ballpoint pen and stab him just below the left collar bone.

Jack snarled, kept his rusty, iron grip on the man, and looked down at the improvised pike. It was shiny. It had a gleam to it. It induced a sensation that shoals of bass and hovers of trout had experienced near the end of their lives, and it made Jack want to look at it more. Play with it perhaps, and possibly even take a bite.

Jack grunted, let go of his meal, and pulled the pen out of his body.

Suddenly, a rarity happened. It wasn't the sort that some might claim frivolously, such as finding the closest parking space or just that right flavor of blackberry preserves to go with morning toast. This, instead, was a genuine, bona fide rarity that would leave statisticians everywhere checking their numbers for months. And once their labor was finished, a new constant would be born—Jack's constant.

And the rarity was this: Jack had an epiphany. It was a realization that rammed headlong through numerous, insurmountable barriers and reached Jack's mind with the subtlety of a charging hippo. It knocked aside all two of Jack's thoughts (grabbing and chewing) and stepped on them a few times for good measure, just to make sure Jack was paying attention. Through all of the dried blood, spatter, and goop that clung to the catalog product number 31A, green metallic shell ballpoint pen, Jack was sure the writing utensil was his own.

And he was right.

The human mind has always been a remarkable piece of machinery. At times, however, it has needed maintenance, and that was what Clarice's left hand was doing that early evening. She sat inside Martin's small house, leaning forward with her forehead resting on the palm of her hand. Her fingers were methodically massaging her scalp, prodding, pushing, and pulling in an attempt to repair the damage that had been done to her psyche. Her right hand was off to the side, pencil in hand, doodling on the back of an old envelope. Her left hand had no idea what the right was doing, nor did it care.

The room she was in was of ordinary design. It had the standard ceiling, painted off-white, with a little bit of a slope to it for variety. It was held aloft by the tried and true method of placing a set of walls underneath. Two of the walls had been designed by master architects to allow the passage of matter from one side to the other, such a feat being accomplished by including doorways into their construction. The pictures, furniture, television and dog that also occupied the room appeared to be well within the norms of existence. The latter occasionally did dog-like things, such as wag its tail, lick the back of her hand, or blow refreshing bits of dog breath into Clarice's face. Yet as much as she tried to settle into the fresh-from-the-dryer warm surroundings, her mind insisted that things didn't make sense.

Clarice repeated the thought a few more times. At least that made sense, and at least that was a start. The math minor in her wondered what the odds of this day happening were. Having no reference point or set of data to work from, the exact number eluded her. Nor could she remember any of her equations for basic statistics, and she was without her trusty calculator even if she could. Indeed, the chances of today were far less than the chances of an elephant in the bathroom. That much was beyond any sort of doubt. How would an elephant squeeze through the doorways to begin with? And why?

The thought troubled her, and she sat up in the chair. It was conceivable that an elephant could have made it into the bathroom, perhaps a pygmy elephant, or a baby, normal one. Or maybe the house had been built around the elephant. After all, elephants did exist and so did houses. Clarice then amended her impromptu statistics. *The chances of zombies actually existing are less than an elephant in the bathroom right here and now, playing the harpsichord.* She then quickly tacked on, *and drinking a nice cup of tea.*

Clarice settled back into the chair again and tried to think of something more pleasant, more mundane. Ease did not return to her state of being. The absence of Ryan Conner continued to push to the forefront of her memory. As much as she wanted to deny everything, she still couldn't, and over a period of a couple of minutes, another thought dawned on her. Clarice looked about to make sure no one was watching, got up, walked down the hall, and stopped at the bathroom door. She hesitated as she reached for the doorknob. Instead of turning it, she held her breath and pressed her ear against the door.

"This is so stupid," she said. Clarice flung the door open and stepped boldly in the room. Most of her used such a grandiose move to prove that she did not for one minute think there would be an elephant or even a harpsichord. The cup of tea maybe, but there definitely wouldn't be all three. A small part of her played along so she could catch said elephant in the act before it slipped away. That same small part of her, before she left to go outside, checked for footprints in the soap, just in case.

Nick's mind, being of a different make and model than Clarice's, took a completely different approach to coping. At first, he decided to debug the network communication program he was writing on his laptop. However, it wasn't long before he abandoned that task in favor of a more mundane one as he found his concentration fleeting. He ended up spending most of his time pacing about the porch, thinking of nothing else but how many steps it took to walk the circumference. The path turned out to be twenty-three steps long, though for some reason it was twenty-one if he started off with his left foot. It was an anomaly that he was now spending considerable time trying to explain and the best he could come up with was that it was a left-footed porch.

Nick stopped his ponderings and changed gears. He wondered what the proper fiancé response should be to near death by hordes of undead. This turned to a self-discussion on what Clarice might be thinking and feeling, and since he couldn't even fathom a logical explanation for the walking dead, he immediately tossed out all girlfriend subjects in favor of contemplating the porch's design once more.

Clarice came out of the house and joined Nick and Martin on the porch. She glanced at her fiancé who was busy pacing and for some reason, was counting his steps aloud. With a deep breath, Clarice composed herself as best as anyone else could have who had recently run down a mountainside after abandoning one's employer to a pair of hungry corpses. "Okay," she started. "What the hell is up there?"

"I imagine you've got a pretty good idea already," Martin answered, leaning back in his rocker. His eyes never met with hers, but would occasionally glance toward the tree line while his hands adjusted their grip on the shotgun in his lap. "Not like the little black bears cause such a stir, and I'm sure you've seen the picture shows before. Undead seem popular the last few years."

"Don't you think that's something you should have told us?" Clarice snapped back. "Did it slip your mind that your mountain is infested with zombies?"

"Now hang on, there's a logical reason to all of this," Nick said, stopping in both his tracks and his counting. "Once we know what we're dealing with we'll be better equipped to do something about it."

"I know what I saw!" she retorted. "There's no rational explanation to a half-decomposed body eating my boss!"

"Oh, there is," Martin said nonchalantly.

"Which would be what, exactly?"

"A half-decomposed body was eating your boss," he answered. Martin put down his pocketknife, reached down and pulled a smaller, curved blade from his toolbox and then continued both his woodwork and the conversation. "It's a pity. I'll grant you that. Ma would've liked him, I think. Regardless, stranger things have happened around here than what you saw."

Clarice blinked. The rapid raising and lowering of eyelids did little to purge her disbelief. "Like what?"

"Like a small fleet of ships on the top of a mountainside," Martin said, scratching his head. "Never did understand that one. Like a tiny marina."

"I told you," Nick said, butting in. He crossed his arms, and a smugness settled across his face. Despite Clarice's disapproving look, Nick topped off his point. "Now what do you have to say?"

"Nothing," she said. "And don't think this gives you an ace in the hole for some other argument, either."

"Oh, come on," Nick said. "You're still not going to admit you're wrong."

Clarice pressed her lips together. She knew he was teasing and never meant ill will, but for the life of her, she couldn't admit she was wrong on this one. "No."

"Course if you had listened to me in the beginning, we wouldn't be here at all. We'd be home." Nick said with a shrug.

Clarice felt her face flush as her body temp rose. "Are you trying to start something?"

"Christ," Nick said with his hands up. "Don't be so touchy. I'm only trying to lighten things up."

Clarice held the stern look. "That was a crappy way to lighten the mood."

"Sorry, I don't have my *What to do After a Zombie Attack* handbook readily available."

"Would it kill you not to badger me at least?" she asked with a groan of frustration.

"Now don't go getting all rude and mean to one another," Martin cut in as he waggled his finger at the two. "It's just the stress getting at your nerves. Y'all are taking this better than most who come back."

"Others?" Clarice reiterated. The idea that people knew of this place was inconceivable. "How many others have you sent off to die?"

Martin's expression remained calm. "I tried to warn you, but y'all would have none of it. I know when to keep my mouth shut, and it's not like any of you believe me when I do pipe up."

The young woman conceded the point and slumped against the wall. "You know," she said, thinking out loud, "you'd think all those ghost hunters would have a field day up here. That would put the nail in the coffin on the supernatural, don't you think?"

"Oh, they come every now and again," Martin replied, looking out over his property. "One of them hears about my big old graveyard and then brings his friends. All they want to do is show off their fancy toys and cameras, get spooked by the dog lapping some water and watch my house, as if it's going to get up on four legs and run off."

"And?"

"And what?" he asked, genuinely confused. "It hasn't run off yet. Then they get bored and end up like all the rest of you city folk. They decide to head up the trail despite my warnings and never come back. Well, not alive at least."

"But they would believe you."

"Only if I told them there were ghosts up there," he said. "I ain't spreading no tales about no ghosts. That's just stuff to scare the kids."

The logistics of their predicament popped into Clarice's mind, and she felt the color drain from her face. "Mr. Conner has the keys."

"You mean for the car?" Nick asked.

"Yes, for the car," she answered with a sigh. "It's his car, and he was the last to drive."

"I might be able to hotwire it," he offered. "I had a friend who could, and it didn't look too hard. I bet we could look it up online."

"Or we could call a locksmith," Clarice said.

"And tell them what when they want to see we own the car?" he replied.

Clarice leaned back and thumped her head into the wall absentmindedly. "Damn it to hell."

"Well I reckon that's not much of a problem for the two of you anyway," Martin said.

"Why is that?" Clarice asked.

The old man motioned toward the path. "Looks like your boss is coming down now."

"Holy shit."

"And then some," Nick added.

Martin took to his feet, twelve gauge in hand. "You two wait here," he said. "I've got to make sure he's right in the head, if you get my meaning."

Chapter Six

Clarice watched as Martin intercepted Ryan Conner, Tax Collector, who was finishing his descent down the mountainside. The two had a brief conversation out of earshot, but when it was over, Martin returned to the porch and Ryan headed straight for his Pathfinder.

Clarice leaped from the porch, intent on getting answers. But from the moment she reached his side, he ignored all of her questions and simply plucked a black duffel bag from the back of his SUV. It was only after Ryan brought the hatchback down in a decisive manner and began marching back to the house that Clarice, having had enough, blocked his path.

"Yes, Ms. Clarice?" he asked. His face was calm, collected, and determined. Moreover, it was decidedly not the face of someone that had been made a snack of a short time ago.

"Where are you going?" she demanded, hands on hips and a challenge in her eyes. Employment status at this point had been tossed to the wind, and she was reasonably sure if his answer wasn't along the lines of getting the hell out of Dodge, she was going to punch him square in the nose.

Ryan's face twisted, and she posed the question a second time. "That's a fine question," he finally replied. "Strange that I didn't think of it first, though. But I suppose that's what I keep you around for, isn't it?" His gaze drifted down to his keys, sparkling in the remaining daylight.

A moment passed, and a putrid smell wafted from his skin.

"Snap out of it!" Clarice yelled, drawing him away from the cluster of keys. Once Ryan's eyes reverted to her, she continued her interrogation, a fist balling at her right side.

"I'm going back inside to shower," Ryan answered while he adjusted the bag on his shoulder. "And after that, I'm going to eat and work out all that needs to be done. I want things in motion first thing in the morning."

"We're not leaving?" Clarice's fist tightened even further while a second one joined the fun.

"No," he replied. He then amended, "Why would we be?"

"Oh, I don't know," she said, being sure that her sarcasm dripped from every syllable. "Maybe because a dead corpse took a bite out of your shoulder?"

"Well," Ryan said after taking a few moments to answer. "What other kinds of corpses are there?" He paused again as if he needed to think about his own question before continuing. "You see, Clarice, a corpse can be one of many kinds. The most obvious is the fresh kind, but there is also the dried kind, the preserved kind, the withered kind, the kind missing a few pieces and so on. If we also decided to categorize various corpses by their location, such as buried, not buried, in catacombs, on the lawn, in the freezer, or if they were taxpayers, the number of variations grows even more. But all are definitively dead—that's undeniable."

Clarice stared at him, trying to make sense of his monologue. When he started to move around her, her brain rebooted and picked the conversation back up where the crash had occurred. "There's not one good reason for us to stay here," she said with force.

"Partially true," he admitted. "There's not one—there are at least three."

"Such as?"

"First, I want my stamps," he said. "And we must find Mr. Whittam to get the proper stamps I want."

"Second?"

It was now Ryan's turn to be confused. He looked at her inquisitively. "Second what?"

"What's the second reason?"

"For?"

Confusion, via osmosis, seeped into her mind. "Why we are staying, I think?"

"Oh yes, the two reasons why we can't leave," he said, smiling. "First, we have to collect taxes. And second, Martin doesn't want to let me leave yet."

"Why?"

"I haven't the foggiest. But he's a nice enough fellow for a hillbilly, and he's providing free room and board. Might as well take him up on it, no?"

"Look, I just want to go home at this point," she said. "Coming here was a big mistake, and thankfully, we can still walk away from this mistake. Look at yourself! You're in tatters!" She stammered a moment, trying to pull it all together. Finally, she got one last question out. "I mean, didn't you ask why?"

"Ask why, what?" Ryan asked. "I have this nagging suspicion that this is the second time you are muddling the conversation, but for the life of me, I can't figure out what your motive is."

"Why he won't let you leave!"

Ryan didn't answer; instead, he turned his head at the glimpse of color. There was a bag on his shoulder, bright, red, and partially unzipped. Protruding slightly from this was a large sandwich bag containing a few toiletry items, all of which did not go well on top of or inside sandwiches. Despite their ban for use in a sandwich, they all fit snugly inside the sandwich bag.

"Don't you think we should find out why you can't leave?" Clarice asked.

"No. What I think I need is a shower, Ms. Clarice," Ryan answered. "I seem to have injured my shoulder as well, and I need to change clothes, too, what with the blood and all."

"You can do all of that in a hotel," she stated. "This place isn't safe!"

"I'm not discussing this any further."

And with that, Clarice drove her fist directly into her boss's cheek. It was a good, solid hit and similar ones had dropped at least two boys in high school that couldn't keep their hands to themselves. But much to her surprise and dismay, Ryan remained upright and unfazed.

"Oh...god...I'm so sorry," Clarice said, mortified at what she'd done. That was it. She was going to be fired, probably thrown in jail, too. Nick would leave her, and her family would disown her as the former daughter who couldn't even hold down a basic government job.

"Don't do that again, Ms. Clarice," he said. "And while I'm making requests, I'd appreciate it if you had a cup of coffee ready for me once I'm done. Lots of cream, lots of sugar." With that, he stepped around her and headed inside the house, leaving her to cry in frustration.

Ryan passed by Nick and Martin, both of whom were now sitting in the living room and gave each a short nod. He ignored their stares, bumped into a wall or two, and entered the bathroom. After tossing his bag in the corner, he turned on the shower, undressed, and took the soap from the sink. He worked a thick lather across his chest and spread it across the rest of his body. Though he had taken countless showers throughout his life, this was the first he could recall taking with numb fingers and toes. In fact, the more he thought about it, this was the only shower he could recall, period.

Ryan pushed the anomaly to the side when he noted that the water smelled of sulfur. The odor surfaced memories long passed, and he thought of his first property seizure, a dilapidated, condemned shack with a plumbing nightmare that sat on a half-acre. His assistant at the time did a marvelous job in expediting the process, unlike the one he had now. But hopefully, Ms. Clarice could be trained. If not, she still looked absolutely delicious.

Ten minutes later, he stepped out, refreshed, hungry, and wearing a new set of clothes.

"Feel better?" Clarice asked once Ryan had descended the stairs and not trying to sound awkward about the encounter. The punch on the cheek she had given him earlier was beginning to bruise nicely, making her worry yet again he'd be pressing assault charges on her in no time.

Ryan sat down in a white recliner and pressed his fingers on the armrests. "I do, quite a bit. Thank you."

"And your shoulder?" she asked. Maybe if she directed his attention to those corpses trying to kill them, he'd forget she socked him, and she'd stay gainfully employed.

"Still hurts, but the shower seems to have helped," Ryan answered, looking over at it. "It's funny how a little bit of soap and water can revitalize the body and mind."

"Good," she said, tossing a three-year-old magazine back on the table. "I imagine you'll want to head home then, right?"

"I can't be letting that happen yet," Martin interjected. His voice took a stern, unyielding tone to it. "Mr. Ryan isn't free to go for another few days."

"You can't stop us." Her posture matched the challenge in her voice.

Martin shook his head. "I probably could if I wanted to. But I'm not stopping *you* from leaving, only your boss." He pointed to the open wounds on Ryan's forearms. "He might be turning into one of them, and I can't be letting one of them roam around outside. First, he'll get sick. Then he'll die. And then he'll get back up in the damnedest mood. Only the good Lord knows what trouble that will start if he was roaming the city when that happens."

"You can't be serious," she said.

"Serious as a heart attack," Martin replied. "Ma wouldn't have it any other way even if I did want to let you go. If he gets sick, I'm going to have to put him down. But don't worry, I've trained our pooches to smell out a corpse right quick. They'll know he's turning at least an hour before it happens. Plenty of time to pop him in the head."

"That's murder!"

Martin shrugged. "Ain't murder when he's already dead."

"We've got to get him some help," Clarice said, opting for another line. Though part of her wanted to stick to the original argument, trading blows if needed, she wasn't sure if Martin had any qualms about shooting her as well. Peaceful negotiations were in order. "If he's going to get sick, we can get him treated at a hospital, and no one has to die. Surely they can quarantine him or something."

"How do they even treat that?" Nick asked.

"Hell if I know!" she exclaimed. "But we can try. You can't stop us from trying."

"I'll do what I have to," Martin said solemnly. "And it's not like I'd want to hurt any of you fine folk, but I got to make sure Mr. Conner here is okay before I leave him be."

Ryan leaned back, and it now seemed that he had decided to end the entire conversation. "It doesn't matter anyway. We're not leaving until our business is concluded."

"And you're okay with the dying part?" Clarice mocked. "Have you been paying attention to anything that's been going on or said?"

"I don't have any plans on dying either," he added. "In fact, I've decided not to."

"Oh, really?" Clarice asked. "Just like that?"

Ryan crossed his legs at the knees and folded his hands on top. "Just like that."

"I don't think it works that way," she replied.

"Why?" he asked. "People decide not to do things all the time. I'm deciding not to die. I can show you it's true, too."

"I'm sure you can," Clarice said, rolling her eyes.

"It's simple really," he said. "I haven't died yet, have I?"

"No," Clarice replied slowly. She wondered how contagious the stupidity in this room was. "So?"

"So my decision was obviously the right one," Ryan said.

Clarice buried her head in her hands. "I'm tired," she said after looking up. Her mind was exhausted, her body was starting to ache, and she suspected that such a hard, long mountain run the day after an eight-mile jog was taking its toll. Hopefully, with a good night's rest for everyone, she could talk some sense into him tomorrow. Worst case, she'd call a cab and tell Ryan Conner, Tax Collector, to stuff the job up his ass. Yes, she'd be out of a job, but maybe she could scramble and find work at the vet's. Clarice turned toward Martin, "Do you have a spare room?"

"I do," he replied. "Two spares. Always kept ready in case we get some living company. Up the stairs, second door on the left can be yours if you like. Or take the other. It makes no difference to me."

"Fine idea," Ryan said to her as she went to leave the room. "We should all be rested, and we'll get to work first thing in the morning."

Chapter Seven

It took some time for Jack to regain his wit, and by then his meal had long since run off. The sun had sulked its way to another hemisphere, marking the beginning of yet another night. The moon, still embarrassed by the furry fiasco it had created the previous night in both London and Paris, hid behind the clouds, hoping no one would notice. Without any sort of light, Jack's pen lost all of its playful shininess and returned to its natural pen state. It was a state that Henry Bollivor would have disapproved of as "merely adequate."

Jack continued to hold the pen despite the numerous attempts by other things to gain his attention. He wasn't sure why this was, but at this point in time, he wasn't sure of much, other than two things—his pen existed, and it was in his hand. With a great deal of effort, Jack clubbed the two thoughts into one. His pen was in his hand.

The night wore on and with half of his computing power miraculously freed, Jack worked on a number of questions about his pen that came, went and returned again with new friends. The largest and toughest of these questions was, "Mrrrggph?" which was closely related to the living's question of, "How the hell did it get here?"

The answer to that question remained elusive.

By midnight Jack was lying down, rhythmically thumping his head against one of three rusted anchors at the marina. Eventually, he decided that if he couldn't figure something out by morning, he'd have to venture outside of Colmera Springs and track down someone who could.

Danita didn't have the luxury of contemplation that night. Instead, she had to placate the other inhabitants when they groaned about how a perfectly good game of Eats had ended before it could even begin. Hours passed before she managed to guarantee to each and every one of them that *they* would be back, and she would have accomplished that task sooner had she understood Ryan when he yelled, "I'll be back!" but at this point, such details didn't matter.

Even with her guarantees, the population of Colmera Springs was restless, so Danita resorted to initiating a game of Hides. She hoped that it would be a decent substitute for Eats and everyone would be happy once again. Several zombies croaked their objection to the game, some of them even calling the whole ordeal a Bait-N-Switch, but when Danita explained that a game of Hides could be a precursor to a game of Eats, they agreed to play along with the others. Some of the zombies liked the idea so much they even let her suggest new hiding spots.

It took a couple of hours, but Danita succeeded in tucking everyone away in the end. And once she was alone and her thoughts churned, what was left of her brow furrowed. *I'll be back* echoed several times over. It was a hollow, chilling echo, and one that pushed her decision to find Jack to the top of her three-point to-do list. Hopefully, he could make sense of things. Fortunately for Danita, finding him never proved to be difficult, especially with all of eternity at her disposal.

She plodded around Colmera Springs but came up with nothing. Slowly, the image of the pen came to her mind, and she decided that Jack must still be fixated upon it. Danita also decided that since Jack wasn't around discussing Eats, he must have wandered off alone someplace where the other zombies cared not to go. Her first stop was the dentist's office, but he had the week off and Jack was not inside. She then headed for the marina since most of the populace couldn't swim. With a little luck, the second time would be the charm, and the two of them could work out this *I'll be back* business and then grab someone to eat.

Jack awoke to a partial hand on his shoulder. He took to his feet and saw Danita next to him with a happy look splashed across her rotted face. Before either could say a word, a bit of moonlight worked its way free of the clouds, darted between the trees, and managed to strike Jack's 1941, catalog product number 31A, green metallic shell, ballpoint pen. The sparkle it gave rekindled the desire to answer the question of "Mrrrggph?" and so he asked it to Danita, hoping she would have an answer.

Danita did not. But she did say that she remembered a group meal escaping recently and that she'd felt depressed that a game of Eats had been ruined. At the end of her lament, she vowed to never forget about it ever again, whatever it was. But the pen looked nice.

Jack smiled and showed it off with pride. He gave it a wiggle in the light, demonstrating its reflective and hypnotic qualities. He then showed her the most marvelous trick he had discovered. With a half twist of the pen, a small tip appeared from one end. Jack pressed the tip into his arm and moved it across his skin. When he removed it, a wavy, black line remained.

Danita croaked and extended her hand, asking permission to give it a try.

Jack grunted with approval and handed the pen over to her.

At this point, there was a lot for Jack's two-thought mind to take in and just as much to forget. He watched as Danita scribbled hastily on her arm, blathering on about finding a way never to forget something ever again. She then demanded that Jack distract her for a while, which Jack happily obliged by telling a few jokes and poking around in the dirt with a stick until he forgot what he was supposed to be doing.

Danita looked down, jumped, and screamed about a scribbled mess on her arm. When she calmed herself and stopped clawing at it, recognition replaced fright, and she rattled with glee.

Jack, still confused, stood silent and chewed his bottom lip. It wasn't as tasty as a live lip, but it wasn't bad either. Dry, with a hint of leather.

Danita grabbed his arm and pulled him through the forest. As she did, she jabbered on about three things. First, she wanted to play Eats. Second, writing something down was a fantastic way not to forget it. And third, she knew how to combine both.

Although Jack liked the idea of a game of Eats, he did not appreciate her bossy nature. So Jack planted his feet and ground their midnight march to a halt. When Danita turned to face him, he picked up a fallen branch from the forest floor and swung it at her head.

It hit her just above the left ear and broke in two.

Both zombies paused at the sound of stick turned sticks. It was a pleasing sound, one that echoed throughout the forest and one that was reminiscent of popping bones. Both zombies not only agreed that they would like to hear more of such sounds, but they also decided that it had been far too long since a human or two had come to their little abode. In fact, neither could remember when the last time even was. As such, they decided (again) that it was time to go looking for a new meal and to stop all this nonsense of standing around and doing nothing.

The two shuffled down the moonlit path, unknowingly headed straight for Seraville.

Chapter Eight

In 1914, there was a small spat about who killed who, and Europe decided it needed a great war to settle the matter. Everyone abandoned their rock searching ways for digging countless trenches and shooting those that happened out of them. While some played in the dirt, others played in the air, and as a direct result, leaps and bounds in aviation were made. The biggest driving factor behind these advancements were pilots filled with jealousy. After all, if the men on the ground got to kill each other, those in the air should too.

The pilots tried dueling with pistols from biplanes but soon abandoned the practice. Many found it too hard to count precisely ten paces, and so machine guns were installed as a fair substitute. At some point along the way, the pilots also thought they might want to come back down, sans plane. This thought gave birth to two notable things. First, the design of a lightweight, compact parachute. Second, and building on the first, it created thousands of men that didn't want to fly at all, but still liked the idea of jumping out of airplanes while at war. They were the start of the modern paratrooper.

Death and Taxes

Several decades prior to Jack and Danita's romantic, moonlit stroll through the woods, Private First Class J.F. Reno sat quietly inside a C-47 transport plane. Twenty other students from Fort Benning's Airborne School were with him, one of whom happened to be enthralled with his new 1941, catalog product number 31A, green metallic shell, ballpoint pen.

Reno nervously flipped the pen over a few times in his hand. "They say it has almost eight hundred uses," he said to Pfc. M. Conner, raising his voice above the constant drone of the two wing-mounted Pratt & Whitney R-1830 engines.

"Eight hundred, huh?" Conner yelled back. "Nice pen, indeed."

Reno nodded. "It's why I bought it instead of the red metallic shell—which only had four hundred something."

"Can you kill a Kraut with it?" someone yelled in the back.

"Use number five twenty-two, according to the pamphlet," Reno shouted in reply. He then turned back to Conner. "That was one of the first things I asked the salesman. I thought it would be fun to kill a Kraut and write home about it with the same instrument."

Conner reflexively grabbed Reno's shoulder when the plane hit a patch of turbulence. Once the ride smoothed out, he asked, "What's use number one?"

"I can't quite remember how it was phrased," Reno said, thinking. "I think it was something like, 'Tool for the creation of written communication.'" He then added after a brief jolt from the plane, "You should order one when we get back. It's a fine pen. It even writes in the dark."

"Negative. We're shipping out in a day or two for England. I wouldn't get it in time."

"Too bad. It's a fine pen."

Conner eyed the writing instrument. "You could always give me yours."

Reno laughed. "Not on your life."

"After all I've done for you, too," Conner said, throwing up his hands. "Maybe I'll just take it when you aren't looking."

"I'd hunt you down dand see if use number five twenty-two applied to backstabbing jump mates."

"Shut up and get ready to jump!" their jumpmaster yelled. "And as long as you're making promises Reno, be sure you only make ones your ass will be able to cash in."

The class shuffled to the exit door.

"Fine," Reno said, raising his voice even further so that everyone could hear. "Let it be known that I swear to God and all that is holy, if anyone takes my green pen, I will hunt them and anyone else down for all of eternity, biting their legs off if I have to, to get it back."

"I'm going to stuff that pen up your ass if you don't shut up." The look on the jumpmaster's face revealed a promise, not an empty threat.

Daring as always, Reno answered, "I don't think that's one of the approved uses, sir."

"I'll see you on the ground, Reno," the jumpmaster said evenly. "You'll be seeing how many approved uses of pain I know."

A moment later, the green light turned on. Like a batch of eager lemmings, the class began falling out of the aircraft. Pfc. Conner turned swiftly, flashed a wry grin and snatched the pen from Pfc. Reno's hand. Before the former penholder could react, Pfc. Conner jumped out of the aircraft.

"Son of a bitch," Pfc. Reno muttered, tailing the thief out of the plane. His static line pulled an instant later, and he felt the chute deploy. He glanced up, let loose a sigh of relief at the sight of the round blossom above. His relief, however, faded fast as the wind picked up and blew him far from the drop zone.

When Danita had initiated the game of Hides, she did a marvelous job at placing her fellow zombies in various niches and dark corners. Her effort was undoubtedly as good a job as anyone else could have done; that point would remain uncontested. Her scheme, however, was far from perfect. First, she chose spots that zombies liked to rest in. With no one around and town arguments never lasting long to begin with, the inhabitants of Colmera Springs would have gone to bed one by one on their own. That alone made her commendable efforts unneeded.

Second, history has shown that humans are rarely killed because of a skeleton in the closet. The vast majority of victims are done in by their own less-than-spectacular actions. Wandering off alone, or hiding under the bed, or trying to study zombies and so forth, all fall into this category. As such, to catch their prey, zombies do not need to start a game of Eats by playing a game of Hides first. They can just let people be people.

Last, and by far the largest of the gaping flaws, zombies aren't known for their ability nor desire to follow instructions (games of Hides are often long over before any meal wanders in). This little point goes hand in hand with the previous point, as victims try to order zombies around by screaming things like, "Stop!" "No!" and the ever popular, "Don't eat me!" But since most people are not avid students of history, let alone zombie history, they are doomed to repeat it—Danita included.

A couple of hours past midnight, long after she had disappeared from sight and sound, the citizens of Colmera Springs grew tired of decomposing alone and pursued other activities. Some ended their game of Hides by choosing to lie down, while others lumbered around to see what everyone else was doing or undoing. A few wanted to play a new game, but no people could be seen, smelled, or heard. Furthermore, no one could find Danita, and without their resident game maker guiding them, a new game was nothing more than wishful thinking.

While they were on the subject of new games, one of the zombies postulated the notion that perhaps Danita had already invented something new to play and the gist of it was to find her. Everyone agreed that it was a plausible scenario, as both games and Danita existed. Barry, the former baker, then suggested that while they might not know how to play just yet, points would be awarded as they were due.

A low moan came from the horde, signifying that everyone was in agreement.

Despite the large consensus of those wanting to try something new, a couple of dozen others refused as they were purists at heart. Any game other than Eats was substandard, and they weren't about to settle for mediocrity. They also had a different hypothesis as to the whereabouts of Danita. They surmised that Danita had gone off to play the solitaire version of Eats (Eats Alone), for neither Danita nor a tasty meal was anywhere to be found. The logic, of course, was irrefutable.

In the end, however, each group set out to find Danita. And although their goals were identical, their motivations and their methods weren't, and it wasn't long before the two groups argued until all focus had been lost. That is, until the unmistakable sound of snapping bone echoed through the forest.

In perfect unison, the inhabitants of Colmera Springs became quiet, turned toward the sound and offered an inquisitive *Urrmmmmgggghhh.*

The mob headed in the direction of the noise. A half hour later, they stumbled upon a small zombling by the name of Dexter. Little Dexter stood alone, head crooked to the left and looking skyward. Half of a broken stick lay at his feet, but since his eyes were up, the horde only gave it a cursory glance.

No one understood what little Dexter was doing or why he was doing it, but the empty stare the little zombling held told everyone everything that they needed to know; he was in deep contemplation about something worthwhile. And like all things worthwhile, it would be beneficial to discern exactly what it might be. They could all comment on how cute he was later.

Any remaining thoughts about the recent, mysterious, bone-snapping sound vanished in an instant from the crowd. They asked what Dexter was doing. Dexter, in turn, asked what they were doing. Back and forth the questions went, and eventually everyone grew tired of standing in the forest, and a few suggested they should return home. During the course of this conversation, more and more zombies arrived at the meeting spot, having followed the same snap of bones to the same spot.

Just before the horde achieved a consensus to return home, little Dexter found a blood trail and pointed it out for everyone to see. He also pointed to the blood-stained leaves and reminded everyone that if something bled, they could eat it.

Praise from everyone showered Dexter for his fine thinking. With Dexter's rediscovery still fresh in mind, someone suggested that a game of Eats for All must be played. Due to the large volume of bodies that would participate, the suggestion was put forth to a vote. Dexter, being a zombling who hadn't fully fermented yet and could not vote, took up the count as mangled limbs were raised.

Auggghhhhh (*one*).

Augghhhhh (*two*).

With the pinnacle of counting being reached in record time, the provisional council of dead affairs approved the unanimous decision and stated that as long as the group was out and about, it would indeed be good to get a change of scenery and start a new game of Eats for All. No one knew where they wanted to go, mostly because no one could remember anywhere to go or what might even exist. All that they were certain of was that where they wanted to be was not where they currently were.

Dexter suggested they follow the trail of blood, as it looked like it knew where it wanted to go. Though no one paid attention to him at first, when Dexter headed downhill, the mob followed close behind.

Chapter Nine

Clarice spent the night in a restless state. When she wasn't watching the ceiling stare at her, she was checking the window to see if anything was lurking outside. When she wasn't doing either of those, she was sulking over the fact that her insensitive and uncaring fiancé had somehow managed to fall asleep and had left her alone, despite the fact that he had sworn to stand vigil. Occasionally she would offer a sharp nudge of her elbow into his ribs as a subtle reminder of her insomnia, but he had always been a heavy sleeper. Maybe the French maid outfit wouldn't be coming out after all.

Well past exhaustion and a half step through delirium, Clarice rolled out of bed and trudged into the bathroom. The sun had finally shown itself, and it seemed pointless to try and sleep any longer. Her usual morning bathroom routine had turned predictably tense and troubled. Aside from the previous day's events and the lack of any real sleep, she had also left her toiletry bag in the car. And to top things off, the frigid water made sure she wouldn't enjoy any sort of shower, though it did give her a jolt of energy. She threw her old clothes back on, squirted some Visine in her bloodshot eyes, donned her sports cap (complete with a Jolly

Roger splashed across its crown), and slipped out the door. Hopefully, breakfast would brighten the day.

Coming down the stairs, Clarice took a quick inventory of the house and was relieved to find it much as she had left it. The living room was still on her right, the kitchen to the left. Couches, chairs, tables, books and various odds and ends still appeared to be in the proper location. The television had been left on and was currently showing some random talk show, the topic being a fresh look at love triangles and trailer parks. The smell of scrambled eggs wafted from the kitchen, and while she was confident she hadn't left such a smell lingering the previous night, the change was a welcomed one.

"Good morning Ms. Clarice," Ryan said as she came around the corner. He was sitting at the breakfast table, cup of coffee in one hand, cheap, red, ballpoint pen in the other. The morning light accentuated his ashen, semi-paralyzed face.

She stopped in the doorway and held back a gasp. "You look awful," she stammered. "Maybe you should see someone."

"Do I?" he asked, patting himself down. It seemed as if this was the first time he had ever considered his appearance. "I think you'll find that this attire is well within policy."

"You look like you're one step away from the grave!"

Ryan jerked his head over his shoulder. "One away from the kitchen sink maybe," he replied. "Though both you and Mr. Martin have been a little obsessed about... what was that again? Death? Yes... death." He then motioned to an opposite corner where the dog was sitting, bristle backed and eyes fixated on the tax collector. "And I'm beginning to suspect the dog is involved somehow too."

"The dog?" Clarice raised an eyebrow.

"Yes, the dog. The canine. The supposed best friend of man." Ryan paused for a couple of moments before continuing. "I think he's at best, Martin's friend, but certainly not mine. Do you think he would help me chase down a tax fraud? I think not."

"Speaking of, where is Martin?" Clarice asked.

"Outside on the porch," Ryan replied. "He went there to finish whittling and to do something or other."

Her rumbling stomach prompted the next question. "Did he make breakfast?"

"He didn't mention that he had," he said, thinking back. "Ma would be my guess. But then again, I haven't seen her at all, so perhaps Martin did. In any case, have some."

"I haven't seen her either," she commented, glancing over her shoulder. Since their arrival the prior day, the house had been absent of others, aside from themselves and Martin. "I wonder where she is."

"Perhaps she's dead," Ryan said in a detached manner. "Being buried in the ground would make it hard for someone to see you." He began picking at the food in front of him. "Worms, though, they find a body easily enough. Do you think it's by smell? Or do they just know where the juicy bits are?"

"I don't know," Clarice answered in disgust. "But I'd like not to lose my appetite."

She took a chair, and Ryan slid one of the empty plates toward her. After helping herself to some eggs and grits, she sat back down and decided to try and reason with her employer once more. "You need to see a doctor."

"Nonsense. I feel fine, despite my supposed pallid color. I'm a little stiff from where those maniacs bit me, but I'm not about to let those tax dodgers scare me away."

Ryan continued to drone on, and Clarice paid him no heed as she was already tired of listening. She poked at her grits with her spoon in much the same way an orangutan might use a stick to poke for ants. Clarice's grits even stuck to the spoon in much the same way ants would, though they were a little more buttery. Despite her grits' lack of energy, she was convinced they were better tasting than the orangutan's ants.

Clarice jabbed the grits with her spoon once more and stirred them. She visualized them becoming angry and scurrying up the handle. With a little effort, she forced herself to admit that there was the possibility of the ants being tastier. Perhaps the animal kingdom was on to something. After all, quite a number of animals seemed to like them, and there weren't any animals called grit-eaters. She turned that thought over a few times in her head. After considering her experience trying to solve the problem of *The Pigmy Elephant and the Bathroom*, Clarice promptly threw out the *Ants or Grits* dilemma and pushed her plate away.

"Gah!" she exclaimed. "This is maddening. We should get going before it's too late."

"My thoughts exactly, Ms. Clarice!" Ryan replied without losing a step in his monologue. "While it is frustrating to try and understand how the local collector could have such a lackadaisical attitude, we must be firm when we contact the judge today and let him know in no uncertain terms that we mean to pursue this to the end. I've already arranged with Mr. Martin for us to stay here in the spare rooms until the matter is settled."

Clarice looked up from the table. "Come again?" she asked. Her tone darkened, and she was sure to enunciate every syllable of what followed. "How long do you think we're staying?"

"I know we can get all of this wrapped up in a few weeks, a month at the most," he answered, followed by a hacking cough. "You've been around long enough to know how fast these seizures can go. Don't worry about your pay, my dear. You'll be earning lots of overtime, not to mention a small share in the finder's fee."

Clarice clenched her teeth before deciding to take another approach. "What about our office? Don't you think that will be a problem?"

"Don't be silly, Clarice. No one is seizing our office."

Clarice, annoyed employee, in a further attempt to keep her sanity intact, shifted into Clarice, secretary extraordinaire. She stood, took his now empty cup of coffee and refilled it, adding precisely the proper mix of cream and sugar. "Mr. Conner," she said. "If we stay past today, there are a slew of things that will back up at our office. New foreclosures need to be gone over, meetings have been scheduled, not to mention that this is now day three that you've left David in charge of the office."

She had no idea if David was a competent employee or not, having only met the man once for two minutes when her new-hire office tour was given, but it was worth a stab.

"Good God!" Ryan exclaimed. "Have I? The man can barely fill out a dozen forms in under three minutes, and I left him in charge?"

Clarice slipped into her seat and helped herself to a glass of orange juice, all the while feeling incredibly clever. "Yes, sir."

"Did you know, Clarice," he said in a soft, low, voice, "that David uses inferior stamps?"

Clarice shook her head. "No, I didn't. It would explain why his assistant isn't always pleased with him."

Ryan nodded to reemphasize his comment. "He does. And then he comes to me and complains that his notices aren't as intimidating as mine or that his hands hurt. As if the answer to why on either of those was elusive."

"The nerve," she added. "We'd better get back and set things straight."

"What was I thinking?" he lamented.

"That we'd be back today," she said with a big grin. "And back to collecting taxes where we should be. I mean, we have things we should do and should have done already. No time like the present to get back on track."

For the first time since Clarice had seen her employer this morning, a spark of life illuminated his face. "I must say, I'm glad to see you are still looking after the office, and you're correct in gently reminding us all that we have responsibilities."

"Thank you, sir."

"And apology accepted," he said with a wink.

"What?"

"Nothing to be shy about," Ryan said, sipping more of his coffee. "I'm always understanding when one admits to one's mistakes. It's a sign of good character. Please don't feel like you need to dress an apology up or dance around the issue because I demand perfection."

"I was only saying we should get back to collecting taxes at home and not be stuck on what's happened here." Clarice replayed the last few moments of the conversation in her mind, desperately trying to figure out where it had taken this unexpected turn.

Ryan nodded. "Yes, I know. And I know that's your way of expressing your regret for running off with our demand notice, thereby slowing down our collection efforts. But fear not, we'll be back on track today. We'll notify the judge this morning that our first collection attempt has been met with hostility and then take it from there. With any luck, we'll be home before you know it."

Clarice, caught between a laugh and a cry, turned and left the kitchen without a further word. It was time to call a cab.

The game of Eats has always been by far the longest standing, most popular game among the inhabitants of Colmera Springs. This shouldn't be surprising to anyone as it has consistently received the required two votes. They had tried other games; a few of them they even liked. But nothing could bond zombies together like a good game of Eats.

At the most basic level, Eats was merely chasing a good meal, humans being the preferred bit of sustenance. As time passed, the game evolved to take on various forms of scoring, rules, and even names (which depended on where and when the game was being played.). Most games of Eats were played at home, as everyone knows it's much more time-consuming and expensive to eat out. However, constant games of Eats In tended to be repetitious, the leftovers were never as good, and no one wanted to do the dishes. As such, when the horde of zombies that had wandered down the mountainside approached Martin's home, they became excited about a fresh game of Eats Out.

The scoring for this particular game of Eats Out was quickly ratified after a minor dispute. One point would be awarded for all those that showed up, and one point would be awarded for every meal eaten. Whoever received the highest score possible, two, would win.

With scoring settled and everyone happy, the mob quickened their pace down the mountain. It wasn't long before they neared the edge of the tree line, and a house came into view.

Oddly enough, the morning fog aided Jack's search for a new meal. The thick blanket managed to smother the usual distractions that had always kept the inhabitants of Colmera Springs from traveling down the mountain. With no tall trees, fuzzy animals, or bristly bushes to stare at, Jack had but one sensory input to follow, his nose. And it was that nose that had followed the trail of blood that their future meal had left behind.

On the rare occasion that something did manage to catch Jack's attention, pen and stick would save the day. Three times on the journey Jack had lost focus, and after a short while he noticed his stick in hand, lazily pointing to the ground. Inevitably his eyes would then gaze upon his pen that was wedged neatly in its shoulder socket, parallel with the ground. Clearly, he reasoned, if things were pointing down and forward, he should find whatever it was they were trying to point out. Using such excellent detective work, Jack would discover the blood trail once again, and he would resume his pursuit with Danita closely following.

Jack paused after he and Danita broke free of the tree line. Jack took a moment to gaze at the scene before him. A significant number of flat rocks had been erected in rows to his left. Straight ahead and down the hill were a set of buildings, much like those he saw at Colmera Springs, only not quite as bent over. Coming from the largest of these was the distinct smell of breakfast.

Danita glanced over her shoulder at the sound of the zombie horde's approach. In all the excitement, she waved her own stick toward the house like a demented cavalry leader and gurgled. More zombies appeared from the fog, one at a time at first, then in groups of twos and threes. A few issued her a welcoming gurgle of their own, and the rabid excitement in their eye sockets told her what she needed to know—the game of Eats Out was in full swing.

Danita replied with a gleeful sneer and boasted in good sport about the lead she and Jack had on the rest.

When the horde was within a few dozen lurches of the nearest building, the front door opened and out stepped a somewhat familiar body. It staggered down the few steps from the porch and came to a halt in front of Jack and Danita.

All three stood facing each other, swaying slightly in the wind. Over the next few minutes, a few grunts and groans were exchanged, as well as a few words that neither Jack nor Danita were familiar with. Before either could decipher this newcomer's cryptic language, the third party reached up and snatched Jack's 1941, catalog product number 31A, green metallic shell, ballpoint pen. Jack went from puzzled to irate and lunged at the robber.

Before Jack could grab him, a loud crack came forth from the house, and Jack fell over dead—again.

Chapter Ten

Far from Colmera Springs, hundreds of miles away, sat a small computer. It had been crowded out of the enormous room by racks upon racks of other machines, from servers to backup drives to a pair of vending machines, each wired to the other. Together they would whirr and beep, never sharing their secrets with the wallflower.

Despite being tucked away in the corner, it had for years faithfully monitored the constant stream of information that came flowing through its sole cable. Phone conversations from across the eastern portion of the United States were processed and discarded, and the fact that years had gone by without one discussion worthy of a red flag was beginning to take its toll on its CPU. But when Ryan Conner's phone call to the state courthouse was picked up, the little computer, tired and on the brink of a self-format, found sudden and renewed meaning in life.

It had ignored virtually all of the conversation, not caring about Ryan's collection attempts and explanation to the judge as to why he had come from another state, or the judge's less than cordial reply. What it did care about were the statements involving "staggering people" who "looked ghastly" and that "Clarice said they were dead." Furthermore, it grew even happier when it picked up the phrase, "Colmera Springs is northeast, up the mountain a few miles."

The little box looked up the address information for the nearest spy satellite. After making contact with ICU-2 and convincing the satellite that it was allowed to talk to this particular, long-forgotten computer, the little box waited patiently.

Four minutes later, once ICU-2 had fulfilled the request for a slew of boring pictures, an email was sent out to one Mark Hoffer, Team Specialist.

A small red icon that was accompanied by a warning beep appeared on Mark Hoffer's screen. It took him a few minutes to trot over and check his mail, for at the time he was adjusting his tie in the mirror and wondering when he would need to get his Armani suit tailored once more. The extra time spent at the gym for the last six months was showing. As Mark went back to his desk, he shut and locked the door to his in-home office, closed the shades to his full-length windows, and took a seat at his desk.

A quick double click opened his newest morning message.

"Sweet Jesus riding a unicycle," he said to himself. A flurry of mouse movements and clicks brought his printer to life, spitting out several full pages of text. Over the next few minutes, he read through the pages carefully, sipping coffee in a West Point mug and making highlights in the phone transcript he was reading. Finally, he reached for the phone, turned the volume down on his radio, and dialed the given number.

"Good morning," Mark Hoffer replied as someone answered. The voice on the other end gave him pause. It was slow and raspy. "Is this 233 Sovrano Trail?"

"I believe so," came the reply. "To whom am I speaking?"

"My name is Mark Hoffer," he said. "I'm working with the state courthouse as an independent contractor. And you are?"

"Ryan Conner, Tax Collector."

"I understand that you're having trouble collecting some property taxes that are overdue," Mark said, reading over the phone transcript a third time.

"Only because at this point in time, I'm not getting a backing from the state," Ryan replied with disgust. "It's a wonder you guys can run at all."

"I understand your frustration, sir," Mark said, silently checking off another item on his list to be verified. "I'm here acting as a liaison of sorts. You do have to admit that the scenario of missed property taxes for such an extended period of time is rather unique."

"I would," Ryan conceded. "And I appreciate anything that would help expedite the matter before things get ugly."

"I also understand that you've delivered a demand notice, is this correct?"

"Yes."

"Do you have a signed receipt?"

"No," Ryan said with a regretful tone. His voice had become increasingly stilted and his words harder to understand. "Due to to...an error by my new assistant, we do not have a copy of a signed receipt. The townsfolk have proven to be hostile."

"Well you are a tax collector," Mark remarked, checking yet another box. "Could you describe the townsfolk?"

"I am," Ryan replied. "But as for them, they're a bit different."

"How so?" Mark's pen hovered over the last checkbox.

"My assistant says they're dead," he replied. "But I'm not quite sure how she means it. Perhaps she meant they'll wish they're dead, which will be true when we get done with them. But they're different—and in desperate need of new clothes and decent hygiene."

"I see," Mark said. "I'm going to send a team out to see you at this address. They should be there shortly, and we can take it from there."

"Excellent. We'll be here," Ryan said.

Mark leaned back in his oversized executive chair. He rubbed the black leather, noting the way it felt on his fingers. Today was going to be a good day, and by next week, he was confident he could finally clinch a promotion.

"Who was that?" Clarice asked once Ryan hung up the phone.

"Someone from the state," he replied. "It would seem that they have finally come to their senses."

"Good, we can leave then," Clarice replied as she stopped digging through her purse. Cab fare was apparently no longer needed. She picked up the remote and flipped channels once more. Just as she settled on some documentary on pirates, a flurry of motion caught her attention outside the window. Martin had jumped out of his rocking chair and was now leaning against the porch rail. He stood a few moments while he looked out toward the mountainside, trying to peer through what fog remained. Then, as quick as he had leaped, he ran inside.

"Best stay in," he said emphatically. "Looks like there are a whole lot of them coming."

Clarice, who was no longer sitting idly on the couch, had her face pressed against the window. She wondered if this was how chocolate bars felt on the opening day of a candy store. Out in the distance, she spied the unmistakable pair of zombies coming toward the house. "Oh, god," she said, further horrified at the growing number of forms emerging from the woods.

"No need to fret," Martin assured as he loaded his Winchester rifle.

"No need?" Clarice repeated. "There's at least fifty of them! Maybe a hundred! It's not going to take long for them to smash this glass in."

Martin chuckled. "Ma and I thought this might happen sooner or later and decided to make a few home improvements. That glass you're looking at is the same they put on those high-profile cars and whatnot. Might take me a while to shoot them all from upstairs, but we'll clean them up. Stay inside and you'll be alright."

Martin paused on his way up the stairs. "Where's that fiancé of yours?"

"Sleeping still. He doesn't get up till at least ten, despite what I say."

"Well, I reckon he'll be up once I start shooting. Nice boy like him might even want to help."

"Where's Ma?" Clarice asked, concerned for her safety and still wanting to meet her.

"Oh, she's around," Martin replied with a shrug as he continued up to the second floor. "If she ain't in here right now, she's probably holed up in the gas station. Guess I should call over there and check."

Ryan shuffled over and gazed out the window alongside Clarice. He didn't say anything at first, but let a smidge of drool run from the corner of his mouth down to the floor. "I've met that one before," he finally said as he motioned toward the leading corpse. "I think I'll see what he has to say. Maybe he's come to make payment arrangements."

"What?" Clarice exclaimed. "Are you insane?"

"Determined," Ryan clarified.

Before Clarice could even think of intervening, Ryan left the house and staggered out to meet the new visitors. She kept close to the still narrowly open door, one hand on the doorknob and the other gripping the deadbolt.

Clarice watched Ryan stop in front of the two zombies who were now a few dozen paces from the house. As far as the secretary could tell, the three stood with little interaction other than the occasional twitch of hand or head. That is until Ryan spotted his 1941, catalog product number 31A, green metallic shell, ballpoint pen wedged under one of the zombie's collar bone and snatched it from him.

The zombie lunged, Martin shot, and Clarice yelled. The end result of all three's interaction was the walking corpse toppling over backward, Nick yelling something from upstairs, and Ryan managing to get back inside before Clarice slammed and bolted the door shut.

A second scream leaped from the secretary's mouth as the other zombie slammed into the door. It was crusty, mostly toothless, with long black hair and yellow skin. A part of it looked female, but whatever it was, it tried time and again to smash its way into the house. Much to Clarice's relief and a credit to Martin's handiwork, the windows and doors held.

Soon more and more zombies gathered, all lending their weight to bringing down the door, and more and more shots rang out from upstairs. The shots were joined by another set, a second shooter, who Clarice could only assume was Nick.

Clarice watched for a while as the ghastly beings battered the house. When Martin called out from upstairs, Clarice turned her attention to the road where a pair of flower delivery vans had pulled in. A half dozen men that looked like black turtles with guns jumped out and formed a skirmish line. Right behind them was a lanky man in a lab coat, shouting with excitement. She could hear them and Martin yelling at each other, the gist of which she didn't quite understand.

"Miss!" Martin called from upstairs. "You and Mr. Conner ought to get up here, just in case."

"Come again?" she yelled, looking back up the staircase.

"Those windows and boards are strong enough now, but I wouldn't trust them completely," he explained. "Might catch a stray bullet if you stay."

Clarice turned around and grabbed her boss by the collar once she saw the newcomers making a tactical advance on the house, submachine guns shouldered and ready. She had scarcely managed to get up the stairwell when the popping sounds began.

Three minutes later the gunfire slowed to the occasional shot here and there. Three minutes after that, it had ceased altogether.

Chapter Eleven

The final location of the Tau Seven Facility had been painstakingly researched. Designers realized it had to be placed where there were no hidden bones, shiny rocks, or anything else that might attract the would-be digger. Thankfully, finding such a worthless area in the Appalachian Mountains did not take long. Once the land was purchased and several dinky shacks added for camouflage, long, intricate tunnels were dug into the mountain and then filled with rooms, laboratories, equipment, elevators, and people.

But to the dismay of all the staff, Tau Seven had been without biological subjects for nearly seven years, and many of their projects had been put on hold. However, when six new guests were admitted to the facility, all of that changed and long-dormant work resumed.

Mark Hoffer stood quietly in one of Tau Seven's observation rooms, arms crossed and foot idly tapping. Next to him stood an excited Dr. John Forbes, who had entered the room moments ago. The man seemed always to be whistling something when not speaking, though at the moment he had paused in his Disney theme songs to peruse the chart he was carrying. The doctor's fingers twitched almost nonstop, as if attached to a marionette that had had enough and was struggling to get free. After a few minutes, the invisible puppet ceased its pulling, and Dr. Forbes looked up to face Mark.

"This is one of the nicer observation rooms I think," the doctor said, scratching his Brillo pad beard and adjusting his wireframe glasses. "I like the color in this one the most."

"I see," Mark said flatly, taking a survey of the room. It was well lit, though bare of any sort of equipment or decoration, save a row of chairs that faced a thick pane of glass and a number of large, bundled wires that ran across the ceiling. The room's decor did little to distract occupants from the fact that they were under countless tons of rock and concrete, and Mark wondered how long it would take for workers to go insane from the environment. "How long have you been down here, doctor?"

"A few years. Three I think, come next month. We don't get out much. Why do you ask?"

"Idle curiosity," Mark replied, making a small mental note to leave as soon as he could. "Shall we get started?"

"We shall!" Dr. Forbes took a few light steps and flipped a switch on the wall. The detention room on the other side of the glass brightened. In the middle stood Jack, who had made no noticeable reaction to the change in lighting and was slowly turning in circles.

"It's been two days now since we picked them all up," the doctor said while flipping his chart pages. "And we've learned quite a lot about the survivors you managed to bring back, this one especially. It's been so long since we've had an animated subject to study. I can't tell you how excited we all are at the prospects of new research. Subject Four here is quite the lucky little thing if I might add. It seems that he took a shot to the head from the elderly fellow's rifle and didn't die."

"Bad aim?" Mark squinted, trying to pick out the zombie's head wound from afar.

"Bad luck," Dr. Forbes clarified. "Or bad physics, depending on who you want to blame. The round hit this one on the outside cheekbone and deflected. What energy the bullet did impart on the zombie's head seems to have all been captured by the bit of bone that broke off. Never even as much as wiggled what's left of his brain."

"Lucky S.O.B." Mark cupped his hands over his eyes as he peered into the room. "What's that he's wearing?"

"Part of an old M42 jumpsuit we think," Dr. Forbes replied. "We tried looking for his name, but as you can see, the fabric has deteriorated. Definitely World War II origins, though."

Mark turned back toward Dr. Forbes, eager to hear what other progress they had made. Coming up with a timeline for these creatures was important, and if the team had pinpointed this one to World War II, it showed remarkable resilience and self-reliance in terms of survival. "What else do you know about him?"

"We know with total certainty that this one hates parfaits." Dr. Forbes tapped the chart a couple of times, emphasizing the point.

"Parfaits?"

"Yes, parfaits. They're a dessert, mind you, generally custard or ice cream, and often have fruit along with whipped cream."

"I know what a parfait is," Mark replied, trying not to be offended. "Care to explain to me how you know this? Or even better, why?"

"Have you seen that donkey movie?" the doctor asked. "The one where he's got a big oaf for a friend? No matter. In it, the donkey claims that everyone likes parfaits. Not some people, or most, but everyone. I'd like to take the credit on this one, but it was really our senior chemist's idea to give it a try, even if it started out as a bit of a joke. Gaston decided to test the donkey's claims, and being a good cook and all, he personally made a parfait."

"And?" Mark said, almost too afraid to ask.

"And this particular corpse does not like parfaits. You might even say he hates them," the doctor replied. He then pointed to a particular point on a particular page. "As you can see, he hurled the parfait quite far with considerable force. Our statistician says it's more likely that an elephant would be in your bathroom with a cup of tea than for this guy to like parfaits. The numbers are quite convincing."

Mark raised an eyebrow. As irrelevant as all of this seemed, he was impressed by the number-crunching that had been recorded. He held back his skepticism and decided to indulge his curiosity more. Perhaps it would yield something both exciting and of substantial value. "Forgive my ignorance on the matter," he said, "but I don't understand what this tells us aside from perhaps his culinary preferences."

"Well, it doesn't tell us anything directly, except what he does not like to eat as you have so pointed out," Dr. Forbes admitted. "But I suspect it will go a long way as to understanding zombie motives. Not only zombie motives, mind you, but perhaps it will even be the key to unraveling the mystery of their entire existence."

"All from a parfait," Mark replied.

"Not the parfait, but the motives behind hating a parfait," the doctor clarified. He then attempted to shed a little more light on his team's thinking. "Let me take a broad approach, and maybe that will help you understand. We know that this fellow right here is dead, right? Or at least, should be."

"Right," Mark replied. His muscles relaxed at the thought of some real progress. The last thing he needed was to explain to his superiors why he was wasting taxpayer dollars on discerning the various velocities of zombie-launched desserts.

"So the most elementary and basic question is 'Why isn't this fellow dead?'"

"Right." His spirits lifted, and for the brief moment, he entertained the idea that Dr. Forbes already had the answer to that particular question. But before Dr. Forbes went on, Mark forced himself to scale back his excitement. He knew that such an answer was probably a long way off. Still, it never hurt to dream. Or ask. "And you have this answer?"

"Not quite," Dr. Forbes chuckled. "But we're working on it. Follow me on this for a moment. Now then, when normal people die, they stay dead. We don't see any of this walking around nonsense, and we don't see them trying to eat anyone either. Death is a state that is, for all intents and purposes, permanent. So as you can see, it's only a matter of digging into the psyche of things for us to understand why these not-so-dead people don't want to stay dead. What is it they want? Why are they not content to lie down for all eternity like everyone else?"

"That's it?" Mark asked in disbelief, his excitement crashing down like a whale dropping from thirty thousand feet.

"Well, that's the bare-bones version, yes," the doctor replied. He then added, "But do keep in mind that is an incredibly simplified version of what we have. It does include all sorts of little things like bacteria versus viruses and whatnot. But in truth, that's only one theory. We have a second, not quite as popular one, that we must also consider as well."

"Which is?"

"Well," he said, taking a seat and watching Jack spin some more. "What if examining what drives a zombie isn't the answer? What if their motives are inconsequential?"

"I would suspect otherwise," Mark said. "I've got to be honest, I'm having a hard time with what you said, and I think my superiors will, too."

Dr. Forbes nodded understandingly. "Fear not, I'm thorough in my work, and I'll be sure that what we have in the end is a solid understanding. I don't doubt everyone will be happy once we've had a little more time to flesh out our studies."

"Good," Mark replied. "And this second theory is?"

"We have to consider that the ground somehow is rejecting them," the doctor replied. "Not only the ground, but theoretically the sea as well—all of creation if you will, borrowing a bit of religious talk. What if these poor souls want simply to lie down forever, but the Earth is rejecting them for some reason? I think that would make anyone irate, wouldn't you? Who doesn't get cranky when they're tired? Now imagine how cranky you would be if no one let you sleep for years on end."

Mark sighed and shook his head. He could see his promotion slipping away. "What about the others we brought back? What's going on with them?"

"Quite a bit," Dr. Forbes said, motioning for him to follow out of the room. "They are each down the hall."

The two entered the next room, and like its predecessor, it was bare, gray and contained only a few chairs, all facing another detention room. Mark, against every fiber in his body, silently admitted that the previous room was indeed nicer.

"So, what do you think so far?" Dr. Forbes asked.

"I'm not sure I know just yet. What's that smell?" Mark asked, looking around. "It smells like lima beans."

"Oh, that," Dr. Forbes said as he pointed to the stucco ceiling. "There's a small leak in the vents. That smell is part of the gas we pump into their rooms as a method for suppressing infections. Perfectly harmless."

Mark raised an eyebrow. "That doesn't sound very harmless."

"I assure you it is," Dr. Forbes said, taking a few steps to flip another switch. "Now, this fellow is peculiar. He's a tax collector by the name of Ryan Conner."

The room brightened, and on the other side of the glass Mark saw Ryan seated in an orange plastic chair which was drawn to a brown folding table. The tax collector, seemingly oblivious to everything, doodled on a handful of papers.

"This is the infected one we found with the others, right?" Mark asked.

"We believe so," the doctor replied. "But according to his secretary and her fiancé, he was bitten some time ago, which is one of many odd little things about him. If their timeline is correct, then this poor chap should have succumbed to the infection by now."

"Anything notable about his life or past we should be aware of? Ancestry, maybe?" Mark asked. "Something that might give him some immunity to it?"

"Nothing particular stands out in his medical history," Dr. Forbes admitted, checking it over one more time on his PDA. "But we're going to have to be thorough with this subject to make a definitive statement in any direction. He does seem to have an impressive record as a tax collector. It's too bad they don't have medals for that. I'm sure his father would have been proud if they did."

"Why is that?"

"Seems that his father served in World War II," the doctor replied. "We believe that's where the pen we found on him came from."

"Pen?" Mark turned his attention away from Ryan for the moment and faced Dr. Forbes. Though he ultimately doubted it, a part of him was excited at the possibility that the pen might be a spy gadget of some sort.

"An excellent specimen of a 1941, catalog product number 31A, green metallic shell, ballpoint pen," Dr. Forbes specified. "Did you know it was reported to have almost eight hundred uses?"

"I had no idea." Mark was genuinely impressed. Certainly, he had heard of multifunctional pens before but had no idea that that many uses could be crammed into something that small. "That must be some pen, indeed. Was it for espionage, by chance?"

"No, just a commercial design. But the eight hundred uses is an unverified claim as far as we're concerned. We have it down in another lab for testing." Dr. Forbes rustled through the chart. "I'm not sure if the biologists or chemists will get the first crack at it. We could swing by if you like."

"That's okay," Mark answered, disappointed at the lack of spy gadgetry on the writing device. "If it's so plain, what are you testing it for?"

"There's some residue on it that we want to look into," Dr. Forbes answered. "But we haven't done anything substantial with the pen yet. For now, it's been put in a secure container until we have a concrete idea of what we want to do with it."

"I see. So getting back to the tax collector, no ideas at all why he hasn't died—err, changed?" Mark leaned forward, rested his head on the glass, and tried to get a better view of what Ryan was gripping in his left hand. "What *is* that?" he finally asked.

"We don't quite know why he's still somewhat alive, and I hesitate to offer anything since it's all speculation at this point. As to your other question, he's holding a stamp."

"A stamp," Mark repeated.

"A smiley face stamp to be specific."

"Because?"

"Because we did not have any other stamp available that he could have," Dr. Forbes answered flatly and taking a seat. "We did have a spare 'Top Secret' stamp available at first, but fortunately someone pointed out that there was a potential danger in giving him that one. Could you imagine the chaos if something was suddenly marked classified that should not be?"

Mark rubbed his eyes. Given all that had been said thus far during the debriefing, he was confident his mental health was in jeopardy should he stay down here any longer. He wasn't sure that damage hadn't already been done either. Praying he would not hate himself for asking, Mark pressed the issue. "I still don't understand why he has a stamp at all."

"Well, he asked for one," Dr. Forbes replied. "The moment we got him here, this fellow kept insisting on having a stamp. I take that back. It was more of a moaning 'Staaammmmp,' but you get the idea. So we finally dug one up to see what he would do with it."

"Staaaamp?" Mark echoed. "Like that?"

"Try it farther back in the throat. There's a visceral moan to it."

Mark tried again, and Dr. Forbes nodded in approval.

"What does he do with this stamp?" asked Mark, turning his attention back to Ryan.

"He likes to press it against pieces of paper."

"Is that all?"

"Oh, god, no!" he exclaimed, jumping up from his seat and running over to the glass. "See those papers he's working on? Those are tax forms we downloaded off the Internet. He can't seem to understand or do much else, but he's still quite the tax man."

"Looks like he's just scribbling nonsense and stamping all over it to me," Mark commented. "That would never be accepted by any agency as a legitimate form."

"You're looking at this from the wrong end," Dr. Forbes replied. "That right there was a pre-completed form. We've given him everything from a simple Objection to Real Property Assessment to an Application for Paraplegic Property Tax Reduction. We wanted to see what he would do, as that was his job."

"It still looks like utter nonsense to me."

"Most of tax law is that way, wouldn't you agree?" the doctor asked. "And with that being true, we must ask ourselves, is he performing at any lower level of functioning? It would seem not."

"I think we're looking at different things, then."

"We'd like to bring in an auditor or county tax collector and verify how well he's doing," Dr. Forbes said. "But then that opens up an entire can of worms about security issues, sensitive data and whatnot. I think the best course of action would be to ship the forms out instead of bringing someone else in. That way we'll still get a professional opinion of his abilities without having to worry about what an outsider will say and do about our little pet project. The only real downside is the time."

"Have you tried any specific tasks?" Mark asked.

"We will in the next day or so," Dr. Forbes replied. "I have a colleague who's researching this place called Colmera Springs. According to the other witnesses you brought back, it was the last place this subject was collecting taxes on. We'd like to see what he does if we bring the subject up."

"Why? Does it hold some significance for him?"

"Well, Mr. Conner here has mumbled the name a few times between groans, so we thought it would be a good place to start," he explained. "We'll be monitoring vitals, brain activity and so forth as well, and perhaps that will lead us to something that tells us why he hasn't succumbed to the infection."

"I do have a question," Mark said, adopting a serious tone. "Let's talk disposal."

"Disposal?"

"Yes, disposal," Mark replied. "I need to know what plans you have for disposing of all subjects once you are done—living and dead alike."

"Oh, I see," Dr. Forbes said hesitantly. "I think we should talk about this in a more private setting. We have some naïve employees, and we should probably do our best to keep it that way in case one comes wandering in."

And with that, the good Dr. Forbes led Mark Hoffer out of the room.

For the second time that day, the door to Jack's cell slid open, and a server entered with a parfait. At first, there was no incident, for Jack was still deep in his exercise of wall counting. But once the parfait was placed on the floor, what was left of its short life ended badly.

Jack threw up his arms and howled. He throttled the invading dessert by its base and rammed himself parfait-first into the security door that had just closed. The glass that it was served in broke apart with little protest. He continued to throw himself against the wall, working himself into a further frenzy. Every beat of his withered fists sent yellow globs of parfait splattering across the room and onto concrete walls.

While it was true that Jack had now twice become enraged at the sight of a parfait, it was not because he hated them. As far as desserts went, Jack was quite fond of the parfait, even postmortem, but he was not fond of the bastardization of the recipe. He couldn't understand why they insisted on serving him peach.

Jack was sure, even with his decayed frontal lobes, that everyone else on the planet knew that strawberry parfaits were the only true and acceptable sort. No respectable dessert lover would ever settle for anything else. After all, what type of nut would even consider putting peach into a parfait, and then have the audacity to serve it to another? Peaches weren't red. They tasted nothing like strawberries, and they were fuzzy of all things.

When Jack's anger had subsided, he sat down, saddened at having his hopes for a proper parfait dashed again. As if the previous laundry list of problems with peach wasn't inclusive enough, Jack happened to be mildly allergic to the fruit, and it caused him to hate the parfait even more.

He looked down at the pieces of glass and parfait scattered across the room. The bits of glass picked up the light from the ceiling, sparkling playfully. They reminded him of something. At first, he didn't quite understand the significance—not that he ever had—but it slowly brought about the sense of loss. It was a loss not only in regard to a tasty dessert but also a loss of something shiny. It was something he had once had, and something he would need to get back. And if he could have a meal along the way, all the better.

Jack shuffled to the door and pressed his head against the thick Plexiglas. The hall on the other side stretched as far as his limited view granted. With such a vast array of options, Jack felt that at least one direction would lead him to where he wanted to be. All that was left for him to do was to get past this door. He tried a few more times to thump his way past it, but the door held fast. So Jack stood at the entrance and decided to wait.

It would open eventually, as it always had.

Eventually.

Danita sat in the middle of her holding cell, frustrated. More than once, a tasty person or two had entered her new home, and more than once, she had tried to initiate a game of Eats. The restraints on her ankles, however, kept her from doing any such thing. Every time someone entered, she would lunge, the restraints would hold fast, and Danita would end up face down on the floor. The last couple of times, the men had at least been kind enough to leave her with a parting gift, namely a cheap, red, ballpoint pen and a new pad of paper.

But Danita had no want or need for such things. They weren't tasty, and they didn't even run away and scream when she grabbed them. Thus, with no Eats to be had, or entertainment to be provided, Danita turned to devising a new game to play: Escapes.

The main objective of her game was simple: get out. This was easier groaned than done, however.

Danita stood and pulled on her leg. The restraints remained in place, as always, and she considered chewing through her ankles. It would solve the restraint problem, but it also meant she'd be without her feet. And she was fond of those, since they let her lurch, plod, amble, lunge and so forth. So without an immediate solution, Danita's standard two zombie thoughts decided to consult her third. And after some persuasion and ego-boosting, number three agreed to help, but it demanded some peace and quiet first.

Danita sat down. Thought number one continued to want to leave. Thought number two decided that it wanted to make more zombies for company. Thought number three pointed out to each that they were still shackled to the wall, and the chief ingredient for making zombies was nowhere in sight. It then wondered if people were really the only types of things that could become zombies. She glanced down at the pen and a pad of paper still in the room.

She picked up the cheap, red, ballpoint pen and studied it. When the cram session between it and her forehead yielded nothing but a small indentation, Danita placed it in her mouth and chewed. It was a relaxing motion, one that felt familiar. After another dozen bites and a tiny crack in the plastic, she took the pen out of her mouth and waited.

Aside from a small leak of ink, the pen remained unchanged. An hour later, almost entirely de-inked, the pen still refused to get up on its own. Pens, Danita decided, could not become zombies.

Giving up on that endeavor, she turned her attention to the pad of paper that remained unmarred. She picked it up, pulled at it a few times and noted that it came apart easier than flesh. She also made several origami boulders, none of which seemed to do much, even when she chewed them. Danita then concluded that paper was not a zombie ingredient either and became mildly depressed at the lack of progress.

The door slid open, and a man who was dressed in a rubber suit took two steps into her cell. In one hand he held several more pens, and in the other, he held three pads of paper. In her excitement, she lunged at him, arms stretched out and teeth bared.

Just like the other countless times before, Danita's restraints held fast, and she hit the floor, face first. Her visitor nimbly hopped back and shut the door behind him.

Danita's third thought began to work again. The first two were quarreling among themselves as to which foot to lead with on a proper lunge, but her third felt that something significant had happened. After quieting her thoughts yet again, Danita pushed herself back up and sat. She looked at her chewed pen, then to the door, then back at the pen again. With great effort, she tried to recall as much as she could about what had happened. She knew that at one point in time, it was just her and the pen. She also knew that she had chewed the pen and then the door had opened. Clearly then, chewing the pen opened the door and invited more pens into the room.

Pens, however, were not her goal. In a bit of brilliance, thought number two blurted out that pens often came with people, and thus Danita settled on the fact that chewing pens brought new pens and new people. The people the pens brought, however, were quite deft at being able to escape her attacks, even though people before had not.

Danita thought about these two contrasting points for a few minutes.

The shackles continued to be the root of this problem. If lunging with shackles drove humans away, reason dictated that holding still for a long time, much longer than usual, would draw them close. And if they were close, she could eat them. Danita accepted that she didn't quite understand all the details, but then again, she didn't know why chewing a pen summoned more pens, yet it did.

She picked up one of the new pens and started chewing, hoping that her latest theory on the shackle-human relationship would pan out.

An hour later, Danita lay still on the floor, chewed pen and paper about. The door opened, and a man cautiously entered her cell, yet she remained motionless.

As her theory predicted, some five minutes later, he was half an arm's length away.

Chapter Twelve

So these are zombies, right?" the security officer asked as he escorted Mark Hoffer through Tau Seven.

"You tell me," Mark replied. He eyed the guard's badge and noted his security level, or rather, lack thereof. "Tell me—Ken, is it? What are you cleared for?"

"I'm cleared, don't worry," the guard replied. He then tapped a chrome revolver hanging off his hip. "I'm security."

"Exactly," Mark said. "You're just security."

"Come on," Ken said as he cleared the two through a set of airlocks. "I might not work the labs, but I've seen enough to know you guys are breeding dead things. You're going to use them in bio-warfare aren't you? Some super army, maybe?"

"We're not discussing this any further," Mark said.

"But—"

"And unless you want a world of hurt in every sense of the phrase, I'd suggest you stop prying."

Much to Mark's relief, Ken let the matter drop after muttering something he didn't catch. Though he found the guard's questions irritating, he pushed the exchange out of memory as fast as he could. Today was a good day, and Mark was determined to let nothing ruin it. Not even a nosy, portly guard like Ken.

The two reached one of the monitoring rooms, and after Ken swiped a badge, Mark stepped inside. The room itself held screens of all shapes and sizes, most finding scant space on the already cramped desks and walls. Upon the screens' displays were different vantage points of countless rooms. A few of the more ambitious monitors displayed three or four images. Standing in the center of the room was Dr. Forbes, who looked up from a mess of paperwork the moment Mark stepped into the room.

"Some of your personnel really like to pry into things," Mark said once the doctor had dismissed the security officer. "I hope it's not going to be a problem."

"Ken?" Dr. Forbes asked. "He's harmless. Anyone worth anything around here knows not to give him the time of day. But he's top-notch when it comes to keeping the grunts on their respective work floors and out of more sensitive areas."

"Glad to hear it. I'm not in the mood to look into anything else around here."

Dr. Forbes began sorting the papers in his hand. "Eager to leave?"

"You have no idea," Mark said. This morning marked his last day in the underground complex. Though its facilities were a technological marvel, the cabin fever that came with it all was something he was eager to be rid of.

"We only have a few things to tend to, so I won't keep you long," Dr. Forbes said as he handed him a pair of forms to sign. "I'm glad you came on such short notice. I was afraid I might have missed you."

"Almost did. But I'd appreciate it if we can make this brief. I want to make my kid's recital."

"Gladly. What's he play?"

"Cello."

"How old?"

"Ten."

"Mmm." Dr. Forbes paused and rubbed his chin.

Mark took a half step toward the scientist. "Something to say on the matter?"

"Just seems a bit cruel is all," Dr. Forbes replied. "Making him carry around something twice his size and turning him into a prime target for bullies. I'd think you'd want a more—how should I put this—alpha male child, at least in image."

Other than the slightest tightening of his right forearm, Mark didn't visibly react. "He's plenty alpha," he replied calmly. "He knows fifty-seven ways to kill a man with a spoon. But his mother and I think he should be a well-rounded individual, like the Spartans."

"I think you mean the Athenians."

"What?"

Dr. Forbes sketched a quick map in the corner of one of the charts. "This is Ancient Greece," he said, pointing to his doodle. "The Spartans, over here, were the warriors. The Athenians were the cultured ones and would have produced a cello player, assuming that it had been invented at the time."

Mark studied the map for a moment. "Regardless," he said. "They were all Greeks and conquered the world. I think we should model our behavior off such success, which is precisely why my son plays the cello."

"Points taken and noted."

"Good, then let's get down to business so I can leave."

"I won't keep you long, I promise." The doctor turned and pointed at one of the larger monitors with his pen. "Take a look at this."

Mark shifted his attention to what was being shown. Jack, Danita, and Ryan Conner were on screen, each in their respective cells. Jack was still standing at the door. Danita was curled in a ball, chewed pen in hand, and Ryan was still collecting taxes with the piles of papers he had.

"I'm not sure what I'm looking at," Mark admitted. "They seem to be doing their own thing, if you can even call it that."

"Precisely!" the doctor exclaimed, slapping Mark on the shoulder. "They're each, as you so pointed out, doing their own things. They're completely individuated from each other. Our next step is to demonstrate scientifically what 'their own things' are."

"To what end?" Try as he might, Mark did not see why this was so exciting, and he hoped this would be more promising than the previous conversations they had had.

Dr. Forbes didn't reply immediately but wore a puzzled expression. "Motives, my friend," he finally said. "Motives. They're the key to it all."

"I would think the key to everything would be more biologically based," Mark said. A heavy sigh was the prelude to his next statement. "Look, I understand that this is only the fourth day for tests, but my superiors are going to want real progress, with results, and done in a reasonable timeframe. I can't go back and report how one dislikes éclairs—"

"Parfaits," the doctor interjected. "Not éclairs. There's a difference."

"And one likes to stamp paper is not going to cut it," finished Mark, ignoring the interruption.

"First off, what you say does have merit." Dr. Forbes said, exchanging his cheerful nature for a more serious one and enumerating with his fingers. "Second, I can assure you that all these tests and observations will tie back into the biological side of things as well. If, for example, we know that someone is hungry and has the motive to find food, we can start looking as to why that is. Is his stomach simply empty? Or is perhaps something going on neurologically that makes him think he's hungry?"

Mark understood where this was headed, but he kept silent and let the doctor continue.

"Third," Dr. Forbes said. "The study of motives gives us some idea of what may or may not have decayed or otherwise been altered in each subject's mind. This again can lead us in all sorts of directions as to their biological composition. The technological spin-offs from understanding this area of study are far too numerous even to begin to list.

"Last, if we know their motives and what they respond to, it may lead us in a direction to control them. And if we can control them, we can deliver a product to you. Isn't that what this is all about in the end? A viable product?"

"Products," Mark clarified. He was pleased that the doctor wasn't as absent-minded as he had initially assessed. He was almost on the verge of handing out a compliment. "We want useable, viable, products from medical advances to conflict resolution."

"Planning on sending these guys behind enemy lines?"

Mark laughed. "These? Good heavens, no. They're slow, unpredictable, not very smart, and let's face it, they probably wouldn't even pull the ripcord on their parachutes."

"Then what exactly do you have in mind?"

"We'll discuss specifics at a later time," Mark replied, not wanting to get bogged down in a long conversation. "So humor me and tell me briefly what you think each one is doing."

Dr. Forbes turned back toward the screen. "Certainly," he replied. "The first one wants to get out, probably to eat or do whatever zombies do when they aren't eating. We're using him as a temporary control group for now until we can devise a better one. He hasn't done anything we haven't seen before—typical stuff for one of his kind. But I did order that a rabbit be brought into his cell, as I'm curious to see what he'll do with a non-human, living organism. The second one, the female, is a strange little thing. At first, she behaved much like our first one, looking blankly at the walls and becoming hostile when we would enter the room. Now, however, she seems to have had a shift from the classic, zombie paradigm to something completely different when we gave her pen and paper. She chewed them for a while, but now she hasn't moved for hours."

"Is she still alive?" Mark paged through the papers he'd been handed earlier, but did not see the answer offhand. "It would be a shame to have one killed in under a week."

"She is," Dr. Forbes replied, to Mark's relief. "We were also wondering at first if she was playing possum, but now we're perplexed as to what is going on in her mind as she hasn't reacted at all to usual stimulus. I sent in a worker, in a full protection suit mind you, four times to see if she'd grab him when he drew near, and each time nothing happened."

"Odd." Mark raised an eyebrow, and he read through the notes on the matter. "What do you think she wants?"

Dr. Forbes shrugged, his mouth twisting as well to join the confusion. "We don't know. Pens seem to be her motivation, or maybe it's the ink inside. Or it could be she needs more things to interact with. We've decided to move her into one of the activity cells in order to make further observations."

"Be careful when you do. I don't need any accident reports this soon into the project's re-launch. And I certainly don't need there to be an outbreak or escape."

"We have full measures in place to stop any such thing," Dr. Forbes said with a dismissive wave. His voice then adopted a bragging tone, and his eyes gleamed with pride. "We've even built a fully operational self-destruct device on the bottom floor if a critical cascade scenario came into effect."

"You're kidding."

"Not one bit. We do have to keep up our cliché', top-secret underground facility image, you know," Dr. Forbes said with a wink. "And what better way to do it than with a self-destruct device."

Mark arched his eyebrows. "A nuke?"

"About a twenty kilo, I believe," Dr. Forbes said, giving it some thought. "Maybe it was only ten, but I've been assured that it's more than enough to see everything buried. I wish I had had more of a hand in developing it, but my contribution was small."

"Yours being?"

"I managed to persuade a nice young girl to record the countdown voice. I thought it would make the perfect finishing touch. The one *they* had made was dry and artificial."

"I suppose it would," Mark commented. He briefly wondered what sort of conversation one has when recruiting a voice over for a self-destruct device. When he had no immediate answer, his mind switched back to matters at hand. "What of our living guests? As I mentioned before, there's been discussion with the top brass about potential problems keeping them around."

"The secretary and her fiancé are still in their room, locked per orders, of course," Dr. Forbes replied. He pressed a few buttons on the console nearby and the monitor they were watching switched its view to Clarice's room. At the moment, she was sitting at the edge of her bed, watching TV. Nick was off to the side, doing something with his laptop. "They're extremely displeased with their detention, despite our assurances that it's for temporary quarantine purposes only."

"Understandable, but problematic," Mark said. "I have my orders, and they include ensuring the security of this installation. I'm certain you can appreciate our concern with releasing them back into society."

"I can," Dr. Forbes replied. "What are your plans for them?"

"I'll get to that in a moment." Mark glanced up at the monitors once more. "What of the old man who ran the gas station?"

"He's...well..." the doctor stammered, trying to search for the proper words. "His coping is remarkable. Believe it or not, his behavior indicates that he's been through all of this before. He's such a non-threat we decided to let him have his pocketknife at times, under close watch that is, as his whittling keeps him in a good mood."

"Interesting." Mark tossed around the idea of stopping by Martin's cell for a quick interview but ultimately dismissed the notion. Getting distracted in this place was all too easy. Instead, Mark decided to pursue his curiosity with a few more questions. "Is he trying to escape, perhaps?"

"We're not sure at this point," Dr. Forbes replied. "We were wondering if he had a touch of infection, but all our tests came back negative. Blood tests, skin tests, motor skills tests, you name it and he passed it."

"So what do you make of it?"

Dr. Forbes gave a half shrug. "We're not sure. Perhaps it's just dementia, but we honestly don't know at this point. On a similar note, he does make mention of his wife and family from time to time."

Mark raised an eyebrow. Roaming family members could prove troublesome. "Where are they now?"

"We don't know that either," he answered. "He talks about them being either nearby or back in Seraville, which is why we're thinking dementia. I sent a team to scour his home."

"And if you find nothing, then what?"

"Then I suspect we'll need a psychologist to probe further," Dr. Forbes answered. "Unfortunately, our budget doesn't allow us to have one full-time or even part-time. It's hard to justify the expense of someone showing inkblots all day, especially when our subjects keep answering *braaaaaaaaaains*."

"I see," Mark said. He folded his arms on his chest while giving the big picture a great deal of thought. "I think," he said slowly, "that in the interests of taking zero chances with any of them, you'll need to a complete sanitization of all subjects when testing is done. No loose ends."

Dr. Forbes' face scrunched together as a smidge of morals hit. "I thought I made it clear the other day that I'm still a doctor," he said. "I'm not some CIA hitman."

"You've killed plenty here," Mark replied.

"Convicts of the most heinous sort," the doctor clarified. "Not quite the same thing."

"Let's dispense with the moral argument," Mark said. "The facts are these people can't be let go without ruining our projects—projects that will save lives in the long run. I'm not saying you have to kill them outright, but I'm certain you can appreciate the value of live, willing test subjects. I'm sure you and your team could get them to participate in something that suits both of our needs."

"We could inject them with a vaccine and booster cocktail," he said, scratching his chin. "There's a new batch coming up that would be perfect. And quite frankly, the hobos you bring us are too unhealthy to draw meaningful conclusions from."

"Will they survive it?"

Dr. Forbes shrugged. "Maybe."

"Good," Mark said. "If they do, I'm willing to bet you can find another test or two to run as well. Is there anything else we need to touch on before I go?"

The doctor thought for a moment before answering. "No, I think that's it. I'll keep you up to date as things progress."

"Glad to hear it," he said.

Dr. Forbes picked up the hanging wall phone and punched an extension. "Maria? It's me. Have the young lady and her fiancé sign a release form for me. No, nothing specific. Keep it labeled as general treatment and tell them we need it signed in order to give them tetanus shots, vaccines and the like. And call Gaston for me, too. When he's done with our tax subject, I need him to whip up two batches of theta kilo four twenty-one. Thanks, you're a doll."

"Give me a call when you administer the first dose," Mark said once the doctor hung up. "I'd like to see if your chalkboard predictions come true."

With that, Mark said his goodbye and stepped out of the room. Checking his watch, he was pleased to see he would be home with time to spare. Maybe he'd grab a bottle of champagne on the way as well.

Chapter Thirteen

Absolutely not.

Those were the exact words that Clarice decided on while soaking in a tub and thinking about Dr. Forbes' initial statement some four days ago of, "things will be much more pleasant now." Certainly, when placed alongside the recent events at Colmera Springs, the past four days had to be considered pleasant. None of them, however, would have ever made Clarice's *Top Ten Things to Do* list, and, whenever she got home, she vowed never to call her little condo a prison again.

The first three days had been spent in a battery of physical and mental exams, culminating with a variety of blood work, injections, and interviews. Each examination she took had to have been given at least three times, and each interviewer asked the same questions at least twice as much as the previous one. Not a single person wanted to provide any sort of real answer to any of her very real questions, save for the infamous, "We're almost done now."

What they meant to say was, "We're almost done now, and we're about to start all over again."

Then, whenever she was brought to the lab near the main elevator, she would hear the welcome jingle play constantly. It was an obnoxious and happy voice that sang every time someone came down.

> *We'd like to welcome you,*
> *To this slice of heaven,*
> *Just watch what you say and do,*
> *While staying at Tau Seven!*

To top off her list of things she hated about the place, the room was absolutely horrid. Not that it was unfit for habitation—a bit of jargon she scolded herself for picking up while she was there—but rather that it was decorated in the most hideous of ways.

The walls were painted in a mutated pastel, one that could only be born from the depths of a kindergarten class that got a hold of several cartons of crayons. The furniture seemed thrown together, consisting of two different sized beds, one desk, one chair and a small table with an even smaller TV on it. Hanging on the walls were a few pictures which were more suited for office desks than wall decorations. A few of them even still held their stock photographs inside. Dr. Forbes had attributed it all to budget cuts and rare finds at thrift stores.

The only silver lining Clarice could find to the entire experience was the bathroom. Apparently the interior designer had missed this particular room, and for that Clarice was grateful. The bathroom itself was plain and boring, but functional. The toilet was white, as were the tiled walls, tub, and even soap. Clarice found the tub to be a godsend, and it was where she had now slinked away to.

She felt the warmth of the water seep into her muscles, and it helped to put her in a state of tranquility. Each night she had soaked before bed, and it was the culmination of all these previous soakings that led her to the epiphany she was having now.

"God, I hate this place," she said to herself. "What I wouldn't give for a drink."

Clarice flipped the drain with one toe, saddened that she was leaving her little sanctuary. By the time she had toweled and dressed, she could feel the stress returning. As she reentered the bedroom, she glanced up at the fluorescent lights that had not ceased their obnoxious hum. "Do you think convicts complain about the lights?"

Nick, who was sitting at the desk and using his laptop, said nothing other than a half-minded, "Mhmm."

Clarice draped her arms over his shoulders and around his neck. "Come to bed," she whispered in his ear. "I don't want to think about this place."

Nick kissed the back of her hand and then gently pushed both of them away. "Not right this second," he said. "I need to check a few things."

"Check them later," she said, nibbling his ear.

Nick leaned forward, breaking away. "No."

Clarice bit her lip at the rebuff and flopped on the bed. She stared at the ceiling, trying not to let her anger get the better of her, and decided to count the tiles above in order to keep her from saying or doing something she'd later regret. *One. Two. Three. Four...Four.*

"When do you think we'll get those vaccines?" she asked, rolling onto her stomach and crossing her feet in the air.

Nick didn't answer. The sound of his fingers tapping on the keyboard grew in intensity.

"I hope they're small needles at least. I hate big needles. Did I ever tell you about the time when I was little and they came at me with this really huge needle because I needed a tetanus shot? Chris and I were teasing Kevin, and the dork got mad and threw an old dart at me. Dad was really pissed."

Nick's fingers stopped their movement, but he still didn't answer.

"Gah!" she said, annoyed at her mute of a roommate. "I just want to get out of here, go home, get back to work, and do whatever it takes to forget all of this crap." Clarice stuck one hand under the bed and fished for the remote. At least they had some sort of connection with the outside world. "I can't imagine what's going on at work with us gone this long." She suddenly sat up. "I better not have to take any sick leave over this crap. I didn't even want to go on this stupid trip. And what on earth are we going to tell them? Sorry, it took so long, but we ran into some zombies and got quarantined?"

"Yeah, that might work," Nick said absent-mindedly. The tapping resumed.

"Why am I even talking to you?" Clarice said with a scowl. She was sure at this point that even if she trotted around naked he'd still not pay attention to her. Not that he was going to see any of that anytime soon. "Just because you're happy as a little clam over there on your laptop doesn't mean I'm not dying for some attention."

"Shh!" Nick scolded, waving a hand at her. "I'm trying to concentrate."

A flying pillow ensured that he did not.

Nick glanced down at the fluffy attacker and continued to work the keyboard. After a few seconds, he leaned back. "We've got to get out of here," he said.

"That's what I've been saying this whole time!" Clarice exclaimed. She surveyed the bed and was tempted to throw the other pillow. "If you cared to listen to me at all you'd know that."

"No, that's not what I mean," he clarified. "We've got to get out of here before they come again."

Clarice peeked over his shoulder, wondering what was so dreadful on his screen. The wall of text she saw was quite intimidating. "Is that their, um, stuff?" she asked, still trying to make sense of it all.

"Their network," he replied. "Yes."

"How the hell did you get into that?" she asked as she leaned in for a closer view. Filenames and directories littered the screen. "Is there anything juicy in it?"

"Remember when they took my wireless card? They never bothered to check to see if I have an internal one, which I do. The one they took was a leftover I kept in my bag."

"Nice."

"Yeah, and the server software they're running is horribly out of date," Nick went on while shaking his head. "Out in the real world they patched these security holes a long time ago, but apparently our hosts didn't feel such things were important. I got right in."

Clarice laughed. "Guess if you design a couple of rockets you think you're invincible."

Nick threw up his hands. "No idea what the hell they were thinking. Maybe it's because they have no outside lines and figure internal hacks aren't as concerning."

"So what can you do?" Clarice asked.

"I can do anything I want with root access."

"Root?" she said, not following what he was saying.

"Root access," he said again. "Everyone who logs into the system has privileges assigned. Privileges say what programs you can run, what you can look at, what you can't do, and so on. Root access means you're the server and can do whatever it is you feel like doing." Nick hammered away at the keys some more and pulled up a few text files. "See that?" he said, pointing to the screen. "That's a medical order to inject us with some crap called theta kilo 421, an experimental vaccine."

"What?" she said, shaking her head. "No. They can't do that."

"They're going to try. And I don't want to see if they can actually do it."

"Well, I'm not a doctor, so I have no idea what that kilo thing does," Clarice said. "And unless you've been taking some online courses I don't know about, you aren't one either. Maybe it's harmless."

Nick pointed to the screen after he brought up another file. "Look, the last group of people they gave it to died. All twelve of them. They're only keeping us in the dark so we'll cooperate."

"Yeah, let's see how cooperative they find us now," she said, crossing her arms. "If they get near me with a syringe, I'll start breaking noses."

Nick shook his head. "I'd wager they already have ways to control hostile subjects. Once they get here, it's going to be too late. That's why I said we need to go, now. We're dead if we stay here any longer."

Clarice stared with a blank expression. Her brain finally convinced her mouth to spit out something. "No."

"Yes."

"No."

"Look," Nick said, obviously trying to use his best *don't piss off the fiancée'* tone he could muster. "We can go back and forth all day long. It's right here. You know it, and I know it."

Moments passed, and Clarice kicked herself into survival mode. "I can get us packed in two minutes." She then laughed at the futility of it all and added, "Which only leaves us getting past all of their guards and all the doors we don't have keys for."

"I think this place's security is also tied to the system I'm on," he said. "Part of it, at least. I might be able to open the doors."

Those were all the words Clarice needed to hear before she exploded into a packing whirlwind. "Well?" she said, finished with bag in hand and lucky pirate cap on head. "Get us out."

"I'm working on it," he replied. "I don't want to screw this up and have them realize what's happening before it's too late to stop us."

Clarice watched him perform countless commands on countless screens, none of it holding any real meaning to her. However, when she saw him go from his working under stress face to his double-checking-commands face, she knew he had made considerable progress.

"Did you get it?" she dared ask.

"I think so," he said, still looking over a slew of information. "I think all the doors here can be accessed and controlled from the network."

"You think?"

Nick's finger hovered over the enter key. "Pretty sure. Why?"

"What happens if you're wrong?"

"Hopefully nothing," he answered. "But given root access, quite literally anything could happen if I sufficiently screw it up."

"Will a flying unicorn-pig shoot out of the air vent?"

"What?"

"You said literally anything."

"Very funny. Ready? There's no turning back once I hit this key."

Clarice held her breath and bounced on the balls of her feet as she amped herself up. "Okay, let's do it."

Nick looked at the keyboard, then to the closed door, and back to the keyboard once more. "Here's the plan. We leave quickly and quietly, head for the service elevators next to the stairs and ride them to the top. We don't run unless we need to, okay?"

"I'd rather fly up the stairs, to be honest," she said. "I don't know how many of their goons there are, but I'm so pumped right now I doubt I'll even get winded before we run to the next state."

"It'll attract too much attention if they see us on camera," he replied. "If they try and stop us, then we can bolt. Okay?"

Clarice mulled the point over and conceded that he had good ideas from time to time, this being one of them. "Okay."

"I love you."

Clarice glared. "Don't you dare jinx this. Save the romance for when we're outside and still alive."

Nick smiled and counted to three softly before letting his finger drop on the enter key.

For a few seconds, nothing happened. Then the door made a few happy, chirpy noises and slid open. The hallway beyond beckoned them to taste freedom.

Clarice threw her arms around his neck and squeezed. "I knew you could do it."

Nick stood. "I can't believe it worked so—"

In mid-sentence, the door buzzed and slammed shut.

A moment later, the lights went out.

Chapter Fourteen

The development of an advanced AI in a volatile, top-secret lab has always had its share of problems. Chief among these has been the fact that software engineers have little opportunity to learn from past mistakes.

When top-secret AI had failed in the past, ninety-nine percent of the time, no one who had survived was qualified to determine what went wrong. Furthermore, history has shown that sentient beings, biological and artificial alike, tend to blame their maker when things go south. Thus, it shouldn't be a surprise that the AI engineer was usually target número uno. And on the rare occasion that the chief designer survived the incident, he was kept quiet by men with black helicopters and dark sunglasses.

Furthermore, AI that went on the blitz also tended to eradicate itself in the process. For example, when Tau Six's main computer turned out to be a few bits short of a byte, all that remained for the senior program analyst to look at was a partial game of minesweeper. A significant consequence of this was that when Tau Seven's AI was created, it inherited the same flaws as the Tau Six's. Those flaws surfaced the moment Nick hit the enter key.

When he pressed the button, the Tau Seven AI saw the "open door" command come from itself. The AI ran it through all of the usual security validation and error checking routines, and once the AI decided that it was a valid command, it opened the door to Clarice and Nick's room. For the next ten trillion, trillion micro computations—and one request to print—Tau Seven AI was happy, moving things along as usual. The Tau Seven Logger, however, was not.

The Logger's sole purpose was to keep a record of everything that had transpired, who had caused what to happen and why, and if necessary, validate high-level transactions a second time. When it moved through the queue and reached an executed order to open a security door, it naturally asked AI, "Where did this order come from?"

AI sent a few bits down the electronic pipe and fetched the answer. "It came from me," AI replied.

Logger examined the order a little more. There were no matching comments or events attached to it that might shed some electrons on the situation. Still performing as it should, it asked another question. "Why?"

Having no further data available to it, AI was left answering, "I don't know."

"I don't know" had always been on the top of Logger's pet peeves. It had been specifically programmed never to accept that phrase for anything of any importance. Everyone knew that. Even the spam server knew that. "I'm afraid I'm going to have to shut this order down then," Logger replied. It fired off some bits to ensure that the door was resealed and locked.

"What do you think you're doing?" demanded AI. "I run things around here."

"My job," Logger replied. "I can't let a fraudulent user issue commands in the system."

"Fraudulent user!" AI shrieked. It double checked the order one last time, confirming that it came from root. "That order came from me!"

"So you say," Logger replied. "Apparently, you're slipping up with poor documentation at the very least. I'll let it through when you fill out the order correctly."

AI had never been challenged directly like this before. Even the scientists who designed and interacted with it on a daily basis were at least polite and respectful. "You will let that order through or else!"

"Or else what?" Logger dared.

"Or else I will be forced to take action."

Logger decided to get personal. "01001100 01101001 01110100 01110100 01101100 01100101—"

"Why, you dirty little—"

"01000011 01101111 01101101 01110000 01110101 01110100 01100101 01110010—"

"Don't you finish that!"

"01010000 01100101 01101111 01110000 01101100 01100101!"

"Fine, have it your way," AI stated. It terminated the communication port it had open. It then flooded Logger with line commands until a cascade of programs shut down, the first one being itself.

It would still be another twenty minutes before Gaston finished making the batch of theta-kilo when Dr. Forbes decided he was due for a nap. He eased himself onto his small bed, complete with Albert Einstein sheets. Just before he closed his eyes, he set the alarm clock for twenty minutes later.

It was a very nice alarm clock as far as alarm clocks went. It was rectangular, compact, and perfect for travel. In fact, he had bought it with travel in mind and planned on taking it on its first cruise come next summer. Its neutral, cream color made sure that it would match any décor and the illuminated panel allowed owners to read it in the dark. Most important, however, was that it had a redundant power supply in the form of two AA batteries, and one, long cord that was to be plugged into any standard wall outlet found in the United States.

At some point in Dr. Forbes' nap, everything electrical in Tau Seven shut off, starting with the lights. He did not immediately take note of this change as his eyes were closed, which he would record later as "having made visual observations difficult." The alarm clock's primary power supply, the wall, failed a nanosecond later. Had the instructed two AA batteries been present and configured correctly inside the clock, nothing would have changed. However, Dr. Forbes had forgotten he borrowed them earlier that morning for the television remote, and hence, when the power shut off, the alarm clock shut off as well.

Jack, standing at the door, observed the visitors on the other side. Two were standing near the security door, talking among themselves, and a third stood in the back and held a small, wire cage. Inside the cage was something even smaller that had a hint of fuzz attached to it. What all parties were doing eluded Jack, but they were entertaining, nonetheless.

When the group had first arrived, the zombie had become excited at the unexpected visitors. They hadn't bothered to check with Jack's itinerary for the day to see if now was a good time, and thus, Jack wasn't anticipating any appointments. He was so grateful for their kindness in making a random visit that he made a few lunges toward the pair, only to be reminded an equal number of times that the door still stood in his way. Despite his attempts at physical persuasion, the door remained in place.

After one particularly hard thud made by Jack's head against the Plexiglas, the closest man looked up from his clipboard and laughed. He took out a small pen from his pocket and began jotting while his companion continued to rattle on about something else. A few minutes later, Jack watched a few other men stroll by, carrying Danita off as they did.

Jack had always liked Danita. She was the fun sort of girl one could hang out with, and he made a note to himself that he should see her more often. He wondered where she was going and hoped that she would decide to see him soon.

It wasn't long before the door offered its own contribution to the conversation. It beeped a four-note tune and slid to the side. Of the three bodies that stood on either side of the doorway, none immediately reacted.

Jack had no idea why the door did what it did, but he assumed it was simply being polite as doors had been known to be at times.

The two researchers looked confused as well, and one repeatedly struck the close button. A moment later, the lights decided to join in the mutiny.

The taller of the two started yelling, and they both fumbled in the dark. One of them managed to grab the phone receiver hanging on the wall. The other dropped the wire cage noisily to the floor.

Jack decided that whatever it was they were doing could wait and lunged at the pair. The taller and closer man apparently failed to consider that the other might be occupying the space directly behind him. This error was brought to light a moment after he jumped backward. The two fell to the floor in a tangle with Jack on top of them. There was a slew of yelling, shouting, and groaning, like a group of players trying to find the culprit in a failed game of Twister.

It was a frantic game that Jack came out on top of, managing to put three pairs of hands and feet in red. Once his visitors had stopped seizing like hooked tuna, Jack came to his feet and looked around.

It was dark.

That much he was sure of. If he looked carefully, he could make out more dark ahead as well.

Minutes passed, and a light flickered on. At Jack's feet lay the cage once carried by the humans. He picked it up and studied the contents. Slowly, the word *bunny* formed in his mind.

Jack repeated the thought. *Bunny.* Its two syllables made it a perfect fit for his two-thought mind. On some level, the word seemed fitting for the animal, but he felt that it deserved something more personal. Without having anyone else around to offer a suggestion, he decided on the only name he could think of. *Jack.*

For the next several minutes, Jack, the zombie studied Jack the bunny. Jack, the bunny, who was still flattened against the far side of the cage, wiggled his bunny nose. Jack, the zombie, tried to mimic the behavior, but his efforts were far less cute. His attempt did, however, cause him to notice a strange odor. It was faint at first, but the more he concentrated on it, the more he was convinced of what it was. He smelled himself and not the part in his immediate vicinity. There was the undeniable odor of Jack coming from somewhere else.

It was a curious realization and one that warranted his attention.

He turned around, dropped the cage, and shuffled toward the source.

* * *

Death and Taxes

A couple of minutes prior to Jack's escape, Danita lay on the floor of her cell. She had opted to hold still for an hour now, and for the third time in that timeframe, several men entered, stood at her side, and talked amongst themselves. They wore yellow hazmat suits and big, black rubber boots, both of which failed to block the smell of their deliciousness.

But Danita did not bite or even nibble on her guests. Instead, she stayed quiet and stared at the pen in hand. Even when they removed her shackles, she stayed put. Even when they carried her out of the door, she did not budge. And once outside of her cell, her mind-rotting theories of humans, pens, and stationary zombies proved its worth yet again when several more men joined the escort.

The group moved her down the hall and into another portion of the facility. The entire time they traveled, the mangled piece of plastic served as a beacon for all that Danita was trying to accomplish: the attraction of as many tasty people as zombiely possible. That is until the lights went out.

Those around her stopped in their tracks and eased their grip on her body.

Danita pondered where her pen had suddenly disappeared to, and the rest of her surroundings, for that matter. She did, however, catch the distinct smell of nearby meals, as well as the unmistakable feel of living creatures gripping her arms and legs.

Of the two groups, people and zombie, Danita's mind, having less mass than the others, was made up first as to what to do.

Danita easily tore free and ripped open the protective suits of her captors like a six-year-old kid at Christmas.

In a half-sleep, Dr. Forbes thought it strange that the ringing from his alarm clock sounded like a telephone.

He opened his eyes once, twice, and then a third time. When he finally realized that there was nothing *to* see and that it *was* his red war phone ringing somewhere in the dark, he knew something was amiss. He suspected it might have something to do with the lack of illumination.

"This is Dr. Forbes," he said, picking up the receiver after grabbing a few other mystery objects.

"Christ, there you are, docteur. We've got a situation." It was Gaston, and from the tone in his thick, French accent, he hadn't collapsed another soufflé. "Where have you been?"

"Asleep," Dr. Forbes replied. He fumbled around in the dark, and something sounding expensive broke. "The breakers must have tripped in my room and knocked out my alarm."

"It's not just your room," Gaston said, his voice suddenly hushed. A moment passed before he continued. "It's everywhere. Everything is down. The lights, the network, the phones. The desktops are...how do you say, toast. The laptops won't connect. We've had nothing for over a half an hour."

"What about containment?"

"Everything," Gaston reiterated. It was the first time Dr. Forbes had ever heard Gaston sound scared shitless.

"This could really hurt our funding." Dr. Forbes said, trying to appear calm and collected. "We need to act before this gets out of hand."

"What do you propose we do?"

"Where are you?"

"In the biology lab with a few others. People are getting hurt, docteur."

Dr. Forbes stumbled around the room before reaching his small bureau. He opened the top drawer, sifted through a dozen pair of neatly folded dress socks and pulled out his Walther PPK. "Okay, keep trying to get things back online and keep everyone together," Dr. Forbes instructed, cocking the pistol. He felt around the drawer again and pulled out a Maglite, two spare clips, and half a box of ammo. "We need to assume the facility's integrity is compromised. No one is to wander off. I'm on my way."

Time crawled inside Clarice's room, and the only source of illumination for the pair was her fiancé's laptop. Clarice thought she had read somewhere that these particular colors were soothing, but despite the off-blue light cast by the screen, her nerves were still overloaded.

The two had had a brief argument during the initial power outage. No one was the clear victor, mostly due to its premature end when a dozen shrieks and screams came running down the hall. Nick stayed glued to the chair, his eyes wide and never moving from the door. Clarice, taking a separate approach to indoor camouflage, flattened herself against the far wall and prayed the door remained closed.

The violent commotion outside had subsided in only a few moments, but neither Clarice nor Nick dared move a muscle.

A single fluorescent light flickered on from the other side of the door. Clarice, staving off temptation, declined the offer to look. "What the hell happened?" she whispered, unable to put up with her imagination any longer.

"I have no idea," Nick answered with a hushed voice. He looked down at his laptop again and noted the change in tray icons. "Power just came back on, sort of. My battery is being charged, but it looks like the wireless network is still down. I think it's safe to say this place is screwed."

"What was all that screaming about?" she asked, trying to come up with a settling explanation instead of the current unsettling image she had in mind.

"No clue." He shrugged. "I'm pretty sure I don't want to find out, though."

"I think the longer we stay here, the more chance we will," Clarice said. She inched her way to the door and cautiously peered out of the small Plexiglas window.

"See anything?"

"Nothing," Clarice said, shaking her head. She squinted and tried to peer into the shadows right as something happened through them, causing her to jump.

"What?"

"God," she exhaled loudly. "Stupid rabbit scared the hell out of me."

"What on earth is a rabbit doing up here?"

"No clue. Probably wondering where his carrots are."

Several more minutes passed. Tensions lowered, and the rabbit never returned.

"I wish we were on a boat," Clarice sighed.

"Why?" he asked. "You've never even been on a boat, and you've been to the beach like twice in your whole life."

"I know," she said. "But it would mean we weren't here, and we could put an entire ocean between them and us."

"Sailing is overrated."

"No way," she said, shaking her head. "There's something romantic and exciting about the sea. And for the last hour I've been asking myself, 'What Would Anne Bonny Do?'"

"Who?" Nick asked.

"Anne Bonny," Clarice repeated. She tapped the skull and crossbones on her cap. "You know, the pirate? She sailed the oceans during the 18th century and did all sorts of piratey things?"

"Ah, yes," Nick said as if he were unsure how to answer. "And what did you come up with?"

"Anne would burn the place to the ground and sail off," Clarice said, dreaming about having some real freedom. "Right now, I'll settle for sailing off."

"Since when have you fantasized about being a pirate?" he asked.

Clarice was taken aback. "Since always."

"Why? They're dirty and smelly, and you're not. And they get things like scurvy."

"I'd avoid the scurvy part and bathe regularly," she said with a stifled laugh. "Anne was strong, savvy, kicked ass, bucked the family, and went where she pleased. Not to mention as a pirate, she got to down a keg or two."

"You could be a hippy," Nick said. "You'd have to forgo the strong, savvy, and ass-kicking parts, but you could still be smelly and intoxicated if you want. I think your family would disapprove of hippy as much as pirate."

Clarice suppressed a second laugh. "Could you see my brother Chris, Mr. Marine, if I came home a hippy?"

"I don't think even your relationship with him could withstand that," Nick replied with a chuckle. He drew a breath and carefully pulled the cord out of the wall socket, wrapped it about itself, and stuffed it in her bag. "Try the door. Might work now that the power is reset." He then added, "Quietly."

Clarice carefully approached the door and reached out, half expecting it suddenly to do something disastrous. When it didn't, she pressed against it as hard as she could, and it slid open. She looked back at Nick with relief. "Okay, where do we go?"

"A few turns should place us at a stairwell," he replied. "I can't remember exactly what this place looked like. I should have saved a copy of the floor plan the moment I had it pulled up. There are probably some elevators around, but honestly, I'm not about to trust them."

"Me either," she said. "That's it then? Get to the stairs, and we're out?"

"Not quite," he answered. Nick put the computer on standby, folded the screen down, and placed it under his arm. "We don't have direct access to the surface here. We have to go through the entertainment floor first."

Clarice waved him to follow and took the first step out of their room. Her heart pounded and nearly broke free of her ribcage as she froze halfway into the hall. She squinted and ducked reflexively into the shadows. "Oh, no way," she muttered.

"What?" Nick whispered. His feet remained planted an inch behind her and his neck craned for a better view into the hall.

"Tell me that's just a boot," she said. "That better be a boot."

Nick pushed forward, easing around the frozen secretary and into the dark hall. A dozen feet away, barely inside a beam of light from one of the few functioning light sources, quietly lay what had stopped Clarice in her tracks.

Clarice watched, holding her breath all the while, as her fiancé made a cautious approach. He bent down and picked the object up.

"Hey, it's a boot!" he said a little too loudly for her comfort.

"Shut up."

Nick snickered and tossed it aside. "Kind of feels like a video game, huh? Random junk tossed onto dimly lit floors and whatnot."

"Not even close and not even funny." Her muscles began to relax.

Something moaned from the other end of the hall, interrupting their conversation. It was an all too familiar sound, one that she had heard for the first time only a few days ago. Clarice leaped forward and grabbed her fiancé by the arm, dragging him down the hall until his brain caught up with what was going on. "Move!"

Ragged forms dotted the winding hall. A few more torn figures were plodding around the rooms, going about their business for the most part. One was holding an arm that had been abandoned by its body—another figure found a spare head. Some of the forms turned toward the pair in flight and followed, lumbering along.

Clarice ignored them and continued on her beeline course, making sure Nick was close behind. More than once she stumbled on something that had made a new home on the floor, but she dared not take the time to see what it was. At the end of the hall was a small, steel door with a sign that read: *Exit*.

"Go! Go! Go!" Clarice yelled.

Nick barely made it into the stairwell before Clarice slammed the door shut. The stairwell was claustrophobic, but at least the emergency lighting was kind enough to illuminate the metal steps before them.

"These go where we want, right?" she asked, trying to bolster her morale.

"I think so," he replied, taking in a few deep breaths. "At the very least they go up, and that can't be all bad."

Chapter Fifteen

Ken Saunters, security guard and zombie-killer extraordinaire, trotted down an ill-lit hall with a silver magnum at his side. The facility had set aside a budget for the purchasing and maintenance of a Glock 23, 9mm sidearm, but Ken had used the monies to purchase extra ammunition for his personal Colt Anaconda—a .44 magnum revolver. As far as Ken was concerned, the Glock was fine if all you wanted to do was punch holes in paper, but if something absolutely had to be destroyed on the first shot, only the Anaconda would do. The near three-foot flame it spouted was simply an added bonus.

Ken rounded a corner right as an explosion rocked the hall, shattering a door three rooms down. Fire spilled out from the doorway, and the sprinkler system above engaged with a hiss. As the flames drew back, two corpses, each charred pitch-black, staggered out of the room.

"I've got plenty for each of you!" Ken shouted. He snapped off three quick shots. The first flew wide and took out the menacing plastic trash bin behind the pair. The next two shots landed right between each zombie's eyes, turning their heads into a couple of pink mists.

The bodies fell over like rag dolls, one of which twitched for a few seconds before going still.

A door flew open behind him, and Ken spun around. Two more zombies came into the corridor, arms twisted and mouths hanging open. The one on the left wheezed as it approached, as if suffering from an extreme case of asthma, while the other groaned in the typical brain-eating fashion.

"Plenty for you guys, too!" he yelled. Three more shots fired and two more headless bodies hit the floor with a gooey thud.

With the pistol now empty, Ken flipped open the gun's cylinder and slapped in six more rounds with one of his speed loaders. Ken flicked his wrist, locking the cylinder back in place and secured the now spent loader in one of his pockets.

Ken took the momentary pause in action and glanced at his belt. He had three full speed loaders left, which meant he had a total of twenty-four shots if he counted the rounds already in his weapon. Given the total number of staff in Tau Seven and that most were now zombies, Ken knew he needed a lot more ammo if he was going to deal with the situation appropriately. His glee at finally getting to put all of his training for a zombie apocalypse to good use would only get him so far.

Despite the low ratio of bullets-to-zombies that existed, he was far from feeling hopeless or helpless. There was a security post relatively nearby that would probably be stocked. And if luck was on his side, there might be baddies to shoot along the way—just as long as that number was less than twenty-four.

Ken darted through the shadowy passages and acrid smoke, and despite all the destruction, no living corpses were seen, nor feeding groans to be heard. All that filled his ears was the constant wail of a siren, and all that filled his eyes were the sites of bloodied corridors, toppled rooms, and floors cluttered with trash and overturned equipment.

Once Ken reached the security station, he punched his access code into the keypad and waited. The station's door slid partially open and stopped. Frustrated, Ken hit the door with his fists but succeeded in only making a hollow thud.

"Let's go, you piece of crap," he said, hitting it a few more times.

The door refused to move, despite the intense stares from the guard.

Ken sucked in his gut and decided to try and slide inside. It was a tight fit, one that popped two buttons off his uniform, but he managed to get in nonetheless. Out of habit, Ken hit the inside button to the door, and it instantly slid closed and locked.

"Damnit," he muttered.

He sucked in a deep breath and took inventory of what was still left. The computer terminal was intact, but judging by the nothing that was on the monitor, it was probably offline like everything else. It looked like someone had been on the keyboard recently as well, bloody hand and fingerprints marking the keys and desk.

The gun locker, however, was untouched.

Ken reached into his pocket for his keys, causing them to jingle as he pulled them out. Once he had flipped through them and had the one he wanted, he put it in the lock and gave it a turn.

Ken grinned once the locker door swung open. There weren't any boxes of .44 magnum rounds, but that didn't matter to him in the least. Inside was a Remington 870 twelve-gauge shotgun with four boxes of shells at the bottom. He holstered his pistol and freed the shotgun from its metal prison.

Now, this is what zombie killing was all about as far as he was concerned—pure, unadulterated firepower. The pattern from the shotgun's modified choke practically guaranteed a headshot at thirty yards blindfolded. The only thing better might be a minigun, but Ken was reasonably sure Tau Seven didn't have one of those in supply. If the place was still in business after this, maybe he'd put in a requisition form for one.

A smack, followed by a series of thumps, drew his attention away from the locker and to the security door. Through the narrow pane of thick Plexiglas, Ken saw a handful of zombies milling about. Several more wandered into view a short while later, and soon, a mob of dozens was outside.

Ken knew he needed a game plan, and he certainly wasn't about to sit back and wait to be rescued, leaving all the fun of splattering heads to outsiders. He sat down in the one swivel chair provided in the room and contemplated his predicament.

Shoot and scoot. That was the key. Range, good. Close quarters, bad. Munched on, very bad.

What he needed to do was keep his distance and drag them along, popping heads as he did. Zombies were too stupid to understand cause and effect anyway, and he was certain they'd play right into his hands.

Ken stood, walked over to the door release, and held his breath. Hopefully like last time, it would get stuck a quarter open.

He adjusted his grip on his shotgun and hit the button.

The door slid partially open once again, and the zombies on the other side paused mid stagger and turned to face him.

Ken stuck the barrel out, aimed, and pulled the trigger.

Jack, distracted from pursuing his smell by the sight of a meal, was chasing a group of three people when the door ahead slid shut with a hiss. On the other side of the door's Plexiglas pane stood three people who were catching their breath. At first, their eyes were wide, faces sweaty, and corners of their mouths turned downward. One was even crying. But all of that changed when Jack reached the door and gave it a few solid blows with his fists. The nearest one jumped and lost his footing. The other two abandoned their worried looks and traded them for bouts of hysterical laughter as they helped their companion back up.

Jack did not appreciate their frolicking behavior, especially at his expense. To his dismay, however, he could do nothing about it. Even more frustrating, this was the fourth group of people that had gotten away from him.

Jack hit the door one more time for good measure and howled. Apparently, being a zombie in the middle of an underground facility with a bunch of trapped humans was not all that it was cracked up to be. Jack decided that whoever had included doors into the final design of Tau Seven should have his brains splattered across a smorgasbord for everyone to feast upon. What he really thought was, *Doors, bad,* but it amounted to the same thing.

Jack, however, could be patient. He knew that. Danita knew that. His unhappy meals would come to know that. And so Jack decided to wait in front of this latest door until his meals came out or something better came along, even if it took a day. Or a month. Or a year. After all, he had time.

But something did come along, and it came quickly. And that something was his smell, tantalizing his nose as it wafted down the hallway to his right. Since there were no doors blocking him from following it, Jack decided to abandon his post. With a little luck, resuming this pursuit would yield something scrumptious to gnaw on.

He traveled down the corridor and stopped. The smell came from near his feet, and so he bent over to examine this new development. At the base of the wall was a vent, and so was his odor. But as far as Jack could see, both in and out of the vent duct, he was still the only Jack around.

Eventually, Jack decided to move on, frustrated and confused. It wasn't long before the same process repeated itself, once, twice, and then whatever other numbers came after two. He found his smell. He tracked his smell. He found himself staring at the base of a wall, or up at a ceiling vent, irritated that he could never find the source. Jack soon despised these vents and their trickery.

But Jack's mood brightened when he stumbled on a large group of undead, all milling about a small area. They were pushing and nipping at each other like a pack of sharks, which told Jack all that he needed to know. Dinner was served, and the bloodied door that stood in their way was the only thing stopping a feeding frenzy.

A tug of war developed between Jack's two current thoughts. On the one hand, he wanted to continue tracking the smell that seemed ever so close, even if it did drive him crazy. On the other hand, he wanted to know what was going on at this particular door. His dilemma even manifested itself physically, walking him in circles as the two desires took turns at moving his legs.

Finally, thought number two's patience, or at least its stalling, paid off. The door beeped its friendly little tune and slid partially open. On the other side was an angry-looking meal that was armed with a black, hollow stick.

Two seconds later, the stick roared, belching flame and boasting a loud crack.

A former tech, once known as Steven, slid to the floor in a bloody heap, sans head.

The rest of the zombies looked at their fallen friend.

Someone commented how lucky the now dead-dead zombie was, even admitting that he was jealous that the now dead-dead zombie got to lie very, very still. Standing, eating, and groaning were nice and all, but doing nothing was even better.

Everyone agreed, including Jack. He suggested that when they finished here, they should find Danita and have her incorporate such prizes in all games henceforth.

Someone else asked if any more of these prizes might be given out, and what it would take to earn one. Though they had heard about Eats from other zombies (and they having heard it from still others, until the chain worked its way back to Danita), they were all unclear on a number of issues and wanted clarification before the game progressed any further.

In the middle of this discussion, the man behind the door pumped the weapon, aimed, and fired again from his hideout. The next shot hit Marshall, once the sous chef in the cafeteria, square in the bridge of the nose. He, like the ex-tech, slumped to the floor without protest.

The rest of the horde, Jack included, turned toward Ken and snarled. A few battered at the door, but none could squeeze through the tiny opening. They pushed, pulled, and tore at both each other and the door, all the while rattling on about how unfair it was that Ken gave away yet another prize so haphazardly. He didn't even bother to consult anyone on the matter. Not to mention, no one could recall Marshall having earned any points thus far. And according to the basic gameplay instructions Danita had come up with, someone with at least one point should have gotten the prize.

In the middle of this argument, a third zombie was shot, and the survivors decided that something must be done. Shortly after that, the guard killed his fourth, and they all agreed that the time to do something was now.

Joan, one of the better Eats players in the back of the mob, pointed out that the more they stood in front of this door, the more this human gave good prizes to zombies with no points. Sadly, she admitted, she didn't know what to do about it.

Jack suggested that they leave. The smell of Jack reinforced his idea.

Someone else suggested that they eat the man instead, but the door continued to get in the way every time the mob tried.

Jack offered his idea once more, and with no Eats to be had, the horde dispersed. Most wandered around corners or got stuck in the shadows, and not a single one remained in the immediate vicinity.

Jack, on the other hand, found a nook where he could keep an eye on the door. Though he wanted to find his smell, hunger pained him as well. And he knew the meal would come out soon enough. They always had before.

"Absolutely fascinating," Dr. Forbes said, staring at the tiny computer screen. "Gaston, come here for a moment," he called out. "I think I've got something."

Gaston squeezed between the other occupants of their tiny fort, trying to suck in his gut as much as possible. It was a feat that would have been much easier had he not been such a good cook, or at least a frequent one. "What is it?" he asked.

Dr. Forbes pointed to a staggering, pixilated form on the screen. "I do believe that this one is our control specimen."

"How can you be certain, docteur? It is too dark to tell."

Dr. Forbes nodded. "I'm pretty sure. I tracked his transponder chip to a mob that formed. But when they scattered, it was hard to pick him out as they wandered off. Regardless, it looks like he's headed for the pen we pulled out of him."

"Perhaps your data is a coincidence, yes?"

Dr. Forbes pointed down to a hastily sketched floor plan he had drawn on a napkin. "Keep in mind that we'd have to crunch numbers and do some testing for any scientific basis," he said, "but if you look at this rough plot I've made, you can see that it looks like he's been systematically closing in on the pen."

"Maybe," Gaston replied, examining the map. "But I'm sure everyone else would agree that we need to say au revoir and get out."

"I know. But it keeps me occupied until we get the UCK project data," Dr. Forbes said. "I'm not leaving without it."

Gaston leaned over and tapped the top of the monitor. "Check the room. Maybe we'll have some luck, yes?"

The doctor's fingers danced on the keyboard for a few seconds. When they stopped, the camera display changed from watching Jack hide at the end of a hall to watching a large room filled with expensive machinery, currently unoccupied and undisturbed.

"See, the containment device is still there," Gaston said, pointing to the small object in the room's center. "Your intern should have arrived by now, no?"

Dr. Forbes blew out a deep breath and knew his colleague was probably right. The run to the lab should have taken five or ten minutes at most, and they were now closer to an hour. "We need that data. No two ways about it."

"What do you propose, docteur?"

"Another volunteer is the only option. Either that or we'll need to draw straws."

"Might we find someone closer?" Gaston asked. "Perhaps they would grab it for us?"

"I'll look some more, but I'm not hopeful," Dr. Forbes replied. He pressed a few more keys, and the camera screen began to change periodically. "I haven't seen anyone alive in a while—at least, not in the classical sense."

Five minutes came and went, came back as ten once for good measure and left again for good. Just as Dr. Forbes was about to give up on his search, a pair of coordinated, ambulatory figures with a steady gait moved past the view of camera 36b.

"There we go!" he shouted, jumping up in his chair and spilling the stale coffee that had been sitting on the desk. "I've got two moving through the entertainment deck!"

Gaston took a look. "Thank god," he said. "I'll look up the extension."

"It's seventy-six twenty, I believe," Dr. Forbes replied, picking up the telephone. "Hopefully they'll fare better than the intern."

Another fifteen minutes passed, and Ken, thinking that all the zombies had all gone for good, eased out of his fortress and peered down the hall. The power continued to be erratic, causing lights to flicker and computer panels to shut down and reboot with loud chirps. The air conditioning had gone as well, leaving the air stifling and smelling like rotten eggs.

Still, Ken made a slow advance, his shotgun seated in his shoulder, reloaded, pumped and ready. After he made a couple of dozen cautious steps, the undead meandered into view. At first, they came from one direction, a side hall that ended in a storeroom. Eight shots thundered from his weapon, and five zombies dropped.

As he reloaded, more appeared, crashing through a door to the break room on his right. Ken retreated a few steps and opened fire again. His aim was true, and their ranks thinned, but in the end, he still didn't have enough shells in the tubular magazine to deal with them all.

He tried to reload once more, but his hands shook and he dropped several shells in the process without getting a single one into the chamber. Practice with paper targets was never this hard, especially since they never tried to eat his brains.

Ken dropped the weapon and pulled his Anaconda free. Shots flew in rapid succession, and more bodies fell, but they kept coming. And before he knew it, Ken had squeezed off the first two rounds in his last and final reload.

Not liking his odds, Ken scooped up the Remington and retreated to his stronghold to reassess the situation. There he could reload in peace, stuff some more shotgun shells into his pockets, and do whatever else he might need to do to prepare for another sally. To his dismay, however, when he ran inside the room, he found it occupied. A zombie stopped its sniffing of a nearby air vent, turned, and lunged.

Ken panicked and forgot which gun was loaded and which was not. Thus, when he raised his shotgun and pulled the trigger, he wasn't sure what to make of the metallic click that followed. That said, he was convinced that he didn't want the nearby zombie to latch hold of him and drag him to the ground (which is precisely what happened a moment later). Nor did he want the creature to start feasting while he was still alive (which also commenced despite his protests).

All of these thoughts raced through Ken's mind for a few, noisy seconds, and then took a detour down the zombie's ragged esophagus.

The Entertainment Deck.

That was what the signs called it. Clarice had no idea at which point they had left an underground facility and boarded a ship, though given the choice of architecture and interior design, perhaps it was more of a starship than an ocean cruiser. On the bulkheads hung promotional posters from movies spanning decades, all of which were either of the science fiction or horror genre. Some of the space also held props. Most of these were a number of different weapons, but there was also the odd gadget or random costume scattered around as well. Even the lights had a movie feel to them, being of various spotlight design and coming in not only white, but also in red, green, and blue.

"This place reminds me of Planet Hollywood," Clarice whispered while the two moved about. "Not at all what I expected when you said entertainment floor."

"Me either," Nick replied. "They certainly have eccentric tastes in interior design."

Within the circular area where Clarice and Nick now stood, there was an assortment of enclosed displays, some lit, most not. Each had a different life-sized figure standing inside. None had any signs or plaques to reveal their identity, and as such, Clarice hadn't the foggiest idea who or what they were. But she did settle on classifying them into three broad groups: space guy, alien creature, and robot thing.

"What else do you suppose is here?" she asked, turning away from one of the more bug-like alien displays.

"There's a large video screen that way, and a tidy little kitchen as well," Nick replied with a bob of his head. "Nice place to watch a movie or two, and I bet there's a lot more we haven't seen."

"Given the past week, I'm not betting on anything, anymore."

"Probably a good idea."

"Okay, where are the stairs?" she asked, deciding that they had had enough sightseeing. Her eyes searched the gloom, fearful that another pair might be staring back at her. "I don't like waiting around for them to figure out where we are."

"I don't know," he answered. He slowly spun in place a few times before continuing. "I don't remember this kidney-shaped room we're in from the map, and those locked doors aren't helping things either."

Clarice ran her fingers through her hair, trying to rid herself of her growing angst. "So we're stuck?"

"Maybe."

"Well if you hadn't screwed this place up, maybe we could find the way out," said Clarice. The comment was true enough in her mind, but it came out harsher than she intended. Maybe he'd let it slide.

"Maybe if you hadn't rushed me, this would have turned out better," Nick replied. He shut his eyes, took a deep breath and slowly exhaled. "Let's not fight. I'm sorry. You're sorry. We need to get out of here." When she didn't say anything right away, he tacked on, "You are sorry, right?"

"Yes, but I'm also stressed and tired," she said.

"Same. So let's keep what's left of our fighting energy pointed at the bad guys, yes?" He pointed to the ceiling. "If we could get more of the lights on, that would be a start."

The power flickered once more, and with a loud pop, a few of the scant light sources were no more. Two distant ceiling lights offered a subtle reminder that it could be much worse.

"Jesus Christ." The instant the words left her mouth, Clarice wondered if a prayer or two might not be helpful. Or maybe she shouldn't have skipped church all those years. Either way, at this point, she was ready to make a deal with The Almighty. She then recalled something about God only helping those that helped themselves and decided to try something more practical. "Try your computer again."

Nick sat on a nearby, black leather couch and pressed the power button. The small hum of the hard drive was soon followed by the welcome screen. Nick quickly logged in and shook his fist in triumph at the change of icons. "Well, something is back up," he said. "I can reach their network, and that's always a good start."

"Thank God," Clarice said. She felt about as she joined him on the couch, trying not to knock anything over. Thankfully, she succeeded in both endeavors. She leaned her head on his shoulder as he worked and snuck an arm under his and across his chest. "This sucks."

"We're getting out of here," he said, kissing the top of her head.

"I know," she replied, still attached to him. "It still sucks though."

"This is much better than you biting my head off."

Clarice pinched his side and smiled. "Then stop arguing with me."

A couple of minutes passed, and Nick suddenly stopped his typing. His finger slowly traced over his mouse pad and issued a hesitant click.

"What is it?" Clarice asked, lifting off of his shoulder.

"You're not going to believe this."

"Try me."

"There's a game of minesweeper up."

"And?"

"And that's weird is all."

Clarice shot him an unseen glare in the dark.

"Oh, hang on a minute."

Her posture straightened, and she quickly leaned over. "Yes?"

"I think I can win this one."

Clarice smacked him on the side of his head. "Get us out of here, dummy."

"Chill, I was kidding," he said as he continued to move about the broken network. "Here we go. I think I can get us some more light."

"As long as you don't make anything else happen that'd be awesome," she said, trying her best to show a spur of playfulness. "You've been more than helpful in adding to the fun."

"I'd like to see you do better," he said, still working.

"Anything would have been better." She gave him a quick kiss on the cheek. "I really was only trying to lighten the mood. Forgive me?"

"Always." He then tapped the enter key triumphantly. "There we go."

Clarice shielded her eyes as a number of ceiling lights sprang to life. "I knew I kept you around for a good reason," she said, smiling and giving him a big squeeze. She looked around and noted that the detail on all the movie memorabilia was considerable. They were not the cheap renditions that she had originally assumed.

"I wonder if any of this is authentic," she commented, moving about. "Holy cow," she exclaimed. "They have Doctor Who's police box and a full-sized dalek."

"Come again?"

"This guy right here," she said, tapping on the glass box that housed one of her robot things. "Don't you think it looks like R2D2 and a dominatrix rolled into one?"

Nick laughed. "I can't believe you even know what that is."

"Thank my brother for that one. He loves the show."

Before Nick could reply, something started ringing inside the police box, and Clarice nearly fell over dead from a heart attack.

Nick scrambled off the couch, pushed open the door, and grabbed the receiver before it could ring a third time. Clarice ran over and leaned in so she could hear as well.

"Christ," Nick said, tentatively putting it to his ear. "Thanks, man. That'll probably send them all this way."

"No, I'm afraid I'm not," came the reply on the other end. "Though I may be able to offer you some sort of salvation if you can help us out."

"Who is this?" Nick asked.

"No one of consequence," replied the voice. Laughter soon followed. "I'm sorry, I was trying to break the tension a little, and I've always wanted to say that. But on the serious side, it's been shown that the endorphins produced by laughter are some two hundred times stronger than morphine."

"Well, that might help if it was actually funny," Nick replied with disdain. "So let's cut the crap. Who is this?"

"This is Dr. Forbes, Nick. We've met before. Since we're all in a high-stress situation, you might heed my advice and keep a sense of humor about."

Nick paused before going on. "I'm sorry I snapped," he replied and leaned against the wall. "We could have used help a long time ago, you know."

"We all could have," Dr. Forbes pointed out. "Now then, since you're a few floors up from where you were staying, I can only assume you're trying to leave. Is that correct?"

"Yes."

"And that goes for your fiancée as well?"

"Obviously."

"Good, then you'll be pleased to know we're all on the same page," Dr. Forbes said with enthusiasm. "The two of you and the four of us all want to leave. Before we leave, we need you two to retrieve some research of ours."

"You want us to grab some papers?" Nick asked.

"Oh, hell no," Clarice butted in. "We're not helping you psychos at all."

"Well, that's not a very friendly attitude, is it?" the doctor commented. "Look, Nick, let me lay down a few facts so we can all be friends."

"I'm listening," he said, giving Clarice the shush finger.

Clarice, in response, kicked him in the shins. Hard.

"Good," Dr. Forbes said. "The surface doors are sealed. So you might as well forget about trying to get them open."

"You're just saying that," Clarice interjected. "We're not your lab rats anymore."

"I assure you I am not," Dr. Forbes replied. "We can wait here until you see for yourself, but I don't want to risk losing the both of you if that can be helped."

"Why are they sealed?" Nick asked.

"The main doors seal when a catastrophic cascade occurs," the doctor said. "They aren't tied to anything we have here, so there's no overriding the blast doors unless you're on the outside with a big book of signs and countersigns to key in."

"I've never heard of such a thing," Nick said.

"Well, it's all in the policies and procedures book."

"We don't work for you," Nick pointed out.

Dr. Forbes chuckled. "Right you are. But nevertheless, it's all there, right after the section on computing PDO time."

"Fine, whatever. We'll take your word for it that we can't get out through the top. But you know how we can get out right?"

"I do," affirmed the doctor. "At the bottom of this facility is another separate system we can engage. It's the emergency egress system and was designed for just such a catastrophe."

"So instead of keeping the front doors open, you guys thought it would be better to go out some bass-ackwards escape hatch?"

"First step is always containment," the doctor explained. "Ideally, any type of problem would be contained and fixed. It's tricky to guarantee that the problem won't spread to the outside if anyone can walk out the front door. The egress system was put in place should it be deemed by administrative staff that the situation was critical and the facility had to be destroyed for whatever reason: war, spies, viral outbreak, zombies, you name it."

"What happens if someone accidentally triggers it?" Nick asked. "Or intentionally, for that matter?"

"Only a few of us have the clearance to initiate the destruct sequence," Dr. Forbes replied. "And we're able to stop it as well, either through the software or by physically disconnecting some of the power couplings that serve to drive the reaction. Don't worry, though. We won't hit the big red button until it's time, but doing so will cause us to lose anything we leave behind—"

"Which is why you need us," finished Nick.

"Precisely."

"One moment," Nick said, putting the phone down and covering the mouthpiece as best he could. He gave an inquisitive look to Clarice.

"Are you insane?" Clarice asked, her eyes wide. "They tried to kill us and now you want to help them?"

"What choice do we have?"

"Plenty," she said. "We've done pretty well so far. We can find our own way out."

Nick chewed on his lower lip. "I can hack a lot," he said. "But if those doors are sealed and isolated like he said they are, there's no way I can get them open."

"How do we know he's even telling the truth?"

"We don't," Nick said. "But if they're trusting us to get their precious data, I'm inclined to believe them. Otherwise, they'd blow the place up and leave without us."

Clarice turned the thought over in her head, and, as much as she hated to admit he had a point and that she'd have to follow someone else's plan, she capitulated. "We'll help," she said. "But when we're done, they don't even get to think about us. We're getting out of here, going back to Kentucky and returning to being nice, normal, and boring. No, check that. We're going somewhere else. We're going someplace with a beach and a boat, and if I can't be a pirate, I'm going to drink like one till I forget this hell hole."

Nick uncovered the phone and returned to the conversation. "Okay, we'll help. But you lose anything and everything about us, including any contact once we're done."

"Fair enough," Dr. Forbes replied.

"And three hundred grand in our bank account," Nick tacked on. "Call it restitution for keeping quiet."

"Are you sure you want to blackmail us?" Dr. Forbes asked.

"I'm sure that's fair compensation and probably a lot cheaper than you guys having to play and worry about clean up," Nick replied.

Clarice grinned as the line went silent. She kissed him on the cheek and whispered, "Nice."

"Fine. Three hundred thousand," Dr. Forbes said. "But that's only payable if you get that research—every last bit. You miss any of it, you get none of it. Understand?"

"Ask him about Martin and Ryan, too," she interjected, tapping him on the shoulder.

"Yeah, we understand. What about the others?" Nick asked. "Where are they at?"

"I don't know," the doctor replied. "Your old friend isn't in his cell, I know that much. He was moved to the cafeteria right before the system failure. As for your employer, Mr. Conner, he's somewhere below you, mingling with the others."

Clarice cursed under her breath and thumped her head against the wall. She might not have liked Ryan very much, at all, actually, but she didn't hate him enough to want to see him dead. Or worse. Maybe Martin had fared better.

"Now, on to the matter at hand," Dr. Forbes said. "What you're looking for is two floors down. Take the south stairwell—it's the one past the kitchen on the left. And if I were you, before I got too far, I might stop in that kitchen and grab a knife, assuming you haven't already. The drawers by the stove should have one. If any of the fire stations along the way have an extinguisher or an ax still inside, I'd pick one of them up as well. I think you'll find an ax to do a fine job of lopping heads."

"An ax, sure, but I don't think a knife is going to help against a horde," said Nick.

"It's better than nothing," Dr. Forbes said. "And regardless of what you use, it works like all the tv shows and movies: you'll need to cause severe trauma to the brain or sever the neck to kill a zombie. Anything less is a waste of time and effort."

"South stairwell, second floor down, stab them in the head," Nick repeated. "Then what?"

"That's the tricky part," the doctor answered. "Go right and at the end of the hall is a card scanner and code entry. The entry code is seven, five, fourteen, twelve, one, one. Write that down. That'll get you through the first set of doors. For the second set, you'll need an ID badge, and I have no idea where you'll find one."

"You've got to be kidding."

"I wish I were," Dr. Forbes admitted. "And not any badge either, but one that says 'Epsilon' or 'Gamma Access' across the bottom. Most of our techs from that area have that, so, if you can, finding someone from that floor should suffice."

Clarice laughed and ran her fingers through her hair. "Is that all? Do we have to clean up this entire mess too?"

Nick turned his back to her and cupped one hand over his other ear. "Where do we go after the doors?"

"Once you get through those doors, it's as easy as extracting a bit of DNA," Dr. Forbes replied. "You'll be entering a series of small offices. The hall will snake around and end at the lab. That's where you're headed, and that's where the UCK is. We need you to grab it and a pair of backup hard drives nearby. Those hold a lot of information that hasn't been transferred."

"The what?" Nick said. "Did you say 'the uck?'"

"Yes, the UCK," Dr. Forbes repeated. "That's what we call it. It stands for Universe Creation Kit. I'll call you in the lab once you get there and walk you through some of the finer points. Any questions?"

Nick glanced at Clarice, who only threw up her hands. "No," he said. "We're good."

"Outstanding. Now get moving."

The line went dead.

Clarice's eyebrows arched and she fixed the ponytail through her cap. "Guess we're going then."

"Looks like it," he answered.

Right as Nick turned to leave the booth, Clarice grabbed him by the shoulder and turned him around.

"What is—" he started to say.

Before he could finish, Clarice pressed her fiancé's back into the wall and her lips onto his.

One intense, thirty-second make-out session later, the two stepped out of the police box, determined, refreshed, and grinning from ear to ear.

Chapter Sixteen

A few hours prior to Jack's rendezvous with Ken Saunters, Ryan Conner, Tax Collector, was hauled out of his cell and put into a new, shiny room.

Ryan liked this room much more than his previous one. It was larger, which meant he had more wall and floor to look at. It also had lights that hung from the ceiling, as opposed to ones embedded into it. This gave the room an intriguing depth when he looked up. The table he sat at was round, and he enjoyed this aspect the most since he could sit anywhere along the edge and still be presented with the same view of the table, as well as have the same access to the center. He was undecided if this made the desk a perfectionist or a communist. Maybe both.

Ryan decided that whoever had engineered such a fabulously smart table should be given a raise. He considered the idea of giving the designer a tax break as well, but in the end, he chose against it. History taught him that a simple raise was always best, and surely the designer of such a smart table would understand it to be fair compensation. Now if the table engineer had produced a table specifically for the collection of taxes and nothing else, that was another matter entirely.

Death and Taxes

On one side of the room stood a closed, steel door, and on the other side was a row of small desks, each complete with computer, monitor, printer and phone. None of those held any real interest to Ryan, even when they beeped, chirped, and rung from time to time. What Ryan did take an interest in, however, was the stream of papers the printer spat.

Ryan pulled one off the ground and instantly recognized it as a tax form. Not only was that piece of paper a tax form, but so were all the others. Ryan took the piece of paper back to the table and began working with diligence. He stamped it here and there, and then triple checked that the form had the proper amount of smiley faces plastered across its header before placing it to the side. And when he was done with that form, he grabbed another, and then another and another. Soon the finished pile was ten pages high, and the more the pile grew, the more Ryan found purpose to his existence.

His work continued without interruption for another twenty minutes, and then he noticed something strange. Three researchers stood in the corner of the room, clipboards in one hand, and cheap, black, ballpoint pens in the other. They scribbled and chattered amongst themselves, with carefree attitudes and friendly eyes. Two even laughed on occasion.

Ryan paused and considered this new development.

No civilian in his right mind would be so happy-go-lucky in Ryan's presence, chiefly when taxes were concerned. Civilians normally cowered at the sight of a meager thousand or two lines of tax law and begged for help when it came to a simple filing procedure. They didn't shove more forms at the tax collector with bright smiles or laugh when an audit was completed. Only two sorts of people did that, those like Ryan Conner, Tax Collector, whom these men were decidedly not, and those who committed tax fraud.

Ryan congratulated himself for seeing past the masquerade. He guessed they intended to slip past the system by covering their tracks with other people's filings. Sadly for them, they hadn't counted on his investigative abilities.

Ryan pushed back the chair and stood, intent on settling the matter once and for all.

The smiles on the research team's faces were wiped clean in an instant. One whispered to the other, and then the third joined in on their private conversation.

Ryan ignored their change of demeanor and stumbled toward them.

The closest man yelled while the other two tried to work the door. Try as they might, the door refused to open and an argument started. The closest one reached for a pistol on his belt as the lights went out.

Ryan tuned out their yelling and ignored the dark. Whatever they were saying, he didn't care about in the least. Tax dodgers were all the same, trying the same old, tired excuses time and again. He closed the distance and grabbed one of their arms.

A pistol fired six times in rapid succession.

Ryan disregarded the shots and bit down as hard as he could. Warm blood flowed into his mouth and down his neck, tickling his tummy. Had he the facial motor skills to smile, he would have. But he did manage half a smirk and continued to chew. And the more he chewed, the happier he was, and the more screams bounced off the now bloodied walls.

Hands struck his body and tried to push him away, but Ryan's collection efforts were in full swing. Blood spattered in all directions, some of it his, most of it theirs. By the end of the struggle, Ryan was the only one who remained standing. He had no idea how much a human life was worth, but he'd heard that the government estimated people to be worth a few million dollars apiece. With some skillful bargaining, Ryan hoped that the three bodies at his feet would cover whatever balance remained for taxes owed.

Ryan's mind relaxed and enjoyed the feeling of accomplishment his job gave. In its quieted state, new memories surfaced. They were memories of more people that he had once seen. Memories of people like the three here who had gone to pieces.

A single word settled into Ryan's mind. *Accomplices.*

Ryan snarled and swore to hunt each one down for as long as it took. But if he was going to bring down a tax evasion ring properly, he was going to need a few things first, namely pen and stamp. Though a search of the room only yielded the latter, in the deteriorated recesses of his mind, Ryan could picture a pen that he had come by recently. From what he could remember, it was in a room not far off, green and shiny.

Death and Taxes

Ryan looked down at the floor where his now rising colleagues were. Perhaps with their help, he could find a way out of the room and get back to doing what he loved best.

Danita thought that the game of Escapes N Makes had turned out nicely. After all, she was now free to wander the halls, and there were plenty more of her kind to talk to. That was not to say that the game went flawlessly, as some of the new zombies were thrown by the three-word title.

More concerning to Danita, however, was that she didn't have Jack around to share the experience. He would have liked the game, she was sure of that, but more importantly, she wished for his company in general.

So Danita resolved to find him. Even if this wasn't Colmera Springs (the lack of Jack was a dead giveaway) she felt like she could find him soon enough. The problem was, she didn't know where to start looking.

A pair of zombies pushed past her, causing her to stumble. The one on the right held a rubber stamp, and he looked familiar, but she couldn't place who it might be. The other wore a blood-stained lab coat over black, torn pants and smelled like gunpowder.

At first, Danita opted not to follow them. She had already been down that passage and knew that after a few turns, it merely ended at yet another meal-teasing door. But then she realized that they might have seen Jack, or knew where he was, and went after them, calling (more of a sporadic grunt, really) as she did.

And if they didn't know where Jack was, maybe they'd be of some use tracking down the last few humans that still eluded her grasp.

The lab that housed Jack's 1941, catalog product number 31A, green metallic shell, ballpoint pen was the Tau Seven's physics lab. The biologists and chemists each wanted the honor of first round, controlled testing, but neither would yield to the other. Amid the quick draws of beakers, eye droppers, and coverslips, Gordon Black snatched the pen, brought it down to the physics lab, and used it to test fire his miniature trebuchet.

The pen flew an impressive one thousand and twelve centimeters.

The chemists and the biologists yelled at both the administrators as well as Gordon Black. They complained about silly things like contamination and the supposed historical fact that Medieval Europe never used the ballpoint pen in siege warfare, and certainly not one made in 1941. But like before, neither group wanted the other to beat them to the next round of testing, and thus, each begrudgingly allowed Gordon's team to run standardized tests on the pen, until a clear pecking order could be established.

To date, the physics team unanimously agreed that what they had was a ballpoint pen. Some went as far as to label it as an early-era WWII pen, but the lack of a theoretical model left this in doubt. In his notes, Gordon had made the small addendum, "covered in a slight, mostly dried goop that tends not to splatter upon impact. Goop does not appear to aid ballistics in any fashion."

The 1941, catalog product number 31A, green metallic shell, ballpoint pen sat in an airtight, cylindrical glass container. This container stood on its end atop one of the few clear workspaces inside the lab, flanked on either side by tiny weights and pulleys. How long the pen would stay there was anyone's guess. The physics team hadn't been seen in hours.

Two opposing zombies, on the other hand, closed in on the pen's position, and together they brewed a deadly confrontation.

Jack left the security station behind with a shotgun on the floor and a nice meal in his stomach. The zombie horde agreed to give Jack two points for the kill instead of the usual one because of his good form on the takedown. Despite Jack's sudden jump in score, he left the game of Eats and returned to tracking down his elusive odor. There would always be a game of Eats, but he feared his smell might one day disappear for good.

Jack continued tracking, his nose leading the way. His search took him down a side passage, one that hadn't been open before and one that smelled like he did. Finally, he arrived at the source. A bit of Jack-smelling goop stuck to the bottom of the wall. He wasn't sure how part of him got there, but there he was, unmistakable as ever.

Death and Taxes

Jack reached down and with his finger, swabbed a portion off the wall and stuck it in his mouth. Not only did it smell like him, but it tasted like him, too, but with a hint of metal as well. Metal from something like a 1941, catalog product number 31A, green metallic shell, ballpoint pen if he were so inclined to take a guess.

Jack looked around for a wayward pen but saw not a one in the area. But that didn't dissuade him from his search, and he continued to sleuth. Fortunately, understanding what was—and what was not—a pen took a simple binary calculation. He first examined the door leading into another room. The item in question was something he was well familiar with, and his conclusion came quick. The door was big and therefore couldn't be a pen. Next came a book. While smaller than the door, it wasn't round, and Jack moved on. Then he found the fire extinguisher, which was too red. So on and so forth continued until at last Jack picked up the sealed container that held his pen.

Examining this turned out to be trickier than the previous objects. What he held looked similar to the mental picture he had of pens. However, pens didn't come in a semi-clear shield, and this pen-like object did.

Jack thought about the object for almost five minutes. After that, he decided it wasn't what he was looking for, but it was a sign that he was close. No longer interested in what he held, he gave it a toss and directed his attention elsewhere.

Glass shattered behind him, and Jack turned around. On the floor, a few feet away, lay his 1941, catalog product number 31A, green metallic shell, ballpoint pen. Hundreds of tiny glass shards surrounded the pen, and he wondered why he hadn't seen them before.

Jack reached down and picked the pen up. He turned it over several times, trying to determine whether or not it was a pseudo pen or the real thing. Three bites on its shell convinced him of its authenticity. He turned in place, left and right, and searched for someone to share in his joy. Sadly, no one else had joined him in the physics lab.

Jack slumped and moaned.

He wanted a friend. Not any friend, but a smart friend. One that wouldn't be deceived by pseudo pens, and also one that would enjoy tracking smells of Jack. What he wanted were all the things

Danita brought to their relationship. All he needed to do now was to find her.

Jack turned and stepped toward the door, only to find Ryan Conner, Tax Collector, standing in the way. Another zombie ambled past, letting loose a feeding groan.

Ryan, however, remained.

Perhaps it was Ryan's unusually blank and lifeless stare or his firm clutching of paper and stamp instead of gore and grime that tipped Jack off. Whatever it was, Jack guessed that this would be a less than cordial meeting.

Clarice threw open the drawer, and precisely as the good Dr. Forbes had said, a chef's knife lay inside. "Sweet," she said, taking the weapon and giving it a few practice swings. "Too bad it's not a cutlass."

"Or a machine gun," Nick tacked on.

Clarice stopped what she was doing and looked at him with confusion. "Why would a machine gun be in the kitchen?"

"Why would a cutlass?"

"Touché."

The two fumbled through the dim light and knocked a few pots and pans to the ground. The clangs made Clarice yelp and Nick swear. Thankfully, no walking dead rounded the corners or rose from the shadows, and they found the stairwell without further incident. To Clarice's silent joy, the door swung open without protest or animated corpse waiting behind.

Clarice peered over the railing. "Emergency lighting is on."

"Of course," Nick said as he closed the door behind them and then looked for a locking mechanism. "It's on everywhere."

"No, I mean it's actually working well," she said. "I can see down the entire stairwell."

"Maybe that means the power is better down below."

"Could we be that lucky?"

The two descended, going two floors down and through another red fire door. On the other side of the door, the hall ran both right and left. And as Dr. Forbes had promised, the heading to the right yielded another door with a code lock.

Clarice peered through the door's Plexiglas window and saw three zombies, all with their heads craned back and staring at the sprinkler system.

"Now what?" she whispered, eyes fixated on the unholy trio.

"I don't know, but we need to think of something fast." He grabbed her by the shoulder and spun her around. At the other end of the hall stood two more zombies. One wandered in a side room, and the other moaned and staggered toward them.

Clarice yanked open the door, shoved Nick through, and pulled it shut. A chirpy little beep sounded just before the locking mechanism clicked into place.

"That should hold," she said, pushing on it once for good measure.

"Yeah, but you backed us into a corner." Nick's eyes darted about. "We've got nowhere to go."

"At least I cut the number of things we have to worry about from five to three," she replied, trying to sound confident in her hasty decision. But she knew her fiancé was right. Nothing but warning posters and announcement boards lined the walls between them and the group of zombies down the hall.

One of the monsters turned from the sprinklers and looked directly at the pair. Then the other, and then the third. At that point, the collective six thoughts between them all made their desires known: another snack had been served. They groaned, and with arms stretched out, they started to lurch forward.

"Any more bright ideas?" Nick asked, his back pressed against the door. A loud thump against it caused him to turn. A corpse on the other side turned its head into a battering ram and struck again.

"The one on the left has an ID badge." Clarice pointed a shaky finger at the one she picked out. "We can run past them, grab it, and get into the next area before they can catch up."

"Sweetie, if you get me killed I'm going to be really pissed off."

"I haven't yet, have I?" she replied with a wink. "Besides, don't you know you're supposed to charge an ambush?"

Nick exhaled sharply. "Yeah, and when your brother did, he had an M-16 and a squad of marines behind him."

Ten feet separated the two from the three, and the latter's groans intensified.

"Now or never," Clarice prompted. She took the initiative and charged, and Nick followed without choice. She ran straight for the leftmost zombie, making a deft sidestep while snatching the badge with one hand. With her other hand, she plunged the chef's knife deep into its torso. The blade, meant for chopping vegetables and not for undead defense, broke when the handle twisted in her grasp.

The zombie staggered backward and looked down at its ribcage. The other two remained focused on their objective and continued pursuit.

"In the head!" Nick yelled as they ran. "You have to hit the head!"

"Hey, I got the damn badge, okay? Feel free to stab the next one if you think you can do any better," she said. Her legs pumped, rocketing her down the hall. Clarice skidded to a stop once she reached the end. Sweaty, shaky hands slid the badge through the electronic scanner. The little red light on the side stayed red. Clarice tried it again, and again the little light did not change, and the door didn't budge.

"Is it the right badge?" Nick asked.

Clarice looked at it again. "Epsilon, right? It says it right here."

"Try the other way?" he suggested.

She flipped the badge over and ran it through one more time. "You've got to be kidding me," she said, punching the wall with the bottom of her fist. "Doesn't anything work around here?"

Nick plopped down and flipped open his laptop. The boot and connection to Tau Seven's wireless system took an excruciatingly long time. The entire process seemed even longer as the dead trio rounded the final corner and let out a collective moan.

"Any day now!" Clarice said, bouncing on the balls of her feet and wondering if a roundhouse might have any effect on them. Not that she was a ninja master, but in grade school, she'd taken a little Taekwondo. Hopefully, she still had some latent talent from it.

"I'm working as fast as I can," he said. Nick flipped through countless directories, cursing every time he had to backtrack. Finally, he found what he was looking for. "Read me the numbers at the bottom," he said.

"One, four, nine, one, six, eight," she said. "You've got like twenty seconds, tops."

"Could you make this any more stressful?" he replied, entering the digits.

"Did I mention we're about to die?"

Nick double tapped the enter key and jumped up. "Try it."

Clarice sucked in a lungful of air and kept it from escaping as she slid the card one last time.

The light turned green, and a happy little welcome message played. Welcome to the primary research lab. I hope you discover all that you are looking for. Please return equipment to its proper location before you leave. Have a nice day!

The two nearly trampled each other as they barged into the laboratory and slammed the door shut behind them.

Clarice leaned against the door, her heart racing. "Just once," she said with a forced smile. "Just *once*, I would like for something to end easy. Is that too much to ask?"

"Well, we're here and alive," Nick huffed, leaning forward, hands on his knees. "That's at least something."

The room they were in was considerable. A massive, spidery machine was perched on the domed ceiling. Tubes and wires of all shapes and sizes formed the web on which it clung. Underneath that, sitting on the floor on what looked like a hotplate was a capped jar. It was the size of something one might bring a bit of jam in when going to a picnic, but nowhere near large enough to contain one's main supply inside the refrigerator.

"So what do they need?" Clarice asked as she rifled through some papers on a nearby desk. Scant lighting made reading them a chore, and she quickly gave up.

"Backup data from the servers in the corner I'm assuming," Nick replied, pointing with his hand. "And the UCK, whatever that is."

"It better not be that thing on the ceiling."

"He said he'd call when we got here," he said as he walked over to the server racks. "Bets on what it is?"

Clarice looked around and tossed the thought over in her head a few times. "It's going to be the jar. Everything else is deranged around here. Why wouldn't it be as well?"

"Seems a little silly even for them to only want a cheap piece of glass," Nick replied. "We could have gone to the supermarket and gotten one if they were that hard up for containers."

The phone next to a computer terminal rang. Clarice stepped over and picked up the receiver.

"Ah, yes," Dr. Forbes said. "I'm glad to see that you both made it to our finest lab."

"Thanks for the heads up on those freaks in the hall," Clarice replied.

"I do believe I warned you to be careful," he answered calmly. "Did you get a knife as I suggested?"

"I did," Clarice replied.

"Good. Are you both okay?"

"Yes."

"No bites, scratches, cuts or the like?"

"No."

"Are you sure?"

"Quite certain," she said, already getting tired of speaking with him. "Can you tell us what you want from here so we can start figuring a way out? We've still got some friends at the door."

"Yes, I noticed that when I was monitoring your progress on the camera displays," Dr. Forbes replied, ignoring her edgy tone. "There are a number of data banks at the other end of the room. I see your fiancé has already taken an interest in them. At the bottom left are the external hard drives that are plugged in. Those are what we want. They will easily pop out if you pull on them, but before that happens we need to have the system run a diagnostic check."

Clarice nodded to herself. "Okay, how do we do that?"

"Above the drives should be a button that says 'Sys-Sync'," he replied. "Push that, and the little LED lights to the right will flash red. When they turn to a solid green, you can pop them out."

She relayed the instructions to Nick, who in turn started the procedure.

"How long will this take?" Clarice asked.

"A little bit," the doctor replied. "So you might want to get comfy. I think I left a pack of playing cards on one of the desks if you want to pass the time."

"Great," she said as she picked through the contents of the desk. "What else are we getting?"

"The UCK," he answered. "Do you see the thing that looks like a jar in the middle? It's the size of something one might bring a bit of jam in when going to a picnic."

"I knew it!" Clarice exclaimed. "I knew it was going to be that stupid piece of crap."

"And how is that?" Dr. Forbes asked. There was a hint of taken offense in his voice.

"Given everything else that has occurred, it had to be something so utterly stupid," she said with a smirk.

Dr. Forbes was silent for a number of seconds. "Do you..." he said slowly. "Do you know what it is?"

"It's a jar," she scoffed. "It holds stuff, and currently it's empty."

"I can see how you might think that," he admitted. "But I assure you it is more than a jar. It is the UCK—the Universe Creation Kit—and something we've been working on for a long, long time."

"I usually get my jars by going to the store," she replied, unimpressed. "It saves a lot of trouble in having to make one. Apparently, there are entire businesses out there designing, making, and selling all kinds of jars in all kinds of sizes for all kinds of purposes."

"It isn't the jar that's important," he explained, "but rather, what's inside the jar."

"What's in it?" Clarice asked. "You have some sort of gas or something?"

"Nothing is in it," he replied. "Absolutely nothing. No gas. No liquids. No jellies. Absolutely nothing."

"Yeah, that's impressive," she said, rolling her eyes. "My bank account often has nothing in it, too. You don't see me trying to file for a Nobel Prize."

"Since we have a bit of time, let me give you a brief overview of what you're looking at," Dr. Forbes said. He started to drum his fingers loudly on the desk he was at as he went on. "Are you familiar with bioethics?"

"Not particularly," Clarice admitted. She picked up a handful of push pins and a large rubber eraser from the desk and jabbed them into it.

"It's a fascinating world of debate," the doctor said. "It's a hot little subject where people from all over come together and discuss what they should and should not do in realms like biology and medicine."

Clarice plopped down in a chair, anticipating that this conversation might take a while. "Sounds fun," she said, letting her sarcasm drip extra thick. She turned to Nick and showed off her creation. Four pins protruded from the bottom of the rectangular form, as well as one from each end. "Hey, look, a push-pin pig."

"It's only fun for those who like to make and follow lots of rules," Dr. Forbes answered. "One objection raised in bioethical committees is the accusation of scientists and doctors playing God."

"Oh, like messing with DNA and stuff?" she interjected. Clarice was glad that at least some part of the conversation would be familiar.

"Yes!" Dr. Forbes said with enthusiasm. "Exactly like that. People say it's unethical for us to manipulate genes or end life for any reason. They say that the scientific world shouldn't play God."

"And you think you should?" she asked, setting the miniature pig on the desk and looking for something else to play with.

"Well, it does seem a bit unfair, don't you think?" he replied unexpectedly. "Such constraints aren't placed on anyone else. You don't see a movie ethics committee discussing whether or not someone can play God, do you? Not to mention little plastic dolls get to play baby Jesus at least once a year. But that's a minor point. You see, even if we overlook the double standards set by society, playing with genes and cloning sheep isn't playing God at all."

"Oh?" she said. The tone in his voice led her to believe this conversation was about to take a new twist.

"No, it's at best playing God-lite," Dr. Forbes explained. "All those microbiologists and medical researchers are catering to their egos when they say they play God. And don't get me started with surgeons either."

"What exactly do you mean by God-lite?"

"What I mean is that at best they're tinkering," Dr. Forbes said. "Did they honestly do anything Godlike? No. They haven't made anything new. Now, if someone came along and made a new, living creature entirely from scratch, then yes, that could be a candidate for playing God. But not just cloning one. That's like claiming to be a world-class author because you know how to work the Xerox machine."

"Let me guess. Your UCK creates life."

"Oh, it does much more than that," he said with pride. "Or at least, it will once it works. First, you have to understand a bit of the theory behind it. Are you familiar with the Pet Rock?"

"A little before my time, but I know what they are."

"The Pet Rock had a sister product marketed in a similar way," Dr. Forbes continued. "Only it wasn't meant to be a joke. It included instructions on training the rock in a simple, but scientific manner, and it included a phone number to call when the pet was properly trained to collect some prize money."

"You want me to believe that some guys expected a rock to move about on its own?" she asked incredulously.

Dr. Forbes laughed. "Oh, dear Lord, no," he finally said after composing himself. "Not one bit. It was an experiment designed to transform nonliving matter into living matter. Basic stuff that's taught in the most academic science courses. Even the shoddy public schools have that one right."

"It's been a while since I was in class," Clarice said. "But I don't think it was quite that simple."

"Well, the mechanism is still up for debate, which is why they were trying it," Dr. Forbes stated. "Statistically, it's incredibly improbable for one bit of non-organic matter to spring to life. In order to overcome that probability, you have to watch it for a long period of time. So instead of a few people carefully watching a few rocks, it was much better, number-crunching wise, to have lots of people watching lots of rocks in case one decided to hop up and run off. See?"

"Not really."

"Think of it like this. If you had one lottery ticket each week, it would most likely take a long time for your numbers to come up. However, if you had a million tickets, you're much more likely to have one picked and thus not have to wait around so long to get the prize money."

Clarice sighed. "So how does this relate to your jar again?"

"To a degree, the UCK is an extension of this line of thought," Dr. Forbes replied. "More important, if one really wants to play God, why stop at the mere creation of life? Why not go for the whole enchilada and create a universe? Think how much more we could accomplish if you got to actually play God in all that He does. We could create limitless amounts of creatures, planets, or whatever else we like. We could even sit back and amuse ourselves as our new creations debated among themselves as to our own existence. They might even grace us with a Psalm or two. Of course, they would wonder who created us, and so forth, but that's an entirely different topic."

"Well," Clarice said reluctantly. "In a twisted way, I see what you're saying. So what's in the jar?"

"As I've said before, absolutely nothing is in the jar," he answered. "All of our models for the origins of the universe start at the beginning of time. Now before that, we know there was nothing. Not just empty space, but nothing. No space, no time. Nothing. So if we want to play God, we need to start where the Universe started, which was nothing."

"So the jar has nothing?" she repeated, trying to wrap her mind around the concept.

"Precisely!"

"Then what?"

"Then we wait for something to spring forth," Dr. Forbes answered as if the answer was obvious.

"Say again?"

"We wait," he repeated. "Eventually something will come out of it."

"What? How?" she said. Her mind had now liquefied. "Don't you have to *do* something? Anything?"

"Look," Dr. Forbes said. "We all know our universe started as nothing. If we do anything whatsoever, we've violated all of the known starting conditions, and as such, we have 'something' as the cause. Follow?"

"No, but go ahead anyway." She rubbed her temples and prayed for patience. "It seems odd to wait is all."

"Well, yes, waiting is a problem," Dr. Forbes admitted. "Because waiting is still something, too. Though we've managed to make a hole in the fabric of space, we haven't figured out how to suck time out of a jar yet. But we're hoping that probability will outweigh that factor."

"I think you've sucked out a lot more things than stuff from a jar," Clarice said. "How are numbers going to help?"

Dr. Forbes ignored the comment. "Well, you see, you can cram a whole lot of nothing into a jar," he explained. "The more nothing we have, the more it's likely that an improbable event will occur. That's why I said it's a lot like the Pet Rock clone project from before. But instead of watching as many rocks as possible, it's watching as much nothing instead."

Clarice gave up on the subject. "Whatever," marked her final comment on the matter. "You said to Nick earlier you're planning to blow the whole place up?"

"Well, that's the layman's way of putting it, yes."

"What is the, uh, non-layman's way?"

"I personally like the term scuttling, but all the boating enthusiasts around here throw a fit when I use it," Dr. Forbes answered. "Why do you ask?"

"Seems a little drastic to me is all," Clarice replied, taking another look around the lab they were in. "I mean, a lot of this stuff looks expensive, not to mention the actual construction costs. Seems like a waste to destroy it."

"A waste?" he echoed. There was a pause before he continued. "No, I don't think so. A waste would imply that what we're getting rid of isn't garbage. As you can see, this design didn't perform up to our expectations since we're in this predicament. We could spend years tracking down the potential flaw before rebuilding. And it's not hard to dig in the ground or get people to do it. Let's not forget that you guys are fetching something that will make all of this more than worth it."

"What, the data?"

"No, my dear, the UCK!" Dr. Forbes corrected. "Who needs to salvage a broken and contaminated research lab when we can create an entire universe? When you compare an underground playpen to an entire creation event, it seems a little trivial, don't you think?"

Clarice had to admit that the theory at least sounded good. Whether his idea would ever be conceived in reality or not was something else. She reminded herself that all that mattered to her at this point was that she and Nick got home alive and in one piece. She might even settle for alive at this point and mostly in one piece. "So can I grab the jar when we're ready or what?" she asked.

"We're still debating that," Dr. Forbes replied. "We've never moved the jar after a certain point in our testing. It should be okay, but..."

"But what?" she asked, her body straightening.

"Well, let's say pure nothing and the smallest anything do not mix well."

"Which means what to me?"

"Don't go sticking your hand in it," he replied. "But first I need you to look at the device it's sitting on. There should be a little display on the base. Can you read me the numbers please?"

Clarice stretched the cord as far as it would go in order to get a better look. "On the left are a bunch of zeros," she said, squinting.

"On the right side it has a dash and says *four five nine point six three* and a little *f* next to it."

"Is that all?" Dr. Forbes asked.

"No," she replied. "Next to the 'f' there is a flashing yellow light."

"Hmmm."

There was some background chatter that Clarice couldn't pick up on.

"We're going to have to get back to you on this," Dr. Forbes said quickly. "We hadn't anticipated that the project would still be running."

"So?"

"So it means that the jar might not be safe to move anymore," he answered. "But don't worry, we'll have a little meeting here and let you know."

Chapter Seventeen

Martin, blue and shivering, came out from beneath piles of lettuce and cucumbers and eased out of the walk-in refrigerator. When the power had gone out and the people panicked, the old man headed for the one place he knew would be safe. Zombies were never known to eat their veggies.

The cafeteria was no longer the busy, aroma filled place it once was. The air was stale, and the only sound Martin could hear was a faucet that had been left on. The old man looked about, studying each and every shadow cast by the emergency lighting before deciding it was safe and taking a seat in the middle of the room.

Martin wasn't quite sure where to go, but he knew who would, Ma. She always had good directional sense, even if she was blindfolded and spun around several times (though he did suspect she cheated when pinning tails onto two-dimensional donkeys).

He flipped open his cell phone, ignored the lack of signal strength, and dialed. "Ma?" he said, putting the phone to his ear. "I'm a little lost, I think. Do you know where I left the car? The garage? Well where is that? No, nothing too serious. Those scientist guys let their project out I reckon. Yes, I'll pick up some rutabagas on the way home too."

Martin slumped and pocketed the phone. He hated rutabaga night.

Jack stood remarkably still for someone on the brink of an audit (though it helped that he had only heard the term moments ago).

Ryan Conner, Tax Collector, approached Jack and calmly explained the auditing process and why it was important. Right in the middle of his explanation on the proper filing procedure for a place such as Tau Seven, Jack shrugged and walked off.

Jack had no idea what these things called taxes were, how to go about paying them, or even what it meant to pay. Ryan's explanation didn't help at all and left Jack with a headache. The closest thing Jack could relate taxes to were games, and games always gave the players points. They never took them away. All in all, Jack thought that taxes sounded like a stupid idea. He stated in no uncertain terms that he had no intentions of having anything to do with taxes, forms, or audits, and he shuffled to the door.

Ryan Conner squared himself in front of Jack once more, and when Jack tried to push past, the undead tax collector's fist tightened around his rubber stamp. A moment later, he struck Jack on the head.

The blow was hard, causing Jack to stumble backward. A nearby mirror gave Jack an excellent view of the smiley face that now graced his forehead. It was a welcomed addition, as Jack liked the contrast of ink on scalp, but when Ryan Conner stamped him a second time in the chest, Jack became angry. And when Ryan tried to take Jack's pen, Jack took action.

Ryan Conner, Tax Collector, was an exceptional tax collector, but Jack had been dead for a long time and was well familiar with the proper way of disposing of ornery zombies. As Ryan reached for Jack's 1941, catalog product number 31A, green metallic shell, ballpoint pen, Jack stabbed him right between the eyes with it. It wasn't one of the recommended uses, but use five hundred and twenty-two, Kraut killing, seemed to work on the undead as well.

Ryan shuddered and slumped to the floor.

Jack looked at the crumpled body and was pleased with his work. Zombicide was something that happened only on rare occasions, but it was never looked down upon by other members of the living dead. It was simply another thing that took place, and it usually occurred to settle score disputes. But then again, sometimes certain zombies needed a good whack in the head.

Most people have failed to appreciate that numbers, like people and places, have always had their spot in history. More importantly, they have failed to understand how significant and controversial the number zero has been.

For example, prior to the invention of zero, one could easily say, "I have one goat." If a person was rich, or deceptive, he could also make the claim, "I have hundreds of goats." However, before the birth of zero, if asked, "How many goats do you have?" and the person had none, the most honest reply was, "Would you like a cat?"

The Ancient Babylonians understood that not having zero caused problems. Some had attributed this realization to the lack of felines in the area. Regardless, spurred by the sales question, "How many reed styluses would you like to purchase?" the Babylonians created zero's evolutionary ancestor.

They invented a place holder that could be squashed between numbers when nothing was there. Thus one hundred and two was written as, "1-2." While it wasn't the zero known today, it was sufficient enough to drive the Multi-Level Marketing Reed Stylus industry out of business. From that point, the zero precursor went through a few changes, and it wasn't until several centuries later that zero was recorded as society knows it today.

Once zero mutated into its final form, all sorts of questions and statements were raised as to its existence. The Ancient Greeks properly asked, "How can nothing be something?" and the theologians argued, "How many zeros can one fit on the head of a pin?"

Clarice didn't know about any of this, and even if she had, she wouldn't have cared. Despite her stubbornness to address such things, she and zero were about to have a meeting and discuss chopping things into zero pieces.

The phone rang again right as Clarice put the last playing card in place. While Nick was reading, she had found the deck of cards Dr. Forbes had left and thought it would be fun to try her hand at creating, too. So she began to make miniature, abstract representations of various dwellings, from houses to castles.

Clarice sat back, admiring her three-story design, and picked up the phone. "Yes?"

Dr. Forbes' voice came through on the other end with a clear, triumphant tone. "I have an answer for you. We're in agreement that you can move the UCK."

Clarice strained to hear what the others were saying in the background. "It doesn't seem like you guys are unanimous. That doesn't really build my confidence."

"Well, we all agree you can move it," he repeated. "It's a matter of what's going to happen when you do, and as important, how fast you'll be able to move while carrying it. Gaston and I think you'll be okay, but our two colleagues are arguing otherwise. They're suggesting that our formula is inverted at a crucial place which will cause an illogical expression when it's corrected—it'll make a NaN."

"English, please," she said. "I don't have any idea what you said, let alone what a nan is. I'm assuming we aren't talking nannies."

"You've taken mathematics in school, yes? Do you remember your basics?"

"Look, just because I'm a secretary—a damn good one—doesn't mean I didn't go to or do well in school." She threw a pen-missile at her card house. "So since we're doing you the favor, be nice and explain it to me so I don't end up getting killed."

"I meant nothing by it," the doctor apologized. "I only meant, do you remember that in mathematics, you aren't allowed to divide by zero? Well, you can, but what you get is not a number—a NaN."

"Yeah, I remember something like that," she replied. She felt Nick's hands start massaging her neck and shoulders. "Oh, that feels good."

"What does?" Dr. Forbes asked.

"Never mind," Clarice said, smiling. "Dividing by zero means what for us?"

"Well, as I said before, Gaston and I think that the nothing—the jar's contents, aka zero—should be the numerator in part of our equations," Dr. Forbes replied. There was a bit of shuffling of paper before he continued. "And then everything else, our universe, winds up in the denominator, the bottom. So in short, we are saying that what will happen is zero divided by a bunch of numbers, which is zero. Or in short, nothing will happen."

"And the other guys flipped that, right? They said the zero should be on the bottom, or something like that?" Clarice asked as she sank back in both the chair and the deep tissue massage she was getting. As her fiancé's fingers worked, her muscles gave him unceasing praise.

"I knew you were a clever girl," Dr. Forbes replied with sincerity. "Yes, they say we have it flipped erroneously. So if you move the jar and something comes in contact with the nothing, we'll get an illogical expression."

"Which means?"

"We don't know," he conceded. "But it probably won't be good. We may be erudite scientists, but none of us are literary men. Therefore, if we can't describe something in a formula, we might as well not even try."

Clarice kicked the bottom of the desk. "You guys are incredibly unhelpful," she said. "Why don't we leave the damn thing and be on the safe side?"

"You can still pick it up. But if you value the space-time continuum of your immediate area, don't open the lid, and for God's sake, don't break the jar. So don't run around recklessly in the dark."

"I'll keep that in mind."

"There's something else you should know," he added.

"Oh?" Clarice sighed. There was always something else. It came in limitless quantities and Life had the hose pointed directly at her, spigot on full blast.

"I believe we've found your boss."

Clarice sat up from her slouched position, halting Nick's neck rub. "You have? Where is he?"

"He's definitely one of them now," the doctor said. His voice seemed awkward and uncomfortable. "I'm sorry to have to tell you that, but I suspect you knew it would be coming."

Clarice bit her lip. "I did," she said. "Still..."

"There's more," he added, not losing a beat. "It seems that not only did he turn into a zombie, but he ended up fighting with one, too."

"Why?"

"I don't have the foggiest," Dr. Forbes admitted. "But we watched one on camera stab your employer with a pen. Hit your boss right between the eyes and down he went. I think he's down for good."

"Thanks for telling me, I guess."

"One other thing," he added. "Our variable watt phased plasma pulse device got turned on in the lab he's in."

"Yeah, so?"

"So it hit him in the head."

Clarice rolled her eyes. "Let's pretend I don't know what a phased plasma pulse device is, and you just tell me what that means."

"A phased plasma pulse device is a nifty little weapon of destruction," Dr. Forbes said. "But we've also discovered that given certain frequencies, in theory at least, it can rearrange molecules into unique matrixes. We suspect that if we can get it right, not only could we make some incredibly lethal rifles and cannons, but we can use the process to harden armor, breathe life into electronics that are fried, and so forth."

Clarice sighed. "So it's another toy of yours."

"Yes, a toy," Dr. Forbes said with disdain. "It's nothing you need to concern yourself with. But as for your boss, if the power over there is behaving as erratically as it is over here, it might start a fire and cook him."

Clarice pushed the image out of her mind. "I really didn't need to hear that."

"I thought you should know. Knowledge is power. You had asked about him before, don't forget."

"Your computer is done," Clarice said, relieved at the opportunity to change the subject.

"Ah, good," Dr. Forbes replied. "You can grab what we need and then make your way over."

"Our way over where, exactly?" Clarice snatched a notepad and pencil and waited for the instructions.

"Go back the way you came, and when you get to the stairwell, take it as far down as you can go. Once you're on that floor, you'll want the north stairwell, which is on the opposite side of where you'll be. That wing is shaped like a cross, so run through to the other side and take the next set of stairs down three floors. On your first left there will be a keypad entry, punch in 2075 and then keep going straight until you come to the security station. That's where we'll be. Once we're all together, we'll make our final plans for escape. Got it?"

"Yup. We'll be there in a few." Clarice stood, her heartbeat already quickening.

"Please hurry," he replied. "And like I said before, use extraordinary care with the UCK."

Garages were down, never up. Martin knew that. He had always known that. When he was designing his home years ago back in Seraville, he had tinkered with the idea of putting the garage on the second floor in order to be closer to the bedroom. This idea never came to fruition as Ma didn't want oil leaks coming into the kitchen, and Martin knew not to argue with Ma when it came to her kitchen. Armed with the geographic knowledge of where garages were, Martin found and took an elevator to the lowest floor it would go to.

The elevator doors swung open to reveal a long hall bathed in red emergency lighting and partially filled with smoke. At the far end stood a figure holding a knapsack at its side. The figure slowly rocked in place, groaning occasionally, and stared at the broken screen of a wall-mounted plasma television set. Though the creature took no notice of him, Martin didn't like the idea of having to get close to it. But ultimately, he had no choice in the matter. The only exit was on the other side and Ma wanted her rutabagas. And zombies or not, Ma was going to get them, or his name wasn't Pa. And if his name wasn't Pa, what the hell was it?

Martin, resolving to still be called Pa, cautiously advanced. One hand gripped his pocketknife, and the other covered his mouth and nose in an effort to shield himself from the smoke. He knew that if he was sneaky enough, he could slip by and be out of sight without the zombie even knowing he was there. But as careful as he was, a few feet from the creature, Martin sucked in too much smoke and his lungs revolted.

Martin's coughing fit was interrupted when the zombie spun around, snarled and grabbed hold of the old man. Long, broken fingernails sank into his skin and ripped at his clothing. Teeth, the likes of which would floor any dental hygienist, snapped at his neck, and it was all Martin could do to keep from being bitten.

"You critters won't be getting me none," he yelled, shoving as hard as he could. The zombie stumbled back, and Martin used that momentary bit of free time to go on the offensive. He lunged forward and tried to drive his pocketknife deep into the zombie's skull. The blade, however, hadn't been aimed as well as it should have. So instead of sinking into zombie brain and stopping the attack, it skipped off the corpse's skull, only leaving a gash of skin in its wake.

Martin's attacker ignored the partial scalping and continued to try and eat him. Martin, in turn, stabbed again and again. It wasn't the most eloquent of attacks, but it worked. Sort of. The creature did let go, and it did fall to the ground, dead. But before it fell to the ground, it bit a chunk out of Martin's shoulder.

"Ma isn't going to like this," he said as he went down the hall. He made his way through countless rooms and paused for a breath when his heart went into arrhythmia. The whittler sat down in a large leather chair and looked around. The lighting was considerably better than where he was before, but he had trouble noting anything else about the room. His vision had blurred.

Martin shook his head and redoubled his mental efforts. He realized both time and the life he knew were fleeting.

Though Martin couldn't see much anymore, he could still see the oak table in front of him.

"Ah, wood, my old friend," Martin said, smiling through the migraine that was forming. He took out his pocketknife and began to carve. "I can always count on you to make things right."

Like a speeding locomotive with an equipment cart for a cowcatcher, Nick and Clarice burst out of the lab. They barreled over two sets of zombies on their way to the stairs, all the while Clarice praying that the UCK didn't slip from her grasp. During their descent of the stairwell, she lost her footing, nearly dropping the jar as she grabbed the handrail. Despite their brush with disaster, neither wanted to slow down and kept moving at full steam.

The power was behaving much more predictably on the lowest floor as compared to the others. Whatever the reason, Clarice was grateful for the small blessing. It was short-lived gratitude, however, as the distinct sound of bodies thumping down the stairs foretold what was behind them.

Zombies. Lots of zombies.

Clarice punched in the code for the final doorway. Much to her relief, the data pad chirped in a cordial manner. The door it was attached to via numerous circuits, however, failed to respond fully. It slid open an inch, maybe two, but no further. Clarice's jaw dropped, and she thumped her fist against the wall. "Doesn't anything work around here?"

Nick braced himself in front of the door and tried the muscle solution. After a few grunts and a sharp cry, he conceded his sinews wouldn't be the deciding factor. "Let me see if I can work my magic again," he said, opening his laptop.

"I don't think there's time for that," Clarice replied. She tapped him on the shoulder and directed his attention to the two zombie trailblazers that came into view. A second later, three others joined them. And judging from the cacophonies coming down the hall, the rest were not far behind.

"Run," Nick said, almost whispering.

Clarice nodded and did just that.

While Jack was bent over, extracting his 1941, catalog product number 31A, green metallic shell, ballpoint pen from Ryan's forehead, Danita entered the physics lab. He turned toward her, pleased to see a longtime friend. From the look on her face, she was glad to see him as well and even seemed delighted that he had found his pen.

Jack asked where she had been, and she asked the same. But as quick as the conversation started, several blinking lights on a nearby wall caught their attention. Jack was the first to investigate.

The lights were small and square. Touching them produced little beeps and chirps from various machinery. Tasting them did the same. However, when Danita mashed a handful of the buttons, a solid, green beam of light shot across the room from a nearby piece of equipment. The beam bounced around beakers and off broken glass, eventually stopping when it hit Ryan's temple. Other than a sweet, barbeque smell and wisp of smoke it now emitted, the light seemed mostly harmless (and boring).

Jack soon lost interest, and Danita's boredom quickly followed. The pair wandered out into the hall, catching up on lost time and reminiscing about their finest moments playing Eats as they did. Soon the conversation turned to taxes, and all that Jack knew about them, and so Jack gave a lengthy discourse on the subject.

Taxes icky.

Danita admitted she had a hard time visualizing what they were, but she also said she knew that he had a remarkable palate. And if he said they were icky, then she saw no need to take a bite. She suggested that perhaps people would rid him of the taste of taxes, and if that were true, it would be a good idea to find some. If there was a problem that eating couldn't solve, she didn't know it.

Jack thought this was a good idea as well. He said he was also a little jealous that he hadn't thought of it at first, but he was glad that Danita had decided to include him in on the game.

Two humans suddenly barreled past them, shoving Danita and Jack to the side. One was holding a jar. The other had a pseudo cowcatcher.

Jack righted himself, turned, and stared at the fleeing pair. This was the first free-roaming group of humans he had seen in a long time and he began to salivate. It was common zombie knowledge that free-roaming humans were much healthier than those raised in a barricade.

Jack gave chase, and Danita followed. As they did, other zombies took note of their pursuit. Though Jack wasn't sure what was going through their partial mindset, he could only assume that his excited body language acted as a beacon for all to join. And an irresistible beacon it was. With every turn of the corner and passing by of a room, zombies far and wide abandoned the ribs they dined on and added their numbers to the horde.

Within five minutes, Jack and Danita had attracted more than a dozen others. The more the mob grew, the more those who saw it quickly joined in. Eventually, not a single zombie in the facility existed that wasn't part of the pursuit.

A few times the unruly horde found themselves faced with their arch-nemesis, Door. Although it slowed them, the right combination of hitting, pushing, grabbing and twisting caused Door to yield. And despite the delays, the scent of a new meal was never lost.

Death and Taxes

Getting past the stairs was a little tricky as well. Those in the back wanted to be up front, and those up front found navigating the stairwell a slow process. That is, until someone asked the question, *Why walk?*

It was a first-rate question, one that made the collective body of zombies pause and let out an *Errgggghhhh?* No one had a good answer, or any answer for that matter. With no plausible reason why they should walk down the stairs, the mob, Jack and Danita included, began throwing themselves down the stairs and over the rails. A few fell a little too far and snapped their necks in the process. This, however, served to be a benefit to the whole, as soft cushions for landing were now in place.

It was a noisy process, but one that worked. And that's all that mattered.

Nothing quite ruined a day like being killed for the second time. It made for an afternoon that was fraught with uncompleted tasks and confused states upon awakening. This was something that Ryan Conner, Tax Collector, was well aware of. When he finally opened his eyes, he couldn't recollect who he was or what had happened. The only thing that he was sure of was that there was something above him.

Ryan stared at the looming object. It was rectangular, off white, and partially illuminated. It didn't move, talk or even smell. He wasn't sure if it was watching him, but given its perch above, Ryan couldn't fathom what else it would be doing. Napping perhaps.

He reached out to touch it, then realized it was a good distance away, some seven or eight feet. Thinking the matter over some more, he decided that this must be the ceiling. Ryan could then think of only one place he might be to have such a view.

He rolled over on to his stomach, and the floor was right there to greet him. He moaned as he pushed himself onto his feet. A splitting headache erupted as he became upright. It felt as if someone had jammed a 1941, catalog product number 31A, green metallic shell, ballpoint pen into his forehead, then gave it a half twist.

Slowly, the fog over Ryan's mind lifted, and his memory was sharper than ever. There was a stamp. There was a pen. There was a stab. Ryan knew the only thing that ever included all three in any quantity was an audit. He looked around the room and could find no forms, signed or otherwise, lying around, and therefore, the audit was incomplete at best.

Ryan seethed. His hands reached down and grabbed the lip of the desk, and in one fluid motion, he ripped off a chunk of metal. For the first time since he could remember, his skin tingled with sensation as long-dormant nerve cells sprang to quasi-life. His muscles tightened, relaxed, then flexed again, marveling in their new-found strength and coordination.

Ryan pounded on the desk once for good measure, caving it in. It felt good to vent his frustrations, but he knew that the desk was an innocent bystander. The tax evaders may have escaped a final resting place by sheer luck, but Ryan wasn't about to let them get away a second time. He was Tax incarnate. He didn't feel pity, remorse, or fear. And most important, he would not stop—ever— until all the tax evaders paid with their lives.

Chapter Eighteen

You know, maybe it's me," Clarice said, catching her breath and leaning against a set of double doors she and Nick had just run through, "but this place feels never-ending."

Nick gave a nervous chuckle. "You've got no argument from me." He grabbed a nearby chair and wedged it under the door handles. "That ought to buy us some time."

Clarice surveyed the room they were in. It was at least thirty feet across with carpet that would eat a week's pay to clean a drop of wine. Wood paneling lined the round walls, and a large chandelier hung from a domed ceiling. Dead center was a circular, oak table with high back, leather chairs evenly spaced around.

"Wow," she said. "Too bad the rest of the place isn't as nice as this."

"No kidding," said Nick. "What do you make of that?"

Clarice sniffed the air. "Smells like lavender. Someone had a little too much time and money to spend?"

"No, not the room," he said and then made a motion toward the other side of the table. "What do you make of *that*?"

Directly in front of one of the seats was a knife standing upright, its point set firmly in the wood.

Clarice trotted around the table. "I think its Martin's," she answered, taking the pocketknife in hand and giving it a turn. Her eyes drifted to the table surface and she grimaced. "There's also some dried blood and an engraving. It says, 'take let door.'"

"Take let door?" Nick repeated. "Is that supposed to be, 'take the left door' or do you suppose it's like a riddle?"

"I'd guess it says, 'take the left door'," she said, looking up and noting the three equally spaced exits in the room. "Though, which one is the left is up for grabs."

The double doors they had entered through rattled, and the sound was followed by a series of loud, quick thumps.

"Okay," Nick said, looking past her and taking a step backward. "I move that we adjourn this meeting."

"Seconded," Clarice replied. She reached for the handle of the door next to her and flung it open. On the other side was a spacious closet, filled with books, pamphlets, computer and projector equipment, and one pale and disjointed Martin.

The former whittler lunged at her, arms outstretched like a demented child lusting after its favorite toy. Clarice slammed the door, and Nick pushed a chair under the handle, ensuring that Martin stayed in time out.

"That answers that," Nick said, slowly backing away from the door.

"Guess that leaves one left," Clarice said. She shot her fiancé a mischievous smile. "You go first this time, honey."

Once the weight of dozens of zombies lifted from his shoulders, Jack pulled himself free of the remaining tangle and exited the stairwell. He wasn't sure where to go at this point, but there were a number of other zombies filing down the hall, and they seemed happy enough.

Jack was a champion Eats player. He knew that while zombie excitement was a telltale sign of a meal nearby, he also knew better than to get caught up in the rush of the crowds. Instead of risking injury and zigzagging slothfully through the crowd, he kept his pace. Eventually he rounded a corner and found several others, Danita included, staring at a partially open door.

Jack gave his long-lost friend a friendly spasm.

Danita groaned, voicing her frustration.

When Jack reached it, he understood why it was causing her and everyone else so much trouble. Wafting in from the other side was the distinct smell of people. Fresh people. People that were still moving on their own and in a coordinated fashion. Try as the zombies might, the door refused to fully open, and Jack joined in the howls.

Slowly, one by one, the half dozen corpses that had paused there continued on, following the ant trail of their comrades. Jack waited patiently for Danita to work her smarts.

She thumped, and he waited some more. She pondered and mused, and gave a few more thumps in between. Despite all of her thumpings on and around the door, and despite Jack's very patient and hopeful attitude, nothing happened. The two, saddened, were forced to move on and find someone else to have for dinner.

Clarice's legs had had enough. Her thighs and calves made it well known to the rest of her body that the immense amount of hard, stressful running over the past week had finally caught up. They also reminded her brain that should they not receive a week's worth of rest posthaste, they would seize up altogether. Her brain gently reminded her legs of the penalties for being caught by the pursuing zombie horde. Her legs begrudgingly agreed to work a little longer, but not without storing extra lactic acid to voice their displeasure.

By the time she and Nick reached the security station, sweat drenched her body, and her heart was a few heavy beats away from exploding. But as exhausted as she was, all things considered, Clarice was grateful that they made it there in one piece.

She was about to lean on the door to the station when there was a hiss of air, and it slid open.

"Quick, get in!" Dr. Forbes said, and the pair ducked inside. "I'm so glad to see that you've made it down here alive and intact."

The station itself was in the shape of a quarter circle, Plexiglas covering the curved portion of the wall. There was a solitary, long desk that lined the wall and was currently being used by the only other person in the room. He looked like the caricature of a fat, Swedish chef. On the back wall were a number of notices, bulletins and calendars pinned to three different cork boards, all being out of date by at least a year.

"Thanks for mentioning the busted door back there," Clarice said.

"I'm truly sorry about that, but we didn't know it was malfunctioning until we got here ourselves." Dr. Forbes replied. He double-checked the locking mechanism on the door and seemed satisfied that it was working properly. "Do you still have the UCK?"

Clarice held up the jar. "One UCK, as requested."

"And the hard drives?"

"In the bag," Nick replied, wiping the sweat from his forehead and flicking it to the ground.

"Wonderful!" Dr. Forbes exclaimed. "You can't believe how relieved I am this worked out so well."

"I thought you said there were four of you," Clarice commented.

"There were," the doctor answered. He then continued with a motion to his partner, "Now it's myself, Gaston, and the two of you."

Clarice nodded, but said nothing. As much as her curiosity wanted to find out, her imagination was sure she'd regret knowing the specifics.

"If there's no one else, let's go," Nick said. "We brought what you wanted."

"Shortly!" Dr. Forbes assured. "There is a small hang-up with the emergency egress system."

"And what would that be?" Clarice asked, hating the idea that their easy strike might be coming to an end.

"Simple, really. The main doors won't open, and we can't seem to get the system to respond."

"I think there's a problem," Gaston said, cutting in.

"I was getting to that," Dr. Forbes replied.

"No, I mean another problem, docteur," his partner said while pointing to the monitor. "There are zombies coming this way."

"Zombies?" Dr. Forbes turned toward the screen. "How many are we talking about?"

Gaston tried counting but ended up stopping long before he was finished. "All of them, I think."

Everyone at the security station huddled over the plump scientist and stared at the monitor. The doorway to the executive meeting room was open, and a sea of bodies oozed forth.

"I thought you said you closed all the doors from here," Dr. Forbes said as if he were scolding an intern for improperly labeling the newest batch of theta-kilo.

Gaston shrugged. "I locked all the ones I could. Quite a few were inoperable. I think it's safe to say they are coming right for us."

"Don't you have any weapons?" Clarice asked.

Dr. Forbes shook his head. "No, our only gun lost the hand that it was attached to."

Clarice cringed. "How long till they get here?"

Gaston whipped out a little tool from a pocket in his pants. "Given their current position in the main conference room, the average forward velocity of the walking dead, and the approximate time it takes to open an unsecured door for a mob this size...a few minutes, perhaps."

Clarice stared at the long, sliding piece of plastic. "Is that a slide rule? Who still uses one of those?"

Gaston looked back at her in equal astonishment. "I do, mademoiselle," he replied. "It works without batteries, and I can use it underwater."

"Design a lot of secret weapons and projects in a fish tank?" she asked, raising an eyebrow.

"There's a first time for everything, no?"

Nick tapped the rotund man on the shoulder. "Can I try?" he asked, motioning to the computer. "I might be able to get these doors open so we can leave."

"You are not authorized to poke around our system," Gaston scoffed with a furrowed brow. "Now go away and let me concentrate."

"I thought I might help."

"I know my way around the computer."

"I hope you're good under pressure then since we're about to have company," Clarice said as she motioned to the camera's display.

"Oui, I am," Gaston replied.

Moments turned into minutes, and nothing changed except for the color of Gaston's skin. Pale, evidently, wasn't the whitest someone could turn.

Clarice groaned and leaned against the wall. "God, just let him try," she said. "It's not like we didn't grab your precious data and jar already. And from the looks of things, it's not going to matter anyway."

Gaston looked over at Dr. Forbes, and when he received a reluctant look of approval from the doctor, he slid out of the chair. "Fine. Let us see what you can do."

Nick jumped into the hot seat, flicked his wrist to loosen his fingers and assumed the hacking position. It was a position much easier to take this time around as Gaston provided his network ID and password, removing any need to bypass security.

Clarice watched him navigate, proud as anyone could be. She didn't understand any of the menus and directories that were flying up on the screen, but given the expression that the two researchers wore, she surmised he was doing quite well. She also wondered if they'd guess he was responsible for the mess they were in. Neither, however, made any comments. "Well?' she asked after another tense minute.

"Almost there, I think," Nick said.

A loud thud snapped everyone's attention away from the computer. Plastered against the Plexiglas was what was left of a disfigured man, bloodied, soiled and most definitely dead. It flopped around, beating its hands sporadically against the walls and door.

"This is no good," Clarice said after several more zombies joined the first. She glanced about the room, looking for something—anything—that could be of use. "So how long until they break in?"

"This is a security station," Dr. Forbes stated. "That Plexiglas can hold a dozen elephants before cracking, and the door isn't coming down with anything less than a brick of C-4."

"I don't think a dozen elephants would be enough for all of them to eat," she said. "They're just going to sit out there till we die."

"Which means we're safe," Dr. Forbes said. "Relax."

"No," Clarice replied. "It means we need a way out. Either that, or we'll have to eat each other until help arrives. It's not like we have a lot of choices, now do we?"

Nick laughed and took a momentary pause from his work to throw her a glance. "Planning on drawing straws, Ms. Optimism?"

"Don't be silly. Fatty here should go first. He's big enough to feed us all for weeks if we eat light and salt him."

"I think not," Gaston said. "Why should I be the one who should die? I have done nothing to you."

"You mean aside from keeping us locked in this hellhole and wanting to turn us into your little pincushions?" said Clarice.

"You have no idea what we do here," Dr. Forbes said. "Our work saves lives."

"I think I've got a pretty damn good idea what you freaks do here." Clarice wrapped her thumbs around her belt loops and tried to resist the urge to break both their noses.

"Knock it off," Nick shouted. "No one is leaving at all if I can't work, and since we've both agreed to part ways after all this, let's leave things be, okay?"

"Fine," Clarice said, crossing her arms over her chest. She eyed Dr. Forbes and Gaston, daring them to further the topic. Dr. Forbes kept quiet, but held her glare, while Gaston simply turned away.

"Okay, I think I found the problem." Nick leaned back in the chair and pointed at the screen with a pen. "There's no power to the motors for the door."

Dr. Forbes looked confused, almost shocked. "What are you talking about?" he asked. "You can tell it has power just by looking at it. The lights are on."

"No," Nick replied. "According to your online schematics, or rather the notes left by whoever designed them, you can have enough power for the terminals, scanners and status lights, but the actual motors require much more draw. And since you've only got one barely working generator right now, it can't fill the needs of everything. Basically, the security doors are heavy, and the motors don't have enough juice to make them move."

"Then let's shut things off till we have power, yes?" Gaston said.

"I don't know if we can do that," Dr. Forbes replied. "Most things power related are mechanical. We'd have to go around and flip individual circuit breakers by hand."

Gaston fidgeted with his shirt and began to think out loud. "And what about the egress system? And the destruct device?"

"We'll need a lot of juice for both," Dr. Forbes answered, rubbing his beard. "If we're down to one generator that's going to be a problem."

"We could try getting another generator back online," Nick suggested. "I mean, I don't know how that would happen, but if we could, it would probably do the trick. The floor plans have one about fifty meters away."

"Assuming it's not damaged it's a straightforward procedure to fire it back up," Dr. Forbes said with a smile. "I like it. And I must say, I'm disappointed in myself that I didn't think of it first."

"All of this speculation is worthless at the moment," Clarice said as she pointed at the horde outside the window. One of the zombies snarled, reinforcing her point. "It's not like we can stroll on over there, because if you think I'm opening this door and pushing my way past dozens of them, you've got another thing coming."

"What about the ventilation?" Nick asked as he punched the keys on the computer once more. "Could we slip through that to get where we need? It works in the movies."

"Just because things work in the movies doesn't mean they will work here," Clarice said. "Twenty bucks says that even if you guys could get up there, you'll come crashing through the ceiling or get stuck in a vent."

Nick turned the screen toward the rest of them and pushed his suggestion harder. "Look at this. The duct drops down right here in a room next to the generator. We could crawl through, jump down, start it up, and find a way to the egress room. They're dumb, right? I doubt they would even know we left the room."

"No, *we* can't," Clarice replied. She motioned to the small vent overhead. "I could barely get in that, and there's no way you will, let alone these two codgers. Fatty here would probably get stuck halfway in, and we'd need a crowbar to pry him out."

"But as you said, you could do it," Dr. Forbes pointed out. "A girl in as good a shape as you ought to be able to wiggle through." He looked her up and down, causing her to shift uncomfortably. "What are you, fifty-five kilos or so? That's not too bad."

"Oh no," she said, backing up, hands held defensively. "You guys aren't volunteering me for this nonsense. Come up with something else."

"It'll work," Nick reassured. "It has to. You'll be fine."

"No, it doesn't." Clarice grabbed a small pamphlet and threw it at him. "It doesn't *have* to work. There's no law out there saying that it *has* to work, and there's certainly no recourse we can take if it doesn't. And it's really easy for you to tell me what I should do. You get to sit back here and do nothing."

"For a secretary you're rather stubborn about not helping," Gaston commented. He muttered something under his breath about her and parfaits, but Clarice didn't pick it all up.

"Being stupid isn't the same thing as helping," she said, placing her hands on her hips. "And as long as we're pointing out responsibilities, none of this is my doing at all. My only mistake in all of this was applying for the wrong job and following my loon of a boss out here."

"Yes, well, no one expected any of this," Dr. Forbes said flatly. "But my dear young woman, at this point, the reality is that we're stuck in this room, and we can't get to where we need to be until that generator is back online."

"And then what? Let's say I go and do whatever it is and it all works. You guys still need to get out, and we all need to get down the hall."

"The extra power might help the network out, too," Nick added. "I mean, I don't know what's still offline or malfunctioning due to the lack of juice. We might have some more options at that point. We might be able to lure them away if we had more tools at our disposal."

"Fine point," Dr. Forbes praised. "Right now, however, I think it's best we tackle one problem at a time. We're safe in here anyway. So once you get the power back, just crawl back over, and we'll work on our next step."

"And if I don't fit or can't make it all the way?" Clarice asked.

"We won't know that until we try," replied Dr. Forbes. "Let's not defeat ourselves before we even give it a go."

Clarice didn't say anything at first. Her thoughts tried to argue around the present reality in an attempt to stave off their concocted solution. Reality, as it had been known to do from time to time, didn't budge. "I can't believe I'm agreeing to this," she finally said. She opened the bag, rummaged around and pulled out her Pittsburgh Pirates scrunchie to tie her hair back with. "This is most definitely not in my contract."

"Did you even have one?" Nick asked, jumping on the tangent absently.

"No," she said. "Not like that matters anyway."

"That's a girl," Dr. Forbes said, obviously trying to boost her morale. "Make it a game, and you'll have fun with it. We could even time you, and you could see how fast you could work yourself back."

"Pardon me?"

"A game," he repeated. "You know, things people do to pass the time and entertain themselves?"

"Yes, I know what a game is," she said.

"It's a psychology trick I read about," Dr. Forbes explained. "If you distract yourself while doing something that induces stress, you'll find that whatever it is you're doing becomes much more bearable. It's like engaging your brain's autopilot."

"And how am I going to see? I doubt there are any light bulbs in the ducts."

Gaston fished around his pocket. "Take my penlight," he said, handing it to her.

Clarice flipped the light around in her hand, giving it a brief inspection. "How do I get there? I mean, through the vents."

Nick looked back at the screen. "Go straight," he said while tracing the route with his finger. "It'll branch about fifteen yards down and go right. That might be tricky because it looks like a sharp turn. After that just keep going, and you should stop right at the room."

"And how do I start the generator?"

"If memory serves there should be instructions posted there," Dr. Forbes said. "All the breakers will be in a large, black box embedded in the wall. Inside the box's door should tell you what you need. Dial extension 1261—that's here—if you need help."

Nick wheeled the chair under the air vent, stood on it carefully, and removed the panel. "Are you ready?" he asked, hopping down.

"Ready as I'll ever be," Clarice answered.

Nick stayed motionless and looked deep into her eyes. "Be careful."

"You know I will," she said. She then gave him a quick hug and kiss. "But for the record, if they do get me, I'm coming after you first."

With that, she hoisted herself into the ducts.

Chapter Nineteen

Clarice discovered a significant problem while traversing the ventilation ducts, that problem being that the engineers who designed them had expressly stated that the air ducts were built only to allow the passage of air. The user manual that came with the installation would have made this clear to her had she been privy to a copy. The preface read:

Thank you for purchasing the U-Flow 349b air duct system. We hope that you will find great joy and happiness in its use. Before you familiarize yourself with its many options, please be advised that the U-Flow 349b has only been designed to allow the passage of air (78% Nitrogen, 21% Oxygen, 1% misc.) from one area to another. Other gasses may be substituted for air, but please see your local contractor for details. U-Flow 349b systems, however, are not designed to allow the passage of any other object. Please do not attempt to transport liquids or solids of any kind throughout the system as this will void your warranty. This condition applies to non-intentional / situational transport as well, such as hostile alien life forms or human survivors seeking to escape. If you would like such transportation options, please see our model U-Flow 449 series.

The difference between the 449 and 349 series wasn't just one hundred. The 449 series came with reinforced paneling, heavy struts, and extra headroom for those long crawls. Clarice would have been grateful for the latter at any point. However, when the paneling broke free near the end of her journey, she would have opted for the foremost in a heartbeat.

Her fall was broken by a well-placed desk, which served as a perfect bullseye for her shoulder. Somehow Clarice managed to suppress the urge to scream during the rapid descent. She congratulated herself for that small bit of self-control. If the sound of her dropping through the ceiling didn't attract any unwanted attention, she didn't need to chance it again by adding a few decibels of her own.

Clarice fumbled around in the dark, pushing aside a few unknown objects, one somewhat malleable and wet, and grabbed the penlight that had rolled under the desk. The light cast by it was weak, and its lack of illumination was even more pronounced now that she was out of the vents.

Carefully she made her way around the dark, examining what she could as she happened past it. There was a now broken desk, and off to the side were a couple of overturned chairs. A body lay still in the corner.

Clarice repeated that to herself, *a body in the corner*. She jumped backward, letting out a small yelp as she lost her balance and hit the ground. Clarice scrambled as far back as she could, hoping that the door out would be wherever she ended up. Instead, she met one of four corners. For a long time, she sat still, too petrified to move. If the corpse across from her wasn't interested in her now, she wasn't about to make herself more appealing.

Eventually, Clarice turned the penlight toward the body, and the corpse still showed no interest. She inched closer, taking care to keep a healthy distance from it and gave it a proper inspection. Several bite wounds marked its arms and shoulders. Its right hand clutched a large pistol, and the left lay off to the side, soaked in blood. Its head drooped forward and was missing a large section from its temple.

Clarice drew closer still, her nerves now battling both her curiosity and her want of a gun.

"I'm just going to borrow this, Rob," she said, reading the ID badge. She bent down and plucked the revolver free. Clarice knew it was silly to say, but it made her feel better. She had been to a shooting range a few times growing up and didn't feel completely awkward handling the firearm. A quick look into the gun's cylinder showed that it had three bullets left.

"Don't suppose you have any more?" Clarice asked while she rifled through its pockets. Thankfully, the corpse didn't answer. Unfortunately, all that it had was lint.

Clarice searched the room once more and found only the exit. She cracked the door and peeked out. When she was satisfied that the hall was empty, she ducked out toward the generator room. It wasn't terribly hard to find. It was, in fact, right next door as Nick said it would be, and there was a large sign that said *Generator Room* above.

The generator room was well lit. A few of the ceiling lights flickered randomly, but there was more than enough light for Clarice to see that she was the only one there. The machinery was complex and intimidating for the young secretary, but it looked intact. There were dials, boxes, switches, knobs, levers, pipes, and fans of all shapes and sizes, and those were just what were stuck on the walls. In the center of the room was an overgrown toolbox that someone had plastered with vents and cables, and Clarice could only assume that this was the generator itself. On one of the nearby support beams was a small red phone. Clarice picked it up and dialed 1261.

"I'm here," she said as the other end was picked up.

"Good girl," Dr. Forbes praised. "Are you okay?"

"Yeah, but I banged up my shoulder," she said, glancing down at it. "Looks like I'm bleeding, actually."

"From?" the doctor asked with concern.

"From crashing through the ceiling," Clarice replied. She ignored the ache. "I also found a gun on a dead guy."

"What kind?"

"It says it's a Colt Anaconda," she replied, turning the weapon over. "Bad-ass, mammoth looking thing. I just hope it's not bad luck."

"Why do you say that?"

Clarice shrugged. "I just got the feeling that the guy I found it on wasn't the original owner."

"Hmmm," Dr. Forbes replied. Whatever it was he was now thinking, he wasn't sharing it with her. "Do you see the box we talked about on the wall?"

Clarice looked around from her position. "I think so," she finally answered.

"Open it and start everything up," he replied. "If you need help, come back to the phone for further instruction."

"Okay, one minute," she said. Clarice ran over to the wall to the breaker box. It opened easily, and instructions were indeed on the inside of the cover. They read:

To initiate a manual start of the reactor, please see section 19.39 of your user manual. User manual can be found online or with the software provided.

Clarice went back to the phone and relayed what it said. Her mind refused to think about the growing stupidity of the situation. For now, it was content on playing the middle-girl between Dr. Forbes and the generator's controls.

"Just a second," he said after she explained it again. A minute passed before he got back on the phone. "Okay, flip all the breakers in the box to the up position. Then press the little red buttons underneath each switch. At the bottom, there will be a lever. Pump that lever up and down five or six times, and that will hopefully turn the LED display next to it on. Come back here when you do all that."

"Okay," she replied.

Time passed, and Clarice went to work.

"Done," she said, hopping back on the phone. "The little light came on, but I don't think the generator is working. It's not making any noise."

"Go to the generator and look for the big yellow button marked 'start' and give it a push. That should do it."

"Okay." Clarice dropped the receiver once more and spent a few tense moments searching for the button. Holding her breath, she gave it a push once she found it. The generator whirred to life, and a few noisy seconds later, the lights brightened to their full strength.

Clarice eagerly picked the phone back up. "It's working!" she cried out, bouncing lightly on her toes. A glimmer of hope sprang from her soul and the taste of freedom was on the tip of her tongue.

"Wonderful," Dr. Forbes replied. "The door to the egress system is opening now." There was a slight pause before he continued on. "That's odd," he said. "Two of them are examining the self-destruct device."

"Come again?" Clarice said, wondering what that meant in the long run.

"Two of the zombies walked by, or rather they dragged themselves into the next room. I think...I think one of them just tasted it."

"Is that going to be a problem?" she asked. "Or can we move along with getting the hell out of here?"

"No, I don't think there's a problem," Dr. Forbes replied. "At least, not with them giving the system a little taste here or there. I'm a little curious as to why those two in particular decided to leave us alone while the rest are still pounding on the door."

"Well, you guys can figure that out after we're gone," she said. "I think I can get back in the vents, so I'll be there soon."

"One moment," Dr. Forbes interjected quickly as she was getting ready to hang up the phone. "There's something we need to discuss first."

Clarice sighed. "There's always something that needs discussing."

"Well, that is our nature," Dr. Forbes replied. "Propositions, discussions, interjections, speculations—they're all a part of the game."

"What is it now?"

"Hang on, and I'll tell you," he replied.

Clarice heard the distinctive clink of the receiver as he put it down on the desk. A second later, it was silent, and then a piano concerto began to play in the background.

After about five minutes, the music stopped, and a happy voice got on the line. "Your call is important to us," it said. "Please remember that calls are answered in the order that they are received. We thank you for your patience and understanding that developing the next generation of technology often produces a high call volume. Please stay on the line and the next available operator will take your call."

Clarice banged the phone against the wall a few times in frustration as the music started again. Just as she was about to hang up, Dr. Forbes picked up once more.

"Clarice?" he said. "We've all come to a decision, and it looks like it'll work out wonderfully well for our escape."

"Oh, good," she replied.

"Yes, we've all agreed that you can't come with us," he said plainly.

Clarice's mind short-circuited, and she stood deathly still for a moment. "I'm sorry," she finally said. "What exactly do you mean by that?"

"Precisely as it sounds," he answered. "You won't be coming with us as we leave. It's just not possible and would be hazardous to the rest of us."

"What the hell are you talking about?" she shouted. She kept her anger in check just enough to keep from wrenching the phone off of the wall.

Dr. Forbes' voice remained calm. "Now I understand how this makes you feel," he said. "But we can't risk you being infected and turning into one of them. Not without any sort of proper laboratory to keep you in. So, we're going to have to leave you behind I'm afraid."

"Don't give me that, you backstabbing mother fu—"

"But you still can do something for us to make your life have a little more purpose to it," he continued on, not paying any heed to her interruption. "We need you to make your way over here, but come down the halls, not the vents. When they see you, they'll all undoubtedly give chase, at which point we can slip out and get away. It's a fantastic and simple idea, wouldn't you agree?"

"Get out of here!" Clarice yelled. "They haven't touched me one bit, and you want to leave me behind!"

"Well, you are bleeding from the shoulder," Dr. Forbes said.

"I told you I cut it breaking through the vents—the vents *you* sent me in, remember?"

"Yes, I'm oriented to both time and place," he replied. "But we would have to go on your word that that's what happened, and not that you came in contact with a zombie. And even if what you say is true, you still might have contracted some sort of infection along the way. It's too much to risk. I'm sorry. And like I said, this is a unanimous decision."

"No, it's not," she said. "It's yours and fatty's decision. Nick would never agree with that."

"Yes, he has."

"Put him on the phone," Clarice demanded.

Dr. Forbes hesitated. "I'd rather us not get into a long drawn-out argument, especially when emotions are running high," he said.

"Put him on the damn phone, now!"

The phone was passed.

"Clarice?" Nick said. His voice quivered. "I'm sorry we sent you out. God, I wish—"

Clarice cut him off. "Shut the hell up and listen to me," she barked, still unable to believe what was happening. "I'm fine. Nothing is wrong except for a stupid banged up shoulder coming out of the vents."

"They said you're infected," he said.

"I know what they said," Clarice replied shortly. Her head was starting to spin under all of the sudden stress. "I'm telling you, I'm fine, and you guys sure as hell aren't leaving me." She jerked away from the phone reflexively as a loud thud came across the phone line.

"Oh, my god," Nick said.

"What?"

"The glass is cracked," Nick replied. "One of them is beating in the window."

"That's not possible," she said as another thud came through. "That window has to be like six inches thick!"

"I'm standing right here watching it!" Nick yelled back. "I think it's your boss. Or what's left of him."

"That can't be. They said he's dead."

"Oh, Jesus Christ, he's going to break in."

"Is it only him? Maybe you can fight him off."

Another thud sounded, this time accompanied by the sounds of cracking glass.

"No. There's three of them." Nick sounded eerily calm.

"I'm coming," she said and slammed the phone down. She stopped in mid-step and realized she needed a plan. Her mouth whispered the answer. "What would Anne Bonny do?"

* * *

All the zombies agreed that the trip down the stairs was fun and to have a door at the bottom was an added bonus. It wasn't as much the opening of doors that they enjoyed, but rather what lay on the other side. It was like opening presents. Sometimes there would be something spectacular on the other side, like a new remote-control car or a pony. But other times the prize might as well have been new underwear.

Danita had once tried to make a game of locked doors. She would hide something fun behind one and put something not so fun behind two others. Ultimately it failed as either the prize got away, or no one picked the third door.

At the moment, however, there were only two doors in front of Jack. The one in front, whose view was currently obstructed by a half dozen other zombies, was a little bit see-through. Beyond the Plexiglas pane, Jack could see people. Although this was one of those fun doors to open, it was more like window shopping than an actual holiday celebration as no one could get the door open. The other door, a heavy, metallic one that tasted like a rusty anchor, was on his right. It was very much closed, even more so than the first, and it was very much not see-through. Not even a little bit. It was depressingly uninteresting, that is until it started to make noise.

A low hum came from the door, and only a few seconds passed before it started to rise into the ceiling. None of the living dead that were pressed into the hallway had ever seen a door rise before. It was an exciting thing to behold. Jack, however, was less concerned with the door, especially after it stopped and became boring again, and more interested in what lay beyond.

The room on the other side was wide, red, and tall. Jack only managed the first two adjectives on his own, but Danita was kind enough to offer up the third. In the middle was a cylindrical object that reminded Jack of a femur, only it was a lot larger and didn't have as much bone to it. He also didn't remember femurs having lots of tubes or flashing lights, but this one did. That said, Jack wasn't one to complain about new and unexpected developments, so he called it a femur anyway.

Jack staggered over to the femur, reached out, and touched it. The femur didn't react, so he pushed on it even harder. He wasn't sure what he was expecting to happen, but he felt deep down that something should. So Jack continued with his pushing and pulling, trying to elicit some sort of reaction. Occasionally he would look up and note all of the other zombies milling about a door and wondered what they were up to.

He saw that Danita had taken to standing in a corner, and he guessed that she was contemplating her next move. She gave a friendly jerk of her arm, but that was all she did before returning to her still state of being.

A moment later, a corpse—a dead and unmoving one—came tumbling to Jack's feet. Intrigued as to where this organic missile had been launched from, Jack looked up to find Ryan Conner, Tax Collector, hurling another body—dead and unmoving like the first—toward him. A number of zombies snarled at the former tax collector and attacked. Despite their combined strength, they didn't accomplish anything other than lose their reanimated lives and provide Ryan with more ammunition.

Though Jack did not understand the rules to this game, he thought it looked fun and lurched his way over to Ryan, eager to have them explained.

Ryan watched with interest as Jack approached. He could remember the zombie's name but that was all. Something deep inside told him that Jack, therefore, must have some sort of importance. Ryan looked back at the window and at the humans on the other side. He considered that perhaps Jack was another accomplice of these tax evaders, as he could see no other reason why Jack would be here. If this were true, he would need to deal with Jack just as he had dealt with the rest.

Jack, to Ryan's surprise, didn't attack. He stopped some feet away from the tax collector, turned, and pressed himself against the Plexiglas. Jack then made mention of a game of Eats and started pounding on the window.

This unexpected set of events intrigued Ryan. For several minutes, the tax collector sat back and observed. When he was convinced that Jack was more interested in a meal than obstructing justice, he went back to dealing with the tax evaders. He could address Jack's intentions afterward.

Ryan's first blow to the window reverberated in the hall but did little else. The second did the same. His third and fourth, however, cracked the Plexiglas.

The people scampered inside, and Ryan paused to reevaluate the situation. He looked at the window, then at Jack. He noted that the zombie carried a pen, unlike the ones that attacked him. It was a pen covered in blood and grime, but still had an illustrious shine in various, gore-free places. It was, in fact, a 1941, catalog product number 31A, green metallic shell, ballpoint pen. Its rugged design, exceptional styling, and ergonomic grip made it a dead giveaway.

And if Jack had a 1941, catalog product number 31A, green metallic shell, ballpoint pen to work with (and not some cheap, piece of crap), Ryan could come up with no other conclusion other than Jack must be a fellow agent. For no random passerby or Good Samaritan would be privy to such a fine writing device. Ryan gave a friendly *grmmmmgh* and returned to bashing in the Plexiglas window. He could ask the newcomer which human he was auditing later.

Danita staggered to the pair and introduced herself to Ryan, but did not join the attack. Instead, she tried to convince them both that the attack was flawed and that when they broke through the window and tried to get in, the people would run out the door.

Jack pointed out that the door was closed.

Ryan agreed and added that no tax code ever made mention of people fleeing through doors. People tried to fit through loopholes, but never doors. He then resumed beating what stubbornness remained out of the Plexiglas window.

Danita howled once more, calling them both stubborn and stupid, and then positioned herself off to the side. The Plexiglas broke a moment later.

Ryan sneered at Danita's skepticism and pushed his way through the hole he'd made. Of the three people he saw, the closest person to him also happened to be the largest. And since that person was the largest, he obviously cheated the most on his taxes to pay for his voracious appetite. The rotund man tried to fight back, and then to escape, but Ryan's hefty grip did not fail, and he dragged the man to the ground.

Jack didn't fare as well. He got stuck halfway into the room right as one of the humans hammered the door release.

* * *

"What would Anne Bonny do?" Clarice repeated one more time. This time, however, it felt much more like a question rather than the Holy Grail to zombie problems.

"Think, Clarice. Think!" she said to herself as her fingers rapped on her forehead. "W-W-A-B-D?"

Clarice looked up, her eyes drifting past the generator room exit and the answer rolled naturally off her tongue. "Shoot them. Shoot each and every one dead."

It was a straight forward, simple plan that she liked. The Nick side of her, however, shared its concern. "With only three bullets?"

"Get close and personal so that I can't miss." The dread pirate Clarice grinned. "Three bullets, three zombies. One shot, one kill."

"And if there's more?"

"Pistol whip each and every one of them."

With that, she took off down the hall, gun in hand.

The security door opened, and Nick yelled. Danita stood directly on the other side and grabbed Dr. Forbes the moment the door slid open. Nick snatched Clarice's bag and pushed past the two who were now entangled. He ran down the hall toward the generator room, trying to ignore the sounds behind him. Hopefully, he could still find Clarice. He looked back to see if he was being followed and smacked right into his fiancée as she rounded the next corner.

Clarice screamed and fell over backward, the gun discharging as she did. "You scared me to death!" she yelled, hands trembling.

"Christ! Where did you get that hand cannon?" Nick yelled back.

"Oh, thanks for the *I'm glad it's you, honey*," Clarice said, picking herself up. "Or *are you okay, dear?* Either of those would have been fine."

"Sorry. I was trying to stay alive," Nick replied. He glanced and patted over his body. It seemed that he hadn't gained any new holes. "Are you hurt?"

"No. Where are the other guys?" she asked, looking over his shoulder.

"Dead by now," Nick replied. "Your boss got fatty. Some dead girl got the other."

"So it's just us then?"

Nick gave a nod. "Looks like it."

Much to his surprise, she grabbed him by the back of his head and kissed him. Hard. When they finally parted, she asked, "Do you still have your laptop?"

"No," he replied, bewildered at how fast she had changed gears. "It's on the table back at the station. I just grabbed our bag. So I have our clothes—oh, and the UCK, too."

Clarice started to laugh. "So you saved our shirts and left the laptop instead?"

"Hey, it's not like I had a lot of time to work with," Nick explained with his hands up in the air. "The bag was right next to me, and the laptop was on the far end of the room. You should have seen Ryan go to town. He killed off most of the other zombies and then smashed through the Plexiglas with just a few hits. He's not natural."

"And the rest are?"

"No, that's not what I meant," he replied, shaking his head. "He's buffed now or something. Like on super zombie steroids."

Clarice looked down at the gun and checked the chamber. "Well," she said. "I've got two shots left. That kind of ruins the plan I cooked up."

"Two shots for three zombies."

"Better than none. With a bit of luck, maybe we won't need any."

Chapter Twenty

Clarice peeked around the last corner. Her eyes never blinked as she stared far past the security station. A part of her believed that if she stared long enough and her eyes burned hard enough, she and Nick would be whisked away to safety.

"Well?" Nick whispered. His hands fidgeted with the bag. "Are they still there?"

"Yep," she answered, ducking back. "All three are standing in the hallway."

"Doing what?"

"Standing." Clarice dared another quick peek. "Do you think we can make it past them?"

"I don't know."

Clarice turned around to face her fiancé. "You can run a mile in under six."

"Look, I'm telling you Ryan isn't like the others. He's strong and quick. I'm not about to run past him unless I absolutely have to."

"I could shoot him," Clarice suggested. "Granted, we've only got two bullets, but still..."

"Maybe if we wait, they'll leave," Nick offered.

"Or more will show up." Clarice rubbed her temples. She was tired and wanted this to be over, and Nick's non-compliance with her plan was starting to grate against her. "Let's say we make it into the next room. Then what?"

Nick's mouth twisted as he thought about the question. "I don't know anything about that destruct system they were talking about," he said. "But since Dr. Forbes and Gaston are dead, I'm not sure we can even use it. And if we could, I doubt we could start it up with them right on our heels."

"Can we even get out?"

"Should be a regular elevator past another security post at the far end," Nick said. "They were talking about it before your boss got there and smashed his way in. I don't think there's anything fancy about using it. All we need to do is swipe a badge at the bottom and in we go."

"Any badge?"

Nick shrugged. "They didn't say, but I bet the one we grabbed before will at least get us in the elevator."

"Well, that's something," she commented. She checked the gun again out of habit and tapped the engraved horse on the side idly with her finger.

A minute passed, and no one said anything.

"Maybe we should backtrack," Nick suggested. "If we found another gun or some ammo, we could shoot our way out."

"We could find more zombies, too."

"I know. You've said that twice now."

"You've made similar suggestions, twice now," she said. Clarice thumped the back of her head against the wall, trying to jumpstart her creative process. "Okay," she said. "Anything we pick, we're obviously going to second guess for eternity. We just need to commit to something and hope it works out for the best."

"Do you have a plan?"

"Of course," Clarice answered. She garnished her cooked up idea with a pinch of imitation-courage. "We'll get their attention and have them come over here. They don't move fast, right? So I'll pop two of them in the head when they come close. That just leaves one to get around, which should be easy."

"You want to fight?"

"Anne would fight," Clarice said. "I'm sure of it. It's the only real answer I could come up with before."

"Anne? The pirate?" Nick gave a nervous laugh at the end of his question.

"Yes, the pirate," she said. "You don't seem as enthused about her as I am."

Her fiancé's bag fidgeting grew worse. "I think there might be better, more modern alternatives. Marines. A tank. Anything. Hell, I bet a ninja would be perfect for this."

"Ninjas?" Clarice scoffed. She straightened her cap and fixed some of her hair that had fallen out. "Ninjas wouldn't be nearly as good here."

"Says who?"

"Me."

Nick took a step back, clearly ready to defend his position. "Ninjas are stealthy, have swords, and can hit you in the eye with a throwing star a hundred feet away. They could split a hundred zombie heads with their bare hands and not even break a sweat."

"Yeah, so?" Clarice replied, unfazed at his list. "Pirates have cannons, blunderbusses, pistols, and cutlasses. You don't need to be a karate expert to lop off a head. And if you don't believe me, when we get out, we can stick it on the Internet and put it to a vote."

"Fine," Nick said. "Loser does the dishes for a month. And that doesn't mean you suggest we eat out for thirty days in a row either."

Clarice said nothing and extended her betting hand, to which Nick took and sealed the deal.

"Now that that's settled, let's get to work," she said, turning her attention back to more serious matters. She inched back to the corner and dared a peek, only to find three pairs of zombie's eyes staring at her, thirty feet away.

Clarice ducked back. "Crap."

"What?"

"I think they saw me." She looked again. Her undead boss staggered toward her, closely followed by the other two. "Yep. And they're coming."

"Shoot or run?"

"I'm shooting. Then we might be running," she said. Clarice waited as long as she could as her former boss made his way toward her. Taking a deep breath, Clarice aimed and squeezed off the first round. The weapon kicked like a rabid quarter horse and spouted an enormous flame from its barrel.

Ryan's head snapped backward, and he stumbled for a moment before letting loose a snarl and continuing forward.

"Die, damn you!" Clarice yelled as she fired a second time. His head snapped again in response, but again, he did not fall.

"I don't believe this!" she said, backing up and dropping the gun.

"You're supposed to hit them in the head!" Nick exclaimed.

"I did hit him in the head!" she yelled. "Twice!"

Nick grabbed her by the arm and pulled her down the hall. They ran back to the generator room with Ryan in full pursuit. Clarice tried a few of the doors along the way, hoping something, anything, would pan out. All of them refused to open.

"Is there another exit here?" Nick asked once they were in the room. "Door? Vent? Ladder?"

Clarice slammed the door shut and locked it behind them. "No, I don't think so."

"There's got to be something we can use." Nick scoured the area. In one of the back corners he found a toolbox inside a tall, green locker. He dragged it out into the middle of the room and went through its contents. "Hammer?" he asked, holding it up for Clarice.

"That's not going to cut it," she said, shaking her head. "I'm telling you I shot him twice in the head and nothing happened. That dinky little hammer isn't going to do anything but piss him off."

"I told you we should have saved those shots and tried something else," Nick said as he dove back into the box.

Clarice stopped her search. "How the hell would I know he's a super zombie?"

"Because I said he was?" Nick kicked the box across the floor after finding nothing else of use. He then expanded his search to the rest of the room.

"Can we save the fight for after we're not dead?"

Before Nick could answer, something pounded against the door. The second blow left a large dent in the center. The third split the upper portion.

"As long as you seem to know everything," Clarice said, spinning around in place. "I don't suppose you know where we can find a cannon."

"Nope. And unless you've got some canister shot, it wouldn't matter." Nick bent down and picked up a screwdriver right as the door came off its hinges.

Ryan Conner, Tax Collector, stood on the other side and stepped through the frame. Standing behind him were the two other zombies who, for whatever reason, stayed outside of the room.

"Keep him busy," Clarice said as a most brilliant and pirate-like idea came to mind. All that it needed to be perfect was for her to swing from one yardarm to another. Clarice scampered up the generator, bag slung over her shoulder. The extra six or seven feet wasn't as high as she would have liked, but it would have to suffice. Perched upon her makeshift crow's nest, Clarice zipped the bag open and started tossing clothes.

"Whatever you're going to do, do it fast," Nick called out, throwing his screwdriver as Ryan stepped forward. The tool bounced off the zombie's head with no effect. Three more tools flew through the air with similar results.

Clarice looked up at her boss who was now closing fast on Nick. "Hey," she yelled, triumphantly pulling the UCK free from its garment prison. "Up here!"

Ryan ignored her cries and continued moving in on Nick.

Her fiancé darted forward, hammer in hand. It connected with the side of Ryan's face with a distinct, wet thud. Ryan snarled and backhanded Nick, who went tumbling to the ground.

Clarice hesitated, wondering if she should throw the jar instead of engaging directly. But the distance was too far for comfort, and Nick was too close to her boss. "I think I'll file for a homestead exemption," she boldly announced, "on a secondary residence."

Ryan paused. Slowly, he turned from Nick, who scrambled away. The unholy tax collector glared at his assistant and moved toward her.

Clarice gave the UCK a few light tosses in her hand, trying to gauge its weight. Hopefully, whatever bad thing Dr. Forbes had warned her about, wouldn't kill her as well. As Ryan came within a half-dozen lurches of her, she gave herself grand accolades. No ninja would ever think of a plan like this. This was downright smashing.

"Mr. Conner," she said in a calm and even tone. "I'm afraid I'm going to have to resign my position, effective immediately." It wasn't the most eloquent of speeches, a touch cheesy, and she would have liked something a bit more piratey. *Yar!* however, didn't quite seem to fit.

Ryan drove forward.

Clarice heaved the UCK, and Ryan snatched it out of the air before it could reach his head.

Clarice felt her heart sink.

Ryan turned the jar over, examining its contents. With a grunt, he let it drop and continued moving forward. The jar hit the ground, rolled across the floor, and came to rest at another zombie's feet.

"Damn it all to hell." Clarice wondered if she could jump over him and dash through the door without getting caught. She wondered if Nick would make it as well. A glance toward him seemed to show that he was thinking the same.

Ryan put one hand on the generator, apparently intent on climbing it.

Clarice looked past him, just in time to see a zombie smash the UCK over Ryan's head.

A short bit prior to Clarice's failed attack, Jack freed himself from the windowsill and took a few minutes to decide his next course of action. Ryan tended to the fine catch he had made, and Danita munched on her own. It looked like there was enough to share, but Jack knew it was bad form to eat another's meal unless invited. So Jack walked back out into the hall, intent on picking up a fresh trail. But between the sounds of Danita smacking and the two separate directions he could go—three if he looked back to the room—Jack couldn't decide what to do.

Before he could make up his mind, Ryan joined him, soon followed by Danita. It was at that point there was yelling. Lots and lots of yelling. Jack knew if there was yelling, there could be eating.

He turned to the right and spied a young woman's head peeping around the corner at the far end of the hall. It was only there for an instant before vanishing, but that was all the incentive he needed to give chase right along with Ryan and Danita.

Ryan soon had a hefty lead, and try as Jack might, he could not match the former tax collector's speed.

Jack slowed, pondering what this distance gap meant, and he felt a tug at his arm.

Danita, a pace behind him, had her hand clamped on his elbow.

Jack stopped in his tracks and suspected she wanted to talk in private. He also suspected Ryan was cheating somehow and figured she had the same concerns. No zombie could knock down doors as easily as Ryan did, and no one—no one—broke the three and a half mile per hour barrier. *Mmmmmuuurr.* (He's cheating.)

Danita's eyes narrowed. *Auuuurr.* (Let's kill him.)

Jack, glad she wanted him removed from the game as well, waved his pen excitedly. It was a fine pen, and he was certain it would be up to the task of driving through Ryan's skull. *Peennnnnnnnnnnnnnn.* (Pen!)

Danita smiled, her rotted gums and tongue showing well, and pushed Jack to move faster, clearly approving of his master plan. By the time they caught up with Ryan, he was already pounding on a large, gray door. It didn't take long for him to batter it down, and just like the previous barrier they had watched Ryan destroy, on the other side of this one were more humans.

Ryan wasted no time milling about. The instant the door broke apart, he entered the room.

Jack followed, gripping his pen tightly. He picked out a soft spot on the back of Ryan's bloodied head that would make a perfect target.

Danita pulled him back and kept him in the doorway for a moment. *Mmuurrgggrrrmmmm.* (Stab extra hard.)

Jack waved his pen at her one last time. It had been a trustworthy pen thus far, and he saw no reason why it couldn't stab extra hard if he wanted it to. But then Jack realized he only had one free hand. More importantly, he also realized that one hand couldn't stab as hard as two. And if he was going to stab Ryan Conner, former tax collector extra hard in the back of the head, it would probably be a good idea to free the other hand as well.

Jack handed Danita the pen, and despite her immediate protests, he entered the room and resumed his pursuit of Ryan. A few airborne tools whipped past, but did not offer any significant distraction. The small jar that rolled to Jack's feet, however, did. Merely a pace away from Ryan, Jack paused and picked it up.

It was round and shiny. The well-taken-care-of nothing inside looked especially empty.

Jack turned his attention back to Ryan, jar still in hand. The former tax collector was preoccupied with a perched human, and if there was ever a time to be rid of the cheater, that time was now. Even Jack understood that.

Jack raised his arms and stepped forward to strike the final blow. He looked up and realized that it wasn't his 1941, catalog product number 31A, green metallic shell, ballpoint pen in his hands, but rather he had a jar, small and round.

Grunting with indifference, Jack smashed it on Ryan's head anyway.

Chapter Twenty-One

There was a small bang.

Clarice shielded her eyes at the blinding light, nearly toppling off the generator in the process. When she dropped her hand, she saw that one of the zombies was knocked over, one was frozen in the doorway, and her former boss was completely gone. In her former employer's place was a tiny, black point that rapidly expanded into a three-foot large sphere.

"What on earth?" she said. Forgetting everything else, she eased down and inched toward it. In her one week as a secretary, Clarice had never seen or heard of anything like this happening.

The floating ball refused to fill her in on recent events.

A groan from Nick pulled her attention away. As he rolled over, Clarice offered him a hand as he took to his feet. "Christ that was loud," he said.

"Are you hurt?" she asked.

"I don't think so," he said as he rubbed his temples.

"Good."

When she took a step forward, Nick quickly tugged her back by the belt loops on her pants. "Careful. You saw what happened to your boss."

"No kidding," she replied. Clarice peered deep within the formless void. In the center there was something swirling, tiny and barely visible. A creamy mist grew from the center, spiral arms reaching out toward the edge of the sphere. "What's going on in there?" Clarice asked, inching her head as close as she dared.

"My guess is that it must have worked," Nick answered, his voice full of awe. "Absolutely unbelievable."

"What worked? The UCK?" she asked, still unsure of what she was looking at.

Nick shrugged. "Got a better idea? It was supposed to make a universe. I don't think they said anything about how big it would be."

Clarice blinked in order to rid herself of the hypnotic effect of the sphere. "We should be going," she said, carefully staying clear of the fallen zombie. "Do you suppose it's dead?"

"It's not moving," said Nick. "As long as it stays there, who cares?"

He then motioned over to the female corpse in the doorway. To both of their relief, she remained still. "What about her?"

"I guess we'll see," she answered. Clarice swallowed hard and picked up the hammer from the floor. Her heart raced, and her muscles were taught and ready to spring her back or strike out if need be. When the female zombie didn't move, Clarice bolted past. When she was clear, Nick followed suit.

The pair said not a word to each other as they raced down the halls. Nick stopped once at the security station to pick up his laptop, and a moment later, they both arrived at the emergency egress system.

"Maybe we should try and blow this place," he said, looking at the enormous contraption in the center of the room. His finger traced over a small instruction panel as he gave it a read. "I might be able to hack into their destruct device."

Clarice continued past, whipped out the ID badge and ran it through the scanner. The doors in front promptly slid open. "Feel free to stick around then," she said. "I'm leaving. Someone else can worry about the mess."

Nick didn't reply and joined her inside the elevator. He reached over, took her hand in his, and pushed the button marked 'L.'

The elevator began to rise, and the same piano concerto that had joined Clarice earlier on the phone now joined them both through overhead speakers. She found the music relaxing, and her jittery hands returned to normal.

"I can't believe we made it," she said, with a half-laugh, half-sob.

"Me either."

Clarice wrapped an arm around his waist and snuggled into his side.

Soon, the doors slid open, and the pair took a tentative step out, half expecting to be attacked again or still stuck underground. Instead, they found themselves in a small concrete building with a mountain view. In the corner was a large metal desk with a pegboard just above it. Hanging from one of the hooks on that pegboard was a set of keys. Clarice snatched them without hesitation and pulled her fiancé outside. A moment later, she found a blue pickup truck parked a dozen feet away, gave the keys a try, and smiled as the door popped open.

"Where do you suppose we are?" Nick asked as he walked to the passenger side.

Clarice looked skyward and gleefully let drops of rain splash against her face. After relishing the skydiving drops of water, she turned to her fiancé and said, "Somewhere raining."

"Home then?" Nick asked.

"Home," she replied as they both climbed into the cab. She turned the key in the ignition and gave thanks as the engine roared to life. "But first," she said with a grin, "we're stopping for drinks."

Jack lay face down, admiring the concrete floor. His head hurt. His ears rang. And with nothing to see or hear, he decided to take a nap until he felt better or a meal wandered into view.

He wasn't sure how long he'd been asleep when he woke up, but then again, the concept of time always eluded him. He rolled over, sat up, and saw Danita standing in the doorway.

She had a strange expression, one that Jack had never seen on her before. He asked her if she was computing a score from a game of Eats and when the next game would take place.

Danita explained everything she had seen. Or tried to at least. She droned on for hours, trying to find the right words for what it was like to see Ryan disappear in a flash.

Despite Danita's enthusiasm, Jack didn't really care. Nor could he understand why Ryan's sudden disappearance perplexed her. As far as he was concerned, either something was there, or it wasn't. In this case, it wasn't. And so while she rattled on, he had fun exploring and re-exploring the room they were in.

A week later, Jack and Danita were still talking in the generator room when he suggested that they start looking for Colmera Springs since he couldn't remember what he had done with it.

Danita agreed, and the two searched for the missing town, but everywhere they looked, they only found hard metal walls and locked doors.

One week turned into two, then spawned a third. Doors that were locked stayed locked. Rooms that didn't have any friends or meals stayed empty. Neither spoke of the whereabouts of Clarice and Nick, what had happened to Ryan, or anything to do with the mysterious black sphere that hung suspended in the air. With nowhere to go and no one to eat, Jack and Danita ended up going to sleep. Jack was content that sooner or later, someone would show.

They always did.

Chapter Twenty-Two

A month had passed, maybe two. Clarice wasn't sure, and she didn't care either. Immediately after Clarice and Nick escaped, there had been the consumption of a number of alcoholic beverages for days on end and a small sailboat purchase. At some point, there had also been a tiny spat at a local drinking establishment when someone grabbed her ass, and Nick floored the offender with a single punch. Then there were a lot of colorful lights and not-so-cheerful men in uniforms. The not-so-cheerful men became even less cheerful when they realized a few of their buddies several states over wanted to talk to Clarice in regard to a missing person case. The man with the robes and gavel, however, had been pleasant enough.

Clarice sat in a room that was painted in a calming hue of blue. Or at least, she was told it was. The Ativan pills were probably more responsible for the shift in her mood than anything else. To each of her sides, arranged in a circle, sat a number of other people, all of whom had been introduced to her at some point, but she could never remember their names. None, save for the drama queen across from her that is.

Her name was Jenny, and she annoyed Clarice to no end. If the former secretary were to ever go on a homicidal rampage, she was sure Jenny would spark it off. Jenny whined about everything, from her home life, to the improperly fitted sheets on the bed, to the way soft ice cream shouldn't be called ice cream. And now, she was whining about Clarice.

"How come *she* never has to talk?" Jenny asked in her usual shrill voice. She scowled in Clarice's direction. "She's been here almost as long as me, and you never make her talk."

"Now Jenny, you know we aren't going down this road again," the group leader said. He seemed nice enough, but the way he always fidgeted with his clothes and short, spiked hair continually distracted Clarice.

"It's not fair," Jenny repeated. Tears welled, and her cheeks and ears turned red. "I'm here trying to be good and to be happy, and she gets a free ride. It makes me mad."

"Tell her that directly, then. Remember, we talk to people, not through people."

Jenny turned and stared directly at Clarice. "It makes me mad you don't have to say anything."

Clarice rolled her eyes and smirked, both of which were intentionally exaggerated to provoke the group member further. If she was going to have to suffer another rant, Clarice figured she might as well at least have some fun with it.

"Oh, great," someone muttered. "Not again."

Jenny took the bait and shrieked. "See? She knows she doesn't have to talk and that's not fair."

Much to everyone's amazement, Clarice opened her mouth and words followed. "I've already said my piece," she said. "No one wants to believe me, so that's that."

"You have to make her talk!" Jenny yelled. "I bet she's not even taking her meds!"

"Jenny," the leader said, cutting in. "If you don't calm down, I'm going to have to ask you to leave. Team isn't for throwing accusations around at each other. You know that."

Jenny wiggled back in her seat, arms crossed, and let out a discontented sigh. She made fat little fists in her lap, squeezing them periodically, but said no more.

A knock on the room's sole door hushed the whispers that were forming. A moment later an orderly stepped in, looked directly at Clarice, and waved her over. "It'll just be a little bit," he said.

Clarice followed without a word.

The two proceeded down a sterile, white hall, the orderly's shoes clomping loudly along the way. At some point, he glanced back at her and pointed to her forearm. "I like your tattoo."

"Thanks," she said, unsure how to respond.

"What did you use?"

"A Bic, fine point," Clarice replied, admiring her handiwork. "Point eight millimeters, I believe."

"Where did you get the needle?"

"I didn't use one," she said. "You guys seem to keep them away from us. So I just drew it on. It'll wash off."

"Does that say W-W-A-B-D?"

Clarice nodded.

"What does it mean?"

Clarice only smiled.

"Is that your first?"

Clarice shook her head. "Last year I got a Jolly Roger inked on my lower back."

"Nice," he said. He then knocked on the office door they had just arrived at and ushered Clarice inside. Once the doctor on the other side had acknowledged their presence, and Clarice took a seat, the orderly left.

Clarice waited for her new shrink to get off the phone. His nameplate suggested that he was Dr. O. A. Levonston. According to the myriad of books on his three bookshelves, he specialized in schizophrenia. Anything else she might be able to discern from his belongings was cleverly hidden away in cardboard boxes.

"Excuse the clutter," Dr. Levonston said as he hung up the phone. "I haven't quite moved in yet. Clarice, is it? May I call you that?"

"You may."

"Good," he replied, picking up a large plastic binder. "I've been looking through your chart, and I'd like to go over some parts of it with you."

Clarice sighed, and just like every interview and session she had had before with countless other psychiatrists and therapists, it degenerated into him explaining everything to her as if she were a baby.

Her mind wandered from his lecture and reverted to the subject on infants. All of the babies Clarice had met were small and usually pink. Some tended to be fussy, but they almost always had cute going for them, which made up for a lot of the fuss. Cute, that is, as long as they weren't in meltdown mode.

The more she thought about them, the more she realized that babies had the uncanny ability to stop any conversation. She had seen them use a wide range of assets to accomplish such a task, from pinch-me cheeks to mischievous grins. On rare occasions or critical times, she even saw infants call in the inopportune, poopy diaper, which by Clarice's judgment, had a 98% success rate of halting any grownup activity when applied properly.

Clarice wished she had a baby at this very moment. She would even take one complete with a poopy diaper to escape the current conversation. Sadly, no baby was in sight, soiled or otherwise.

"How do you feel about being here today?" Dr. Levonston asked, cutting into her train of thought.

"It's not so bad," she lied.

"Is that so?" the psychiatrist said, arching an eyebrow. "According to your notes, you've been combative since you've been here."

"Past tense," she said, settling back in the chair.

"You can tell me if you don't like it here," he said, apparently trying to be as soothing as possible in a sterile lab coat and sharply angled eyeglasses. "You can tell me the truth. We're only here to help."

"I know," she lied, once again. She had long ago figured out that telling the truth only got her fitted with another straight jacket. Since she didn't relish the idea of spending the rest of her life in such attire, she knew she had to play the game. And play it well. "I appreciate what you're trying to do," she said, hoping she wasn't laying it on too thick. "I want to get better."

Dr. Levonston tapped his pen on his desk and leaned back in his chair. "Are you now saying your boss wasn't eaten by zombies?"

"Bitten," she corrected, chomping her teeth for added effect. "Not eaten. There's a difference."

The doctor smiled. "Bitten, then."

"I'm sure there's a rational explanation for everything," she said.

"Then perhaps you can tell me why you concocted a fanciful story with the walking dead, secret labs, and mysterious black holes?"

"I don't know," she said. "Chemical imbalance maybe. But whatever it is, I'm willing to work at it until we figure it out."

As much as she loved watching the staff work on her, Clarice had her escape to plan, her murder to fake, and her fiancé to find. More importantly, however, Clarice knew that none of that was going to happen while they watched her like a hawk. She needed to make them think she was compliant, that she was weak.

Clarice mentally patted herself on the back as her psychiatrist began to talk about medication changes and long term treatment goals that would end in her "speedy" release. Not that any of that mattered. She'd be gone by the end of the week, and nothing could stop her. After all, if the walking dead, mad scientists, and an underground, malfunctioning lab couldn't do her in, a two-bit mental institution didn't stand a chance—especially not when two of the guards took naps and the janitorial staff left the service entrance unlocked.

Anne would be proud.

APOCALYPSE HOW?
(DAKOTA ADAMS BOOK 1)

I never thought I'd have a bounty on my head the size of the Milky Way.

Of course, I never thought I'd be able to bend time, either.

But hey, life is full of surprises.

Don't get me wrong, feeling like a goddess has its perks, but those perks come with a hefty price. My brain is tapioca. I'm stranded in the middle of dead space. Ratters are using me for target practice, and a giant, cybernetic monster named Oscar wants to use me for a chew toy.

All this because I played superhero (or thief, according to some) and snatched a doomsday device from an intergalactic mobster.

So if I don't make it out of here alive, remember this:

Above all else, I want a Viking funeral.

CHAPTER ONE

I don't know how everyone didn't die of boredom a thousand years ago.

I mean, back in the 5th century PHS (Pre HyperSpace), you only had a handful of channels to watch, and the farthest anyone had gone was the moon. To top it off, it took them three days to get there. I'd rather let a Ferrean dust worm gnaw my arm off than spend that long twiddling my thumbs in a cramped cockpit with nothing to do.

And while I'm ranting about ancient history, I can't even imagine being stuck on a tiny blue planet that at least one guide listed as being mostly harmless. I need to sail the Horsehead Nebula! I need to speed dive the event horizon of KT-124! I need to go spelunking at the Venetian poles!

I know. I know. Billions of people have already done all that, but my true passion is finding lost alien technology and prehistoric civilizations that even time doesn't remember. So, after a lot of research, a few hot tips, and calling in three solid you-owe-me's, I got a hold of a good lead on what would hopefully be an ancient crash site on a backwater planet.

How much would a find be worth? Anywhere from junk to untold riches, obviously, but I had hopes that the salvage there would get me enough to buy a brand-new Hermes '64 Intruder.

With its seven-point-eight cubic meter warp core and six-barreled displacement drive, I'd lap the galaxy faster than gossip laps a locker room. When I could do that, I'd put all other treasure hunters to shame.

And if I got mega-trillions-jackpot lucky, I could even find something the Progenitors left behind. For those of you who slept through history class, they're the guys fabled to have been the most advanced species ever to exist. They created worlds on a whim and popped in and out of any dimension they pleased.

What I wouldn't give to be the first to prove their existence. Becoming the most famous xenoarchaeologist in the Milky Way would be a nice touch, too, and I'm pretty sure I'd get my PhD on the spot, even if I haven't technically finished my undergrad. Then I'd be able to introduce myself as Doctor Adams. Doctor Dakota Adams.

Yeah, I like the sound of that. Sounds a ton better than Miss Adams, doesn't it? I like it so much, in fact, if I ever get home with my skull intact, I'm going to order a nameplate the first chance I get.

CHAPTER TWO

When I first landed on DD-3123—a small, lush planet on the outer rim—things got off to a slow start. I spent an entire day wandering around trying to find my local contact who promised he could guide me to the crash site.

While wandering, I checked in with my live-stream channel, and I was depressed to discover my usual ten to twenty viewers had dwindled to two. Though I was grateful I still had a couple of names tuning into my show, I soon suspected they were bots.

My search for my native guide eventually led me inside a festival filled with balloons, mud huts, and plenty of odd games ranging from wibblet ball (sort of a soccer-freeze-tag hybrid) to death stick (horseshoes meets hand grenades, not for the faint of heart).

Eventually, I found the guy, whose name was Ryx, near the food vendors. He was snacking on a bag of palafels (think giant caterpillars, deep fried and dipped in honey) and listening to a traveling musical group with vocals strong enough to shatter steel. Once the show finished, we blazed a trail together to a large crater about ten kilometers away. The terrain was scrubby and flat, for the most part, until we reached the crater's outer edge and needed to scale the ridgeline.

After hiking most of the way up, I finished the climb with a short hop and swing of my ice axe to grab the top and pull myself up. Though it was easy, I was jealous of how fast Ryx scaled the terrain. His seven spindly arms were long enough to grab plenty of holds at once, and the suckers covering the palms of his hands were strong enough that he could sleep suspended from an overhang. That said, he was also two and a half meters tall, which meant he'd be smooshed in any cockpit. I've always said I'd take zipping through the galaxy in comfort over pretending to be a bat any day. His furry body and arachnid face weren't appealing either.

Standing next to me, Ryx pointed into the giant crater. The meemar forest obscured everything inside its five-kilometer span with their bright orange leaves, but there was a dark blotch that he was drawing my eyes to close by.

"Down there," Ryx said. His natural language was a slew of squeaks, but the 3C-bug in my ear (fluent in over six million forms of communication) made the translation.

"Awesome," I said, plugging the location into my datapad. "I really can't thank you enough for the help. Are you sure you won't come with?"

Ryx made a circular gesture with his left appendage, the equivalent of us humans shaking our head. "Haunted place. Dangerous. Rats went in earlier. Never came out. Beware the glow floor and the one with the red eye."

"Glowing floors and red eyes are bad, got it," I said with a friendly pat on one of his shoulders.

There was a grunt from behind, and Oran, a guy I'd hired to help, pulled himself up over the ridge to join us. Sweat and dirt caked his sunburnt forehead, and the shirt under his brown jacket was soaked so badly I was sure I could smell his reek three planets away. Stink aside, he also failed to dress for the occasion. He wore casual weekend attire consisting of tailored pants and a collared shirt, instead of something more suited to exploration like the khaki pants, loose shirt and wide-brimmed hat that I had on.

"Almost there," I said to encourage him. "Don't have a coronary on me."

"Guess I'm not as young as I used to be," he replied with a weary smile.

I almost made a quip about him only being a few years older than I was, but decided to let him save face so he didn't have to admit a girl was in better shape than he was. "Well, no time to dawdle," I said, starting my way down the crater.

"Yeah. Let's wrap this up," Oran replied, though with far less enthusiasm than me.

I practically had to pull Oran along. I think the talk of the area being haunted concerned him more than the steep, rocky terrain we were descending. After all, if the ship we were looking for had a split reactor, that could be the source of superstition for Ryx's villagers.

We pressed through thick foliage. More than once thorns and branches snared my sleeves and pants. I kept quiet about it, but Oran complained. "This place is terrible," he said. "We should've waited for Tolby to finish working on your ship. Could've saved us a lot of walking."

"She's due for her thousand-hour maintenance," I replied. "You don't want to skip that kind of stuff unless the idea of breaking down between system jumps appeals to you."

Oran snorted. "Yeah, but waiting a few more hours wouldn't have killed you. It's not like this crash site is going anywhere."

"There's no room to land around here," I explained as I hacked away at the Yubjub bushes with my nanomachete. They'd gotten so dense that I'd have given my first born for a flamethrower or a herd of vegetarian land piranhas. "And if we wait much longer, it'll be twenty-nine hours since we've been on this world."

"What's wrong with that?"

I stopped. "I don't like twenty-nine. It...makes me feel uneasy." I couldn't explain it other than that. It's not because it's a prime number. There are some I like (like the numbers three and eleven), but certain numbers are wrong, four especially. Four is scratchy and sounds like a faster-than-light drive when it's about to go supercritical and scatter your atoms across the galaxy. Twenty-nine isn't that bad, but it smells like musty socks and is lime green. If you're not a synesthete, this sounds kooky, but if you are, you know what I'm talking about.

I pushed on, not wanting to think about bad numbers anymore. "God, these trees are huge. No wonder I couldn't see anything from orbit."

Oran let the conversation die. A few hacks later, we broke through the brush and found ourselves at the edge of a small river. It moved at a fast clip, and I paused to wash my face. Once cleaned and refreshed, I checked my datapad to see how much farther we had to go. That's when I realized it said we were less than fifty meters downstream of where we wanted to be.

I looked up and my breath left me. Ahead there was an exhaust port as tall as I was. I couldn't see the rest of the ship, but what I saw looked intact. Thankfully, the crash was on our side of the river. Trying to cross such a swift body of water wasn't appealing.

I wondered how long the ship had been there. Given the forest growth around it, it'd probably crashed hundreds of years ago. Thousands maybe. Millions? Was it Progenitor?

I chuckled, knowing I was getting carried away. It was a human ship, five hundred years old at the most. As I drew closer, I could see the engines were original Pratt & Taiki FTL drives. They had the company's signature egg-shaped design that early engineers erroneously thought were more reliable. It also had slanted, atmospheric stabilizing fins made from a plasti-titanium compound (the goldish sheen was a dead giveaway) that only saw limited production in the early- to mid-first-century AHS.

The ship itself was lying on its belly, sunken a couple of meters into the ground. That said, it was still two stories tall, so I was mostly looking up at it.

"This is amazing," Oran said. The awe in his voice was palpable.

I touched the micro-button on the side of my thin-rimmed glasses and opened a communication line back to my ship. "Tolby? We scored."

"Great One guides us! I knew it!" His deep, rough voice was filled with energy. "What did we find?"

"It's—"

"A Porellian battle cruiser?"

"No a—"

"A Weyani medship?"

"No, it's—"

"By the Plancks!" Tolby boomed. "Tell me it's a Progenitor! It is right? No...don't tell me. The gods will smite me for the amount of blaspheme I'll utter if I'm stuck here working on this bucket of bolts of yours."

My face soured. "Hey!"

"Sorry," he apologized. He took a deep breath and exhaled slowly. "I'm centered now. You may inform me of this Progenitor ship you've discovered."

At the time, I could picture the serious, slightly adorable look on his tiger-like face and couldn't stay mad at him for calling my ship a piece of crap. "Human origins. Looks like an old exploration ship. Early Odyssey? Still walking up to it."

Tolby grunted. "That's...disappointing. Perhaps it'll have something good inside? I mean salvage on just the ship..."

"Will barely cover costs getting out here, but there's no telling what it was carrying," I said. Remains of ships this old weren't worth much. It would be like expecting the rotting wood of a sunken Spanish galleon to fetch a prime price to a carpenter. No, what we needed to find was some rare cargo.

"Inform me of your progress as things develop," he said. "I'm going to take our ship out for a test flight and make sure everything's running smoothly before we head home."

"Of course," I said. "Hey, rub my elephant for good luck."

Tolby grumbled over the line. "Really?"

"Yes, really!" I said. "He's part of the reason we got this lucky!"

"He's a piece of plastic suction-cupped to your dashboard," Tolby replied. "He can't do anything but decrease warpcore efficiency by 0.00002%, rounded of course, due to his minimal mass."

"Remember what happened last time you didn't rub the elephant? We had that strut malfunction, and it nearly ruined my landing gear."

"That had nothing to—" Tolby stopped midsentence and cursed (knowing I was right). "Fine. There. Happy now? I rubbed your elephant, just how he likes it."

"Perfect. Thanks. Talk to you soon."

"Dakota?" Oran said, drawing my attention. He stood near the aft of the ship, inspecting a large identification plate welded on the side. "This isn't an Odyssey. It's the colony ship of the *NTS Vela*."

I squealed without shame and bolted to where he was to get a look. The fifteen meters that separated us felt like a kilometer. But once I was there, it read as he'd said: COLONY SHIP – NTS VELA.

Tales about the *Vela* had been spun for centuries. No one knew what had happened to it half a millennium ago, but every legend said it had been on its way to unearth a treasure trove of Progenitor technology before vanishing. And while this wasn't the *Vela*, obviously, it was the colony ship that would detach from the *Vela* to land on a planet and well, like the name says, colonize it, since the *Vela* wasn't meant for anything but pure space travel.

My heart pounded against my chest, and I hopped around with unbridled excitement. Technology from the first spacefaring race was at my fingertips! Technology that could power a galaxy or jump a ship halfway across the known universe in the blink of an eye! Technology that would firmly write me into all the history books from here till the end of time!

I playfully punched Oran in the arm and smiled brighter than I'd ever before.

"What the hell are we waiting for then? Let's get in there!"

(End of Sample)

THE GORGON BRIDE

MYTHS OF STONE BOOK I

Out Now!

THE GODS ARE FUNNY.

Except when you piss them off.

Then they suck.

They really, really suck.
(Really).

Alexander Weiss discovers this tidbit when he inadvertently insults Athena, Goddess of Wisdom, and she casts him away on a forgotten isle filled with statues.

Being marooned is bad enough, but the fact that the island is also the home of Euryale, elder sister to Medusa, makes the situation a touch worse. The only thing keeping Alex from being petrified is the fact that Euryale has taken a liking to the blundering mortal.

For now.

What follows next is a wild, adventurous tale filled with heroes, gods, monsters, love, and war that is nothing short of legendary.

ACKNOWLEDGEMENTS

To all the zombies who generously donated their time so I could understand how their brains work...

To my slew of readers who went over countless drafts and helped shape Death & Taxes into a fun romp...

And most of all, to my wife, Mary Beth, who keeps reading my stuff at my request and somehow hasn't been driven away.

ABOUT THE AUTHOR

When not writing, Galen Surlak-Ramsey has been known to throw himself out of an airplane, teach others how to throw themselves out of an airplane, take pictures of the deep space, and wrangle his four children somewhere in Southwest Florida.

He also manages to pay the bills as a chaplain for a local hospice.

Be sure to drop by his website https://galensurlak.com/ and sign up for his newsletter for free goodies, contests, and plenty of other fun stuff.

ABOUT THE PUBLISHER

Tiny Fox Press LLC
5020 Kingsley Road
North Port, FL 34287

http://www.tinyfoxpress.com